ZEN

and

GONE

Also by the Author

Signs of You

ZEN

and

GONE

EMILY FRANCE

SOHO TEEN

Published in the United States by Soho Teen
an imprint of Soho Press, Inc.
853 Broadway
New York, NY 10003

Library of Congress Cataloging-in-Publication Data

France, Emily.
Zen and gone / Emily France.
1. Sisters—Fiction. 2. Missing children—Fiction. 3. Dating (Social customs)—Fiction.
4. Mothers and daughters—Fiction. 5. Marijuana—Fiction. 6. Zen Buddhism—Fiction.
7. Boulder (Colo.)—Fiction. I. Title

PZ7.1.F73 Zen DDC [Fic]—dc23 2017055381

ISBN 978-1-61695-857-2
eISBN 978-1-61695-858-9

Interior art by Nathan Burton
Interior design by Janine Agro, Soho Press, Inc.

Printed in the United States of America

10 9 8 7 6 5 4 3 2 1

For my son.

May I be with you every precious moment I'm with you.

ZEN

and

GONE

PART I

THE FIRST NOBLE TRUTH:

Duhkha exists.

Duhkha (thoohkh), noun. Sanskrit. Direct English translation unavailable. Derived from a word meaning "wheel out of kilter."

The persistent, recurring feeling that life doesn't feel like it should; it's uncomfortable and painful in a million different ways. It never really satisfies. You don't get what you want. Or you get what want, and you don't want it anymore. You want things to stay the same, and they change. Or you want things to change, and they stay the same. You want to feel stable, grounded, safe, happy. You want things to be better and different. You want to feel good. You want to feel high.

*Sometimes you've got it. For a moment.
It's all just right.
And then it slips away.
Good and bad. Here and gone.
Over and over.*

And you suffer.

That's duhkha.

June 23

3 A.M.

1

ESSA

It was her job to keep Puck safe.

Puck—Essa's nine-year-old sister, the budding genius, the girl she lived for. The royal pain in the ass who wasn't supposed to be on this trip in the first place. It was Essa's job to keep an ear out, an eye out, to be aware of any danger. It always had been. But it was especially true up here. Especially true tonight.

Essa bolted upright, her eyes wide. She saw nothing but consuming blackness.

Was that a noise?

Footsteps?

It couldn't be the deadfall; they hadn't reset it after they'd caught a mouse. Essa rubbed her hands together for warmth, wiggled her icy toes inside her boots, pulled her knees to her chest. Her eyes adjusted to the night, and she could see snippets of moonlight sneaking through gaps in the walls of their tiny brush shelter. A stiff mountain wind whistled through the pine boughs and dead leaves they'd layered to keep the weather out. They'd been stuck in the storm for hours; everything had gotten wet. Even though it was June, Essa was cold. She knew it couldn't be true, but she felt like it had dipped into the thirties.

She shifted on the forest floor. They'd forgotten to cover it with a layer of brush to insulate them before they went to sleep. All night, a chill had been reaching up from the ground, climbing through her thin hiking pants, sliding down her legs, wrapping around her ankles and toes. It felt like it had a mind of its own, the cold. Like it was out for her, thrilled that they were here, ten thousand feet up in the Mummy Range, lost, with barely the clothes on their backs. Like it was determined to make one thing understood:

If you make it out of here alive, don't come back.

She heard it again.

Snap.

Louder this time. She couldn't tell if it was coming from inside or outside. She looked up at their shelter roof, but couldn't see well enough to check the large tree branch they'd used as the main support beam. She hoped her bowline knot was holding.

Shuffle. Snap.

She heard it again, and this time, she was sure it was outside the shelter. She told herself it was a raccoon sniffing around their camp. She told herself it wasn't a bear that was about to rip through the sides of their pitiful homemade walls and attack. That it wasn't the random creepy guy they saw earlier walking through the woods. That he wasn't out there, stalking them in the darkness, lurking with an ax.

She tried to calm down and picture herself back in the Zendo in Boulder, meditating on a cushion. She imagined that the sounds outside the shelter were nothing but the gentle shuffling of her Zen teacher's robes as he settled just before zazen. It was one of her favorite sounds.

Silently she recited the gatha she'd crafted with her teacher:

Breathing in, I know my breath is the wheel of the ship.

Breathing out, I know the storm will pass.

Her mind didn't stay with her breathing. It did what it normally did: it reached for thoughts like a frantic monkey, grasping at one random idea after the other, feeding on disorder, on chaos. She thought about her mom back down in Boulder, more out of control by the day. About her best friend Micah, gently snoring next to her. How annoying he'd been at the party two weeks ago with the weed gummies he'd snatched from Pure Buds. She thought about sitting by the campfire last night, outside their shelter, after everyone else had gone to sleep. Exhausted. Wet. Cold. Her belly aching with hunger, getting nothing from a granola bar and a few sips of pine needle tea. Afraid to eat the food they'd brought, not sure how long it was going to have to last. She thought about the soft firelight on Oliver's skin. Oliver, the boy from Chicago she'd met not even a month ago. The one who felt so familiar, so fast. The one with the sister who was sick; the one who seemed to understand. The one who had pulled her close and kissed her . . .

She tried to return to her breath.

To another gatha.

Fears are clouds drifting by a mountain.

Watch them. Tend to them.

But know

You're the mountain.

Another sound split the night.

Crack.

It was even closer. Something or someone was out there. She reached over and nudged Micah. "Hey," she hissed. "Get up. I hear something."

"Dude," Micah groaned. He snorted briefly and rolled over and went back to sleep. She shook him again.

"Wake up. Seriously." When he didn't move, she grabbed a handful of his thick black hair and gave it a few firm tugs.

"What the hell?"

"I hear something," she hissed again. "Outside."

Micah propped himself on one arm to listen. Just outside the shelter, off to their right, she heard it again. Movement. Footsteps. Or something being dragged along the ground.

"Probably just a raccoon," Micah mumbled. But he didn't sound convinced. "We have no food in here for a bear to come after. It's all outside. Unless you count the mouse I roasted last night. And man, this ground is *ice cold.*"

"We smell like *people*," she said. "That's all the incentive a bear needs."

Crack. Snap.

The sounds rang through the darkness. Her mind flashed to the guide Oliver left back in the car. They were in the Comanche Peak Wilderness. Full of bears, mountain lions, coyotes. Fear sent her mind racing through other things that could be out there: Serial killers? Runaway felons? Ghosts?

"What if it's that guy we saw?" she whispered.

She noticed for the first time that she was shivering. Her arms and chest quaked as she thought about the random guy they'd seen in the woods before they'd realized they were lost. He wasn't wearing stuff hikers or hunters wore. He was in baggy black cotton pants. A preppy blue sweater. A straw fedora. Rubbery black plastic clogs and white socks. He looked wildly out of place, like a snake in the bottom of a kid's toy chest. A knife tangled up in your bedsheets. He claimed he was out looking for the site of a plane crash. Essa knew there was a trail to an old WWII B17 crash site somewhere in the area. But the man claimed the plane had been his grandfather's, that it had been full of valuable Japanese antiques. He said he'd been searching the woods for years, looking for any that might have survived the crash. He said no one believed him.

Essa didn't, either.

She shivered again and wondered if it was the cold or the fear making her core temperature drop. "You think he could've followed us?"

"Dude. Chill," Micah said. "That guy was harmless. Just a crazy dude out for a hike."

Goosebumps tumbled down Essa's spine, and instinctively, she leaned over and reached for Puck. Last night, Puck had gone to sleep at her side, Essa's face nuzzled in her sister's tangled blonde hair, the smell of Puck's cherry lollipop dinner wafting up her nose. Now she gently felt in the darkness for the reassurance of Puck's tiny, warm body.

Her hand landed on cold ground.

She groped in the dark a little farther to the left. And then to the right.

"Puck?"

Silence.

"Puck!" Essa hissed, frantically searching. "Puck!"

Her breath hitched in the back of her throat, but she tried to stay calm. Maybe Puck had rolled over to a new spot in the night. Essa strained her eyes in the darkness, but she couldn't see. "Micah? Is she next to you?"

She heard Micah search the shelter around him. "No. I don't feel her."

"Nudge Oliver awake," Essa said.

"He's not over here, either."

"Oliver? Puck?"

No one answered. A cold wind hissed through the shelter wall next to her. She knocked into Micah as she scrambled onto all fours, searching every inch of their tiny home, running her hands along the ground, up the walls. She felt Puck's backpack.

"That's probably what we heard outside," Micah said. "They probably got up to go to the bathroom or—"

Essa didn't wait to hear the end of his sentence. She bolted out the small exit hole of the shelter and got to her feet.

"Puck!" she called into the dark woods. It felt like her voice was swallowed by the rushing wind around her. It died down for just a moment. "Puck! Oliver?"

Silence.

She looked into the sky, searching for the moon, begging it to shine down on their camp, to light up Puck's stringy blonde hair, her blueberry eyes, her lips that were perpetually candy-stained red. But the moon was nearly doused, obscured by clouds and a muddy, stubborn blackness.

Puck was gone.

And so was Oliver.

June 5

2

ESSA

Essa was down on Pearl Street listening to a band called My Brother's Keeper. The guitarist sucked, and he'd pinned a long, real fur tail to his pants. As he strummed, the tail quivered and shook. The guy on the banjo wore a tiny tambourine around the toe of his shoe, and he tap, tap, tapped. The lead singer had a scruffy beard, and he was wearing a flowing tie-dyed skirt. It was a typical Boulder band, and Essa was about to bail on music altogether and search Pearl for a decent magician or maybe for the contortionist who could squeeze himself into a tiny glass box. Or maybe for the guy she saw last week who'd set up a little table, a typewriter, and a sign: POETRY ON DEMAND. But then the band started a new song, and the lyrics caught her, like good lyrics did, and she found herself swaying back and forth, back and forth. Sometimes music was like a strong wind. Invisible and without warning, it *moved* her.

She was distracted by the woman in front of her. Dreadlocks rested on top of the woman's head like so many intertwined, sleeping snakes. Thin lines of marijuana smoke rose from her joint and settled around the snake pile like an incoming fog. She swayed to the music like Essa had, her gauzy dress revealing her threadbare bra. She took another long drag off her joint and blew the smoke straight up in the air this time. An actual wind kicked up, and the smoke drifted into Essa's face.

Annoyed, Essa tapped her shoulder. "Hey," she said. "Mom. Blow *that* way."

"Sorry, Essa." Her mom smiled a slow, stoned smile, like she knew a complicated secret she wasn't sharing. "You want?"

Essa looked at the glowing cherry, beckoning, promising escape. Like a magical doorway made of smoke, opening right there on Pearl Street.

All I'd have to do is inhale to go through. To somewhere else. To wherever my mom is most of the time, blissed out, and just . . . not here.

But she'd never smoked. She couldn't. She had to stay put, stuck in what she sometimes feared was the crappier reality on *this* side of her mom's magical smoke doorway. Because of Puck. She needed Essa, the one person in the family who had her shit together.

She stared at the joint again, sniffed its weedy, swampy smoke. She thought about the Zen priest; hoped he was right. A line from one of her favorite Dharma talks flooded her mind; she held onto it, steadied herself with it.

Escape doesn't work. It doesn't cure duhkha.

Stay in this moment. Present moment.

"You know I don't want," Essa said.

Her mom shrugged and gave her a red eye roll. "Essence McKree. Oldest teenager I know."

Whatever.

She was almost late for work. And so was her mom. They both had jobs in Pearl Street shops that were a few doors down from each other. And Essa hated to be late for the thing that funded nearly everything in her life: her job at a little kite shop called Above the Clouds.

"Time to go," Essa said, standing and offering her mom a hand. Her mother's lips melted into a little frown, but she reached out. Essa pulled, and her mom's body slid up, all gooey and easy like a piece of warm caramel. She was smiling.

"You're a peach," her mom said.

They strolled down the wide brick street, and her mom dug

in her faded patchwork purse for a cigarette. She lit it and took a drag. A sweet, dry mountain breeze twirled her dress and then Essa's. They passed jugglers, fiddlers, dancers, and poets. They dotted Pearl like tie-dyed roses, each one a burst of color, a reward for all the shoppers who'd come to this open-air plaza of indie stores.

"Shit," her mom said. She tossed her cigarette on the uneven bricks and mashed it with her sandal. "Beth's in there."

They were in front of her mom's work now. The sign above them creaked in the wind: PURE BUDS, 100% ORGANIC CANNABIS. It was the first legal pot shop to go organic in Boulder. Essa looked in the big glass windows at the sleek interior of the store. No hippie crap here. Behind beautiful reclaimed wooden shelves, the walls were painted a fresh apple green. Big mason jars full of buds sported black labels with names written in chalk: *Bubba Kush, Pineapple Express, Skywalker OG.* Behind the register, bright glass cabinets showcased the edibles: marijuana-infused cookies, multicolored lollipops, shiny gummies, thick fudge brownies. It looked like a high-end bakery.

Beth, the owner of the store and her mom's boss, came out to meet them. She didn't look happy. "Was that a cigarette?" she asked. Essa's mom looked at the ground and nodded in shame. "They're so *bad for you*," Beth whined.

Beth didn't say any more, but her judgment oozed around them like a melting marijuana gummy. She looked Essa's mom up and down, surveying her dreadlocks, her gauzy dress. Beth was wearing the exact opposite: sleek black stretchy pants, a gray wrap-around top. Essa's mom called Beth's style "Smart Yoga" or, alternatively, "Make Me Puke." Beth gave Essa's mom a job baking edibles. In the back.

"I'll be in in just a second," her mom said.

Beth nodded and gave Essa a *you poor kid* smile. "Good to see you, Essa." Then she went back into Pure Buds.

Essa's mom rolled her eyes. "I thought Beth was mad because I messed up a batch of gummy pineapples. I made them with

Willie Nelson's new brand—Willie's Reserve. They came out looking more like ducks than fruit." She smiled, but it faded quickly. "Fucking potrepreneurs." Essa's mom thought all the East Coast business people who were moving to Colorado and taking over the old-school pot scene were a real drag. She always said that they were changing the culture.

Essa just didn't want to be late for work. "I don't get off until six," she said. "You're five-thirty?"

Her mom nodded. "I don't really know. Can't remember. Just come straight home after."

Essa raised her eyebrows.

"There's someone I want you to meet," her mom said. "We'll have dinner at the house."

Another new one?

Essa didn't say it out loud, but she made a face. Her mom instantly broke into salesperson mode. "He's really great, Essa," she said. "Really. I think you'll like him. His name is Ronnie."

"Hope springs eternal, Mom."

Her mother rolled her eyes again. "Don't be an asshole." But she said it lovingly. She stepped close, ran a hand through Essa's hair, making her butterfly hairclip slide askew. "Why don't you bring a date? You must have a crush on *someone*. One of your camping buddies? A guy? A girl? I don't care which. You know that."

Essa straightened her butterfly clip and swatted her mom away like a persistent fly. Actually, her mom wasn't like a fly at all. She was more like a butterfly. Wispy. Colorful. Hard to catch.

"We don't really *camp*. We do orienteering up there. It's different," Essa said. "And you know I don't date."

Her mom shook her head. "Have it your way," she sighed. "Just be home for dinner, okay?"

3

OLIVER

"Maybe you'll fall in love with this place."

His mom knew that the likelihood of this happening was some very small fraction of zero. But she was trying to be upbeat. To encourage him. It was obvious that he was two nanoseconds away from bailing on this plan to live with Aunt Sophie in Boulder for the summer. It wasn't his plan, anyway; he hadn't really been given a choice.

Oliver looked out the window, through his aunt's dangling Tibetan prayer flags, at the car that was waiting to take his mom back to the airport and back to Chicago. He felt terrible for agreeing to come here. Like the worst person in the world.

"She got you an internship at a tech startup. How great is that? Maybe they'll turn out to be the next Google? You never know. Plus, you need this," his mom urged. "What happened with Lilly was—"

"Can I have my bag?" He cut her off. He couldn't stand to think about that night a few weeks ago. What he did to his sister. The sound of his parents fighting. The sound of his voice when he totally and completely lost his shit. The sound of Lilly's screams when the paramedics came. How she called him a traitor. He took his last duffel bag from his mom's hands. And felt like a coward.

"Your room is almost ready!" Aunt Sophie called from down the hall.

"Promise me you won't try pot," his mom whispered. "Boulder is a little . . . *bohemian*." She gently ran a hand against his cheek, and her gold watch slid down her arm toward her elbow.

"But it's legal here. I don't see a problem." Oliver grinned for the first time in weeks. Maybe months.

"Oliver." She wasn't seriously worried. He was Oliver Burnham, the good kid. The one who wouldn't even take a sip of ouzo at New Year's Eve dinner at YaYa's house. Even though it offended his Greek grandmother, he didn't drink. He didn't do anything. Oliver was the kid who—at least until a few weeks ago—had been trying not to cause any problems. They had enough of those in their family already.

"Maybe you can hike or something," his mom added. "I think they do a lot of that here."

"Yeah, sure," Oliver lied. Like he would ever actually choose to trek off into the woods or opt to be outside more than was absolutely necessary. He tossed his duffel on his aunt's sofa. "Lots of hiking. No getting wasted."

And even though that had always been his policy—never getting wasted—that last night with his sister, he would've had an entire bottle of ouzo if he'd had the chance. After it was all over, after Lilly was admitted to the hospital, his mom and dad kept fighting. About his sister. About Oliver. About the fact that his dad had filed for divorce. After what had happened that night, he didn't know what to do with himself. His dad left, and his mom poured herself a giant glass of red wine. The curvy glass seemed almost as big as her head. As big as a fishbowl. Oliver sat there across from her. After a few long sips, her breath got a little slower. A little deeper. He caught himself staring at her wine in this weird way. It looked good. Really good.

But he didn't drink. Instead, he got a Coke out of the fridge and went to his room. He tried to forget what he'd done. He tried to journal like their family therapist had told them to, but he couldn't. He remembered throwing the empty diary across the room. He remembered doing this half-choking, half-crying thing he'd never done before. He remembered nearly breaking his fist against the wall. Over and over. His mom called his aunt Sophie in Colorado and cried into the phone. She announced the Boulder summer plan the next morning.

"Your room's all done," Sophie said, breezing in. She flipped her long black braid over her shoulder and linked an arm with his. Oliver nearly choked. She smelled like flowers. And lemons. And herbs. She seemed so *eager* to have him here. He knew he should be grateful and all. Instead, he was annoyed.

His mom moved on to Sophie. "Thank you so much," she said, hugging her sister. "For getting him the internship. For everything."

The tech internship that Sophie had gotten him was what had ultimately convinced Oliver to come out here. So he could put that last episode with Lilly out of his mind. So he could "cool off" and "settle down." So he could put the job on his college applications and try to get into a decent school so he could . . . he didn't really know what. Or why.

"I'm happy to have him," Sophie said, her feather earrings brushing his mom's shoulder. Oliver's mom always said that Sophie got all the creative genes. That Sophie was the only one genetically capable of having fun in the family. He suspected his mom had always envied her. "And when you get home, don't let Bill yell at you anymore."

"I'll try. I canceled that stupid dinner party. I had a deposition. A huge trial coming up. What was I going to do? *That's* the last straw?"

Sophie kept hugging Oliver's mom. Didn't say anything.

Finally, his mom pulled away and flashed Oliver a goodbye smile. Like he was a baton she'd handed off to the next racer. Like the next leg wasn't up to her. Like she wanted to forget this last part of the race altogether. She teetered out the door and down the sidewalk on her high heels.

"Mom," Oliver called after her, holding the door open. She

stopped and looked back. Held a hand over her eyes to see her son better. The sun was so bright, the sky so blistering blue in Boulder. To Oliver, it felt like a different sun, a different sky. "Tell Lilly I'm sorry."

His mom looked lost for a second. "I don't think I should say anything about . . . It's too soon, I—"

"For leaving. Just tell her I'm sorry for leaving."

Oliver could tell it made her sad. What he said. Really, really sad. She nodded and then headed for the car. The driver held the back passenger door open, and his mom checked her cell as she slid in. If she looked back or waved one more time, Oliver couldn't see it. The windows were tinted.

The car disappeared around the corner, and he stepped outside. A mountain range loomed in the skyline above the town. As he squinted at the craggy peaks, he felt like he was on some hostile planet. And his sister was back on earth. He panicked then, breathed too fast. He knew it was more than the thin mountain air. It was the light-years between his sister and him. Light-years.

He tried to calm down, and his fingers itched for his phone. He'd downloaded a mountain locator app before he flew here, so he held his phone up to the mountains and got a result: the Flatirons. It said he was looking at the "small foothills of the Rocky Mountains."

Small?

The bigger Rockies were farther off in the distance, covered by clouds. The screen loaded with names of peaks like Green and Bear. The only other time he'd visited Sophie in Boulder was when he was six years old. He didn't remember the mountains looking so huge. So empty. He thought about home. Riding the L every day. The clacking trains. The skyscrapers. The pavement and the people and the noise. There was hardly any traffic around Sophie's house. Not by Chicago standards, anyway. He watched three cars rumble down the street. He noticed their tags, one by one:

PHD-390
PHD-723
MPO-147

Then it was quiet again. All he could hear was the wind.

He'd read that Boulder had the highest PhDs per capita in the country. But did they all have to be asshats and put it on their license plates?

He missed Chicago.

He went back inside.

"You okay?" Sophie asked. She was at the stove. "I'm making chai. Want some?"

"No, thanks," he said. "And why does everybody have to brag that they have a PhD here?"

"What?"

"License plates. I saw two in a row with 'PHD' on them."

Sophie smiled as a spicy smell filled the condo. The sun beat through the colored cloth squares of the prayer flags in the window. "They're not bragging. That's just how Colorado tags are. Three letters. Three numbers. Doesn't mean anything." She stirred her tea. "But the town is *full* of smart people. It's a little intimidating."

Oliver shrugged and flopped onto Sophie's couch. Everything felt so neat in the apartment. Oliver couldn't decide if he liked it or if it was creepy, but everything was . . . peaceful or something. There was a big pot of bamboo in one corner; water tinkled over a small stone fountain in another. The sofa was white. The big chair was white. Bookshelves were dotted with little black bowls full of moss and smooth rocks. On the back wall, there was a simple wooden table that kind of looked like an altar. On it, there was a two-foot white stone Buddha statue. A little red bowl of sand with a single stick of incense jutting out. A tall, skinny vase with a single white flower. And a framed white sign that read in curly, thick black letters:

ALL WE WANT IS TO WAKE UP.

Oliver had no idea what that meant. He read it again.

Does Sophie have a hard time staying awake? And even if she does, why does she need an altar dedicated to not falling asleep?

Super weird.

A text came in then, and he hoped it was his mom. He wanted her to say that she was turning the driver around, that she was coming to get him—that this whole Boulder summer plan was off.

And it was from his mom. But it didn't say any of that.

It was a warning. A really annoying Mom Warning:

Be a good houseguest.

4

ESSA

After dropping her mom at Pure Buds, Essa made her way up Pearl Street toward Above the Clouds. If a carnival and a windstorm had a baby, it would be this store. It had been her favorite since she was a kid. Kites of all shapes and sizes hung from every inch of the ceiling. The center of the store was a jumble: marbles, meditation stones, mini catapults, wooden labyrinths. Zodiac games to guide your love life. Bags of runes to tell your fortune. And a million toys and trinkets to keep you occupied in the meantime.

But as she got closer to the shop, she realized something was wrong: the windows were dark. The OPEN sign was flipped to CLOSED.

Dammit, Micah.

He was a rising sophomore at the University of Colorado and was *supposed* to open today. He hadn't even called to let her know he wasn't going to make it. He was typically on top of things, but he hadn't been himself the last few months. He was always late. Frazzled. Unfocused.

She peered inside. Even in the darkness, she could see the kites hanging from the ceiling. A green dragon kite in the back breathed bright orange canvas fire; his yellow spiked tail swayed under the air conditioning vent. Next to him hung a toad with a long fluttering tongue, then a princess, a train, a caterpillar. The back row of kites that hung over the cash register were the boring ones. One-dimensional triangles and simple boxy shapes. But she loved even those. For their simplicity. For how they refused to try to be cool.

She pulled a wad of keys out of her bag and opened the door. The bells above it jingled like mad, and a gust of incoming air sent the kites fluttering and pulling against their anchored strings. Wind chimes in the middle of the store clanged all at once; Japanese paper lanterns rocked and bumped against one another like people in a crowd. She stepped inside, flipped the sign to OPEN.

She hated opening. It was always crazy dark, and the light switches were way in the back in the storage room. She took a deep breath and sped through the store. She rounded the rack of juggling sticks, and her shoulder brushed against a stash of peacock feathers that arched out of a large vase. But then she stopped. Under the dragon kite. He seemed to be hanging crooked, his diamond-shaped eyes looking straight at her. And he was lower than he should be.

Did someone take him down yesterday?

A tickle ran along the back of her neck like the end of a kite string sliding along her skin. She passed the cash register and the wall of kite supplies. Everything there looked just like she left it. The spools of creamy string were all in their places. As were the dowel rods, bottles of glue, and reams of canvas for do-it-yourselfers. The wind socks on the back wall were all in order. They hung still and lifeless on the end of long sticks: flags and fish and wildflowers like Colorado columbine.

Then she heard a noise. A *thump*. She froze.

"Hello?" she asked.

Silence.

She scolded herself: *Don't be stupid. Who would break into a kite store?* Her heart raced as she pushed against the swinging door to the storage room and ran past overflowing shelves. Out of breath, she reached for the light switches and flipped all three at once. She pinched her eyes shut as the buzz of electricity filled the shop. *One. Two. Three.* It always took a minute for the cold fluorescent lights to heat up and turn on.

The storage room flooded with light, and she opened her eyes. No one was there. In the storage room, at least. She grabbed the feather duster hanging on a nail, thinking she could use the stick end as a weapon, and slowly tiptoed out to the main shop floor. She wound her way through the various displays, making sure everything was in place.

It was all fine. No one was there.

She inhaled and exhaled a few times. Slowly letting the adrenaline in her veins drain away. Since she had the duster, she started dusting. It was like a circus in the middle of the store. She started with the bins of rubber bouncy balls made with swirls of color and glitter. Then the cartons of tiny plastic animals, each no bigger than a penny. She dusted the labels above each bin: *Mini-Unicorns, Mini-Pigs, Mini-Bison, Mini-Butterflies.* And on and on. She loved them all. They made her want to take hand-fuls, line her windowsills, line her locker. She'd collected almost every one, and she worried it was childish. She was seventeen years old, not ten. But she just—

"Boo."

She jumped. Her heart crashed out of her chest as she spun around.

"Did I scare you?"

Standing there, with long, stringy blonde hair and lips stained blue from a lollipop, was her nine-year-old sister.

"*Dammit,* Puck." Essa picked up a Mini-Octopus and zinged her sister with it. Puck smiled and squealed, took off running. Essa chased after her. Puck rounded the bin of Mini-Monkeys and then madly grabbed a wind-sock fish that was stuck to the end of a long stick. She wielded it like a sword.

"Aren't you supposed to be at play practice?" Essa swatted at her with the feather duster, but Puck deftly blocked her with the fish. "And how did I not hear you come in? You're wearing *tap shoes.*"

"I'm sneaky." Puck giggled. The shoes broke Essa's heart; Puck found them at Goodwill, but didn't take tap lessons. They couldn't afford them. "And Mrs. Connelly's sick," Puck said. "The whole day of drama camp is canceled. I walked over."

Essa felt a tug in her chest at the mention of Mrs. Connelly's name. She'd let Puck enroll in the camp for free. "You're supposed to call me when that happens," Essa groaned. She spun around and swatted at Puck again with the duster. But Puck was too quick for her. She stealthily tapped sideways and poked Essa in the stomach with the wind-sock stick.

"Okay, okay," Essa said. She held the duster above her head. "I'll surrender if you tell me how you got in here."

Puck lit up with victory. "The little storage room window. If you tap on it just right, it pops open." As Puck's blue eyes sparkled, it occurred to Essa that her sister was just like one of the tiny plastic animals in the bins—so small, so perfect, so colorful; Essa wanted to hold her in her hand. She wanted to carry Puck around in her pocket. Always.

"That's technically breaking and entering, you know."

"Sorry," Puck whined. But it was unconvincing. "Can I?" She pointed to the storage room.

Essa sighed. "Go ahead." Puck took off running, her shoes tapping the whole way, and disappeared behind the swinging door.

A truth that embarrassed them: Essa and Puck didn't have a computer at their house. Their mom liked to be "off the grid" as much as possible. Which Essa thought was fine for her mom, because all she did was bake weed edibles in a pot shop and listen to old Grateful Dead shows in her free time. But Essa and her sister were *real people*. And real people needed the Internet. But Essa didn't want to spend all her paychecks from the store on a data plan, so that meant they only got to surf the Net when they were at school, at a friend's house, or at the computer that lived in the kite store storage room. Which is why Puck always wanted to go in there.

Two customers walked in. Essa dealt with the white-haired lady first. "Can I help you?"

"I'm looking for a kite for my granddaughter," the woman said. She was wearing dark blue jeans that had actually been ironed. A crease ran up the center of both pant legs.

"How about this castle kite?" Essa pointed up to a boxy gray kite above her. The woman didn't know it, but Essa was gently steering her away from gender stereotyping. "It even has little flags that run along the top of the tower. She'll love it."

"Well . . ." The woman's eyes went dark. She hated it.

"How about this awesome snake kite?" Essa was pointing again. And sounding way too eager. "He even has fangs."

The woman wandered across the floor, looking up. Then she stopped. "I'll take that one."

It was a pink princess kite. Essa sighed and headed for the stepladder. At least she'd tried.

After Essa rang her up, she moved on to the middle-aged guy who was clicking around the store in his road-bike clip shoes. He was wearing super tight spandex bike shorts with the padding on the butt that made it look like he was wearing a diaper. His bike jersey had a giant sun and a beer mug on the back—the local Sunshine Brewery logo. To Essa, it felt like every third adult in Boulder was into locally made craft beer. She pegged this guy as a do-it-yourselfer right away.

"May I help you?" she asked.

"Yeah. How much is your canvas per yard? And your dowel rods?"

I knew it.

He told Essa he wanted to build a kite that looked like a giant bicycle wheel for his son, and he wanted the spokes to be wooden rods. Essa tried to explain the weight and balancing issues he'd have if he went that route, but he wasn't listening.

After he left, the customer flow died down. She headed to the back to pull Puck off the computer. She'd been on

it long enough. Essa pushed on the swinging door and saw
Puck sitting on the high stool in front of the screen. Just as
Essa stepped into the room, Puck quickly closed her browser
window.

"Hi," Puck said, spinning around. There were two empty lollipop wrappers on the desk. Now Puck's lips were not only blue,
but also red and green.

"What were you looking at?"

"Nothing," Puck said way too fast.

"You know the rules. Scoot over." Puck slid off the stool, and
Essa opened up the browser to see what the last window was. But
it opened to the Above the Clouds homepage. Essa hit the BACK
button. And got nothing. "How'd you do that?"

Puck shrugged.

"Seriously," Essa said. She gave Puck the Older Sister Eyes.
"You shouldn't be able to delete your browser history. I disabled
it. How'd you hide your last page?"

Puck twisted a chunk of her not-brushed-in-days hair around
a finger. "I don't know." She dragged out her answer in a high-
pitched, singsongy voice.

"Mom is going to be so mad if I tell her you're hiding stuff
again." Last year, Puck managed to buy a year's subscription to
a Candy of the Month club without a credit card. She'd gotten
busted when Essa found several five-pound boxes of candy in
Puck's room. And a letter from a collection agency in their
mailbox.

Puck's eyes pooled with tears. Essa suspected her little sister
was stalling. But still. The tears were real. "Mom won't care,"
Puck said. "She won't even notice. She's too busy making out
with half of Boulder. And you'll probably fall in love with Micah
any minute."

It was a low blow. Essa's chest filled with the falling feeling
she got whenever Puck was sad, like her heart was a mountain
climber who'd carelessly forgotten to clip in and had just slipped
over the side. Essa got off the stool and bent down so she was

face-to-face with Puck. She looked directly into her sister's eyes. They weren't sparkling anymore.

"No, I won't," Essa said. First of all, Micah was just a friend. Second, Essa didn't date. Ever. Puck knew this. "I'm here for you. Always." Puck glanced at the floor. "Look at me, Pucky." She did. "And no matter what Mom does, we'll be okay. You and me. We're solid. No matter what. Okay?"

"Promise?"

"Promise." Essa licked her thumb and tried to wipe some of the candy stain off Puck's face. It didn't work. Puck flinched and pulled away. But at least she was grinning a little.

"Then let me come with you sometime," Puck said. She was so sneaky. And using her Tiny Begging Voice. It was a killer. The closest thing to it Essa had ever heard was the sound a baby marmot makes when it crawls on top of a rock and calls for its mom. Essa nearly buckled every time Puck used it.

"No," Essa said firmly.

"Pretty please? I've been reading about it. All the orienteering stuff. I'm great with a compass. And survival. Did you know you can make a Band-Aid out of pine bark? I'd be a good teammate. You'll see."

Recently Puck had been begging to go on one of the wilderness orienteering treks with Essa's friends. They had to find their way from Point A to Point B in the backcountry with nothing but a topographic map and a compass.

"Absolutely not. It's too dangerous. Maybe when you're older."

A pout clouded Puck's face like a quick-moving summer storm. "Pretty please with sprinkles on top?"

"No. We go for three days. You can go on one of our day trips. Close to town."

"Meanie," Puck said. Then she stormed off.

But just before she made it through the storage room door, Essa remembered. "Hey. Seriously. What were you looking at on the computer?"

The sparkle returned to her sister's eyes. "Just a game. With kites. Really pretty kites. But you're too *old* to play it. You wouldn't understand. Maybe if you were *younger*." A devilish smile spread across Puck's face, and she ran off, leaving the door swinging in her wake.

5

OLIVER

"Hey, Sleeping Beauty."

Aunt Sophie was touching his shoulder. He was in the guest room. He'd come in here to unpack his stuff and ended up sprawled on the bed asleep. There was a long line of dried drool on the side of his face, and he tried to sit up, but couldn't; he was tangled in a blanket, and his left arm was completely asleep.

Sophie leaned in, flipping her braid over her shoulder. He closed his eyes as she kissed his cheek, her feather earrings tickling his nose. When he opened them again, he caught a view down her top and got an eyeful of middle-aged-aunt boob. Which was about the worst thing ever. Then he felt like a sick weirdo for even looking.

"I have a surprise for you," she said. "Wait here."

She disappeared down the hallway but came back a minute later and plopped something in his lap. At first, he thought it was a dark green football, but when he tried to pull it out of the folds of the blanket, it was hard. *Really* hard.

And then he saw a leg.

"Get it off!" he screamed. He backed up and tried to shove whatever the hell it was off the bed.

"Go easy," Sophie said. She swooped in and gently grabbed the green-legged football. She held it up. "Oliver, meet True. True, meet Oliver."

It was a turtle. He had mostly retreated into his shell, but he was peering at Oliver with his beady black eyes. All four scaly legs were moving on either side of Sophie's hand, like he was trying to air-paddle away from the reality of his life. Oliver didn't blame him.

"Oh," Oliver said, trying to act cool. "Hey, True."

Sophie pulled a hot pink ribbon out of her pocket. She gently put True on the floor and wrapped the ribbon around his shell, tying a large bow on top. "That's so you don't step on him," she said. Like it was a totally obvious thing that Oliver had seen a million times before.

"So he . . . roams the house?"

"Truth is everywhere," she said, flashing a thousand-kilowatt Boulder-sun smile. "And it's slow moving."

Oliver raised his eyebrows.

"He's a Buddhist," Sophie added.

She wrapped her legs like a pretzel underneath her, settling on the soft white fuzzy carpet. She patted the spot next to her, motioning for Oliver to come down and sit. He couldn't make his legs bend like hers did. It kind of creeped him out. But he slid off the bed and sat down. Legs straight.

They both watched as True the Buddhist Turtle slowly made a circle on the carpet, leaving a path of tiny little turtle shits the whole way. Oliver looked at his aunt, who remained completely unconcerned about what was happening to her carpet. She just lovingly smiled at the circling reptile. It was obvious to Oliver that his aunt was sweet and all, but still. He felt like the turtle taking a dump on the floor highlighted the magnitude of his mistake. *I have to get back to Lilly. I have to explain what I did. I have to make things right.*

Sophie left the room and came back with a rag. "Let's go check on dinner," she said as she cleaned up after True. She scooped him up and headed for the kitchen. Reluctantly, Oliver followed.

The minute he hit the hallway, he was whacked in the face with the scent of dinner. Which smelled roughly like a thousand boiling skunks. Sophie had covered the kitchen counter with an epic amount of crap. There were metal bins full of vegetables, glass bowls of spices, jars of chopped-up mystery items. She informed him that she didn't use plastic of any kind. That it was full of some evil chemical called BPA that acted like a hormone in the body. Oliver briefly wondered if the plastic soda bottles he frequently drank out of could explain the inordinate amount of time he spent thinking about sex. (Which he'd never had.) But he was pretty sure that was due to the fact that he was seventeen, not to the fact that he drank insane amounts of Mountain Dew.

"Smell this," Sophie said, waving a chunky brown stick in his face. "It's burdock root. It'll help your acne."

He put a hand to his bumpy face, which felt like it was hovering around five hundred degrees, scorched by humiliation. "Um, thanks?"

"Don't be embarrassed." She shredded the root into whatever horrible pot of horribleness she was cooking on the stovetop.

Easy for her to say. Her face didn't intermittently look like a crime scene. Then he remembered his mom's ominous warning: *be a good houseguest.* He told himself that he needed to be on his best behavior so he could get Sophie on his side and have her convince his mom to fly him home ASAP. "Can I, um, help set the table?"

"You're so sweet." She ruffled his hair. Which brought his scorched cheeks back. "But we eat on pillows here."

And they did. She pulled these giant pillows into the center of the living room, handed him a bowl of Steaming Organic Hell, and told him to sit.

He was so uncomfortable. And it wasn't just the pillows. Sophie started asking him questions. About his life. About Lilly. About the divorce. They didn't do this at his house—eating and talking about real stuff. His mom never cooked and usually wasn't home from her law firm until eight or nine o'clock on a good day. Even if they all miraculously ended up eating a meal together, they didn't actually *talk* about anything.

"Has it gotten worse? Since he filed?" Sophie was still on the divorce.

"Yeah." He didn't look up from his bowl.

"That must be hard."

Oliver shifted on his Dinner Pillow.

"The divorce," she continued. "And Lilly. And next year is senior year for you." She paused and looked him right in the eye. "I understand what happened, Oliver. You can't blame yourself forever—"

"Dinner was good," Oliver interrupted her with a lie.

She took the hint and changed the subject. She put her empty bowl on the carpet and started playing with one of her feather earrings. "Listen, I know I'm your boring old aunt, but I really, really want you to have an awesome summer here, okay? You deserve it. After . . . everything. So I have a surprise for you."

Oliver braced himself and expected her to pull out another reptile. A lizard named Lie. A snake named Bullshit.

Oliver, meet Bullshit. Bullshit, meet Oliver.

"I didn't get you an internship at a startup, like I promised your mom. I got you a job. A paying one."

Now Oliver was listening.

"Where?"

"At a really cool shop in the middle of Boulder," she said. "On Pearl Street. Which is sort of like the social heart of things."

Oliver scooted off his pillow, careful to make sure he didn't see a pink-beribboned turtle anywhere nearby. Or a ring of turtle turds. "What's the shop?"

"My friend owns it. It's a kite store. Above the Clouds."

"A *kite store?*" he asked. Sophie nodded and smiled like she had just delivered the greatest news he'd ever heard. "I can't work at a *kite store*. I was supposed to do a tech thing. So I could put it on my college app—"

"I know, I know. But kites sort of take technology . . . physics? Engineering? I mean, you have to know how to build them so they fly right."

"Um, no," Oliver said. "Just, no. Gluing kites together is *not* a tech internship."

"I'm worried, Oliver." Sophie stopped fiddling with her earring and leaned in a little. Her eyes looked watery. "I think you need some *fun*. Some *lightness*. You know? With all you've been through . . ."

Oh, right. Because the cure for the nervous breakdown I'm pretty sure I had before I left Chicago is to become a kite salesman.

Sophie stood and held out a hand to help him up. "And there are kids your age who work there. Including girls. Very. Cute. Boulder girls." She sported another *isn't this great* smile.

Chicago Oliver. With a Boulder girl.

Yeah, right.

6

ESSA

After Puck and Essa got home from Above the Clouds, they waited in dread for Mom's new guy to show. He didn't. Their mom claimed he got caught up at work and couldn't make it. The details she gave about his supposed employment were *extremely* vague. Something about weed yoga studios. How if you do yoga high, you have all sorts of realizations.

Or something.

Essa didn't bother to ask for clarification. She and Puck were happy to eat frozen pizza and watch TV.

Around one in the morning, a tap on Essa's bedroom door woke her. She lifted one eyelid. Her door was open just a crack, a slice of yellow light cutting through her room. She sat up.

"Wake up. I think that guy is here." It was a whisper. Essa reached for the lamp and clicked it on. Puck crawled onto the end of the bed, her red pajama pants bunched around her legs. Her blonde hair was pulled back in a knotted, messy bun. She looked excited, like she'd just started a Spy Club, and she was sending them on their first mission.

"Who?" Essa asked, rubbing her eyes.

"I think it's the new guy who was supposed to come for dinner. Come see."

She clambered over the bedspread and took Essa's hand. Puck's was soft and warm and small. Essa gripped it gently and followed her little sister down the hall toward the living room, her own too-long pajama pants dragging the floor. She heard voices, so she stopped and peered around the corner. It was a good thing Essa wasn't wearing her favorite old nightgown that had become half see-through because there was a guy sitting cross-legged on the floor. A middle-aged guy in ripped-up jeans and a gauzy linen shirt. He and Essa's mom were next to each other on the ratty orange carpet. Her mom was leaning against the couch, and he was handing her something.

"Dried chan seeds," he said. "Sacred. From Costa Rica. They ward off evil spirits. And relieve constipation."

"Really?" her mom asked, popping a few in her mouth. She chewed thoughtfully. Then wrinkled her nose. "They're not very good."

Essa could tell Puck was trying to keep it together at the mention of constipation, but she lost it. Her shoulders started shaking, and she made it another five seconds until her giggles exploded.

"Girls?" They were busted. Essa kept Puck close to her as they emerged into the living room.

"Hey there," said Seed Guy.

"Hello," Essa said. He glanced at Essa, but then looked back to Puck.

"Girls, this is Ronnie," their mom said. "Ronnie, that's Puck and Essa." She pointed to them one at a time.

Ronnie reached for the bowl of seeds again. "You want one?" he asked as he held the bowl in Puck's direction. He shook it a little, and the seeds rustled together. Before Essa could react, Puck was gone from her grip, like a slippery little ghost. She was at his side, taking a few seeds out of the bowl.

"No, Puck," Essa blurted out. She stepped forward. "Don't eat that."

"Relax, Essa," her mom said slowly. She tucked a stray dreadlock behind her ear. "They're just *seeds*. They're healthy. They don't mess you up or anything. They're like flax. Or chia. That I put in our bread."

Puck popped a few into her mouth.

"Ronnie is an expert on seeds," her mom went on with a dreamy look her in eye. Ronnie watched Puck chew. He smiled as the seeds crunched and popped in her mouth. Essa hated his smile. It was fake somehow. Like it was a smile on the outside but something totally different on the inside. Then again, she hated all her mom's boyfriends.

"I studied with a shaman in Costa Rica," he said. "He taught me about all the seeds there. Seeds are power, you know. If you have seeds, you have everything. You have the world." His dirty blond hair fell in his eyes a little. But he wasn't looking at Essa. He was still looking at Puck. "Do you know what that is? A shaman?"

Essa grabbed Puck's arm and pulled her close. "Yeah, it's like a medicine man," Essa answered. "We've gotta go back to bed."

"Bummer," he said, shrugging.

Before Puck could do or say anything else, Essa shepherded her down the hallway and into her bedroom. Essa flipped on the overhead light and closed the door behind them. She pressed her back against the cool wooden door, relieved to be away from the whole situation. "Ugh," she grunted. "Creepy guy. Right?"

Puck flopped onto her bed and stared at the ceiling. Essa looked at the kites Puck had hung there: a monarch butterfly, a soaring heron, an owl, a pirate ship. The owl was blue and yellow with gigantic white eyes. Instead of wise and chill, he looked spooked. Sort of shocked or terrified, like he'd seen something horrible that had silenced his hoot.

"I don't know," Puck said, shrugging. "Seems okay to me. The seeds were nasty, though." She reached for a cup of bright red Kool-Aid by her bed—which she wasn't supposed to have so late at night—and gulped it down. Essa furrowed her brow in disapproval, and Puck gave her a super innocent, giant red Kool-Aid grin.

"You realize you get everything you want?" Essa asked. "You get that, right?"

Puck shrugged like she didn't agree, but maintained her stained-lip smile. She leaned over the side of her bed and pulled something out from underneath it. She sat up and started fiddling with it in her lap. Essa took a step closer to see what she was holding. It was a Puzzle Kite, Puck's favorite thing from Above the Clouds. It was a honey-colored wooden box that functioned as a puzzle. The outside was covered with little pieces of wood that had to be moved around just right until the box snapped open. Inside was a kite to put together. Every puzzle and every kite was different, and the shop had twenty-five Puzzle Kites in all. But they were pricey. Like, fifty bucks a pop.

"Did you take this from the store?" Essa asked. She sat down on the bed next to Puck. "Seriously, you're going to get me fired."

"I'm just *borrowing* it," Puck said, her hands sliding over the wooden puzzle pieces. They gently clicked as she shifted them into place. Her bright red tongue snuck out the side of her mouth as she concentrated. "I've been telling Mom forever that I wanted a new one. She never listens."

Her little hands danced over the puzzle pieces like ballerinas. She was good at these. She was good at everything. The walls of her room were loaded with awards and certificates that proved it. Spelling bee champion two years in a row. First place in the reading challenge. First place at the social studies fair for her project on Eastern religions. "I'll tell Jan to take it out of my next paycheck," Essa sighed. "But you have to pay me back. By helping me at the store. Okay?"

Puck was still laser-focused on the box. "I wonder what this one will be," she said. Her tongue shifted to the other side of her mouth. "I'm hoping it's the horse kite. I *really* want the horse."

Essa kicked her legs onto the bed and stretched out on her back. After a few more pieces clicked into place, Puck stopped fiddling with the puzzle box and curled up next to her big sister. They snuggled close on top of her lumpy purple comforter.

"Puck?" Essa asked. A strand of Puck's hair had fallen out of her bun. Essa twirled it around one of her fingers. She breathed in Puck's scent. She always smelled like candy. Like gummy bears. Like cherry lollipops. "Don't keep secrets, okay? Like the computer today. And taking the Puzzle Kite." Essa twirled her sister's hair. And twirled and twirled. "Tell me stuff. Tell me everything. Every little thing. I want to know. Okay?"

Puck didn't say anything at first. But finally, "Okay."

"Promise?"

"Let me come with you to the woods this weekend?" Puck was using the baby marmot squeak again. She never gave up. On anything.

"No. But you have to promise to tell me everything anyway."

Puck exhaled a tiny puff of a sigh and pressed a little closer against Essa, curling into a ball and gently nodding against her big sister's chest.

June 8

7

OLIVER

"What have you done today?"

It was 3 P.M., and Sophie had just arrived home from her afternoon yoga class. She raised the blinds. The too-bright sun poured into the room, highlighting the fact that Oliver was sprawled on the sofa with a (now empty) bag of veggie chips, a few cans of "all natural" ginger ale he found in the fridge, and his cell phone. Which was about a thousand degrees in his hand because he'd been streaming videos on it. And playing games with his friends back in Chicago. All day. For three days. He'd also been waiting for his mom to tell him Lilly was stable enough for a phone call. So far, she wasn't.

He blinked in the painful light. And shrugged. "Stuff."

"Have you even been outside? On the trail I told you about?" She set a cloth bag of groceries on the kitchen table and lit a stick of incense.

Oliver shook his head.

"You're in the *Rocky Mountains*," she continued. She pointed out the window, past the incense smoke that was snaking into the air. There was a trail right across the street and a winding dirt path that disappeared into wide-open nothingness at the foot of the Flatirons. He knew he was supposed to want to get out there, like he was in a granola bar commercial, but something about the emptiness was creepy. He liked it better inside. Always had.

"In Boulder, people like to go *outside*. It's good for you," she said as if she'd just read his mind. She took what appeared to be several hundred thousand vegetables out of her Whole Foods bag and put them into their respective bins in the refrigerator.

"I'm not really a nature-type guy." Oliver turned up one of the ginger ale cans, and a few last burning drops of ginger landed on his tongue. "And this stuff sucks."

Sophie rolled her eyes. "After I get these put away, we're going out. Down to Pearl Street. I'll introduce you at the kite store."

He sat up. The veggie chip bag crinkled underneath him, and the empty cans of ginger ale tumbled onto the white carpet. "About that," he said. "I was thinking. I don't think I really want to. You know. Work there."

"You were thinking, huh?" Her voice was muffled. She was still bent over a vegetable bin, her head fully in the refrigerator.

"Yeah. That maybe I should just—"

"There's a saying." She straightened up, returned to the cloth bag, and pulled out a vegetable that looked like a large, bloated comma. Oliver guessed it was an eggplant. Or maybe an exotic squash that had magical healing powers. She waved it in the air as she talked. "You can't *think* your way into happiness. You have to *act* your way there." She turned and tossed the shiny purple comma into the fridge.

"Huh?"

She sighed. "It means we're taking action. We're going out. And please take a shower. It smells like teenager in here."

How she could smell *anything* over the incense haze that was rapidly blurring Oliver's vision was beyond him. But he knew he'd be a fool to stand behind the argument that he didn't stink.

"Okay," he said, tossing the blanket on the floor. "I'll shower. And go to Pearl Street. But that's it. No kite stores, okay?"

Sophie grinned, but didn't say a word.

● ● ●

Oliver found the People of Boulder. They were teeming down Pearl Street. All kinds. He expected to see a mass of all-natural types like his aunt, but he didn't. He felt like a lot of these people could be straight out of Chicago neighborhoods. He saw a group of mainstream girls in huge sunglasses who were very Lincoln Park. Older people who looked stuck-up and rich. Kind of Gold Coast. A high school artsy type pushed past him, carrying a wooden case with paintbrushes sticking out. And people decked out in college swag dotted the crowd. University of Colorado. Regis. Naropa U.

"What's Naropa?" he asked Sophie. He pointed to a guy in jeans and a T-shirt: *Too Zen to Deal With Your Bullshit. Naropa U.*

"Buddhist university a few blocks from here." She was eyeing a pile of crusty handmade soaps in a shop window. "A lot of famous writers hang around there. They've got the Jack Kerouac School of Disembodied Poetics."

"Disembodied poetics?"

"They take a contemplative approach," she said. Which helped Oliver understand exactly zero. Sophie moved past the soap shop, and they walked along the wide brick street. "You into poetry?"

"No way," he said.

"You sure?" She looked at Oliver like she knew something about him that he didn't.

"Yep. Real sure."

Like his mom, he hated poetry. It was one of the first things Lilly started doing that had given them a clue something wasn't right. She showed Oliver her first poem when she was sixteen. It made no sense. He was fourteen at the time, so it would be logical for it to be over his head, but it wasn't an age gap in comprehension levels that was the problem. The poem actually made no sense. As in, the words didn't go together in any conceivable way. It was gibberish. Word salad. She explained it to Oliver, which only made it worse; he could tell she understood it perfectly. He showed his mom, and she chalked it up to his sister being in a confusing teen phase.

She was wrong. Way wrong.

Sophie shrugged. "It's a shame. There are amazing poets around here."

They kept walking. They passed all sorts of stores: ice cream, falafel, yoga gear, handmade books, Native American art. There were street performers, too. Everywhere. A barefoot dude in a ratty red blazer played a fiddle. He smiled and bounced as he sang. He looked out of it, but also like the most intensely stoked human being Oliver had ever seen. He stared. He couldn't help it.

A girl jumped in front of him, blocking his view of the fiddle guy. She was holding a ratty cardboard sign, FREE HUGS. Her sequin pants were too long; they were frayed and dragged the ground. And her hair was down to her butt. She paused, looked in Oliver's eyes, asking. He shrugged. And she hugged him.

"Love," she said as he was enveloped in her cloud of BO and flowers. Except she held him too long. Her hips pressed into his, and his face started the burning thing again.

"Let's go, Oliver," Sophie said like she was singing it. She tugged on Oliver's arm and quickly escorted him away. He turned and glanced back, but the girl wasn't looking. She was staring up into a giant tree in the middle of the plaza. Her eyes were wide, like she had seen the most amazing thing in the branches. A giant bird. An angel. A miracle.

Oliver looked.

And saw leaves.

"Check your wallet," Sophie said. "Some are out for love. Some are out for your debit card."

He slapped a hand against his back pocket and thankfully, his wallet was there. "People just . . . hug people like that?" he asked. "Is that normal?"

"Welcome to the People's Republic of Boulder," Sophie said. "It's an emotive place."

Oliver shook his head and looked down the street, checking for more Random Huggers headed his way. He didn't see any, but something else caught his eye. In a row of shop windows filled with boring sage green and beige, one store was blaring with bright colors. It was all reds and blues and yellows. He went closer. And stopped in front of the store.

It was full of kites.

If he had seen this store when he was ten, he would've freaked out. And begged to move to Boulder so he could go there every day. Below the kites, there was endless stuff: plastic dragons, remote-controlled snakes, pirate map puzzles in bottles, solar-powered waving Einsteins. Hover racers, rocket launchers, mini catapults.

But still, it was a *kite store*. And he was seventeen—not ten.

Sophie stood next to him with a signature *I told you so* smile.

"I'm just going in," he said. "Don't introduce me or anything. Okay?"

"Sure." The smile was still there.

"I'm serious." He tried to put emphasis on the word *serious*, hoping to get his point across. He didn't like the way Sophie kept looking at him like he was her project for the summer. Like she was super confident that she could fix something he didn't even know was broken.

He opened the door and headed straight for the hover racers. He was checking out the most expensive one when he heard someone laugh. A little girl.

He turned. She was eight or so. She was peeking around the display of dragon figurines, and she had a red lollipop in her hand. "Hello," she said. She was still giggling.

"Hello."

She had this long, tangled blonde hair, and her shoes were black and shiny like little tap shoes. Her blue eyes practically glowed in the store light, and Oliver's throat felt tight. She was so small. So cute. She reminded him of old photos of Lilly. When he was way younger and so was she. When they felt like pirates in the same crew. When he'd never heard the words "schizophrenic" or "paranoid delusions" or "for life."

"I have a secret to tell you." The girl rounded the dragon shelves and came closer, her shoes clicking with each step. They *were* tap shoes.

He bent down. "Okay," he said. "Is it a secret about the dragons?"

"No," she said. "But you know which one is my favorite?"

He surveyed the shelves and took a guess. "Him?" He pointed to the bright orange one.

"Nope," she said. She pointed to a large blue dragon with her lollipop. "*Her.*"

Oliver walked over and picked up the dragon. It was about five inches tall and painted a flaming hot blue. And it had these awesomely huge wings that were wide open. "He—I mean she—looks pretty cool . . ."

"Her name is Badass."

"Badass the Dragon?"

She nodded. "And you want to know the secret?"

"Sure."

"Your fly is open." Her giggles erupted, and she took off running, filling the store with the sound of rapid taps.

Oliver looked down. She was right. His fly was gaping open. Roughly a third of him died of embarrassment as he zipped up and prayed that no one—

"Sorry about that."

It was a girl. But not the little one from before. This was a *girl* girl. In a long, green sundress. She had a name tag—*Essa*—pinned just beside her right boob. Her lacy black bra was showing.

And Oliver's face was five thousand degrees.

"My sister Puck," she said. "She *loves* telling customers when their flies are open. Or when there's toilet paper stuck to their shoes. Stuff like that."

A tattoo was just below her collarbone. It was simple. One

word: *SANCTUARY*. With a single blade of green grass beside it. She caught Oliver looking.

"It's from my favorite . . . story," she said. She gently tapped it, like she was touching a memory. Or maybe a dream. "Hard to explain."

Oliver's first thought: *She seems half-annoying. A carefree kite girl with zero problems and an insanely cute—and perfectly healthy—little sister in tow.*

Must be nice.

But still, a hundred questions slammed into his head. He wanted to ask her what it was like to live in Boulder. What she did on the weekends. Why the word *SANCTUARY* was beside a blade of grass. Why it was hard to explain. Why he felt like he could stare at her for ten days straight without food or water. But all he could manage was:

"Cool."

Much to his horror, Sophie joined them. She leaned in and read Essa's name tag. "Essa, I'm Sophie, and this is my nephew Oliver from Illinois. I talked to Jan about hiring him for the summer?"

Oliver glared at Sophie as the temperature of his face doubled to a scorching ten thousand degrees. He was pretty sure he could melt metal on it. "Um, I'm stuck here for the summer," he blurted out. "But I don't really think I—"

"You're *stuck* here?" Essa cut him off. Her eyebrows went up. "From Illinois? Because *that's* such a badass place."

Now he knew where her little sister got her word choices.

"I didn't mean it like that." Oliver absentmindedly grabbed a Mini-Penguin out of a bin and started fiddling with its little arms. "I'm just used to a real city . . . I mean, where there's real stuff to do." Essa looked even more pissed. And he didn't even understand what was coming out of his mouth. He was talking like he was some dude who spent all his time clubbing every other night in Chicago. Or previewing the latest exhibit at the Art Institute. Mostly he played video games in his room.

So shut up, Oliver. Shut. The fuck. Up.

Essa rolled her eyes and tucked a strand of her long brown hair into the butterfly clip just above her right ear. "The penguins are twenty-five cents. And my boss Jan will be in tomorrow. You can talk to her about working here. But I really don't think we need any more help."

Other than the fact that she seemed like a carefree Boulder kite girl, one thing was inescapably obvious:

She hates me.

"Can you at least tell her I stopped by?"

Oliver was 99 percent sure that he'd actually said this out loud, and he was 100 percent confused by it. He was now begging the Boulder girl who hated him to help him get a job she clearly didn't want him to have and which he didn't even want. It was like his awkwardness was going through some process of rapid cell division and multiplying at an unstoppable rate.

"Sure. I'll tell her," Essa said, unconvincingly and most likely out of sympathy. Then she bailed. And in her wake, Oliver smelled coconuts. And something he couldn't place. Something spicy, like Sophie's incense. But instead of choking on it, he caught himself sucking in a deep breath, wanting more. Like a maniac.

Maniac.

He reminded himself that he shouldn't use that word. That's what he called his sister that night. But really, at this moment, he felt like he was the one who deserved that title.

"That didn't go so well," Sophie said, crinkling her forehead.

"Why'd you say *Illinois*?" he hissed, tossing the Mini-Penguin in with the Mini-Monkeys. "Say, *Chicago*."

He headed for the door. But just before he reached it, he caught Puck out of the corner of his eye. She had this sneaky smile going, and she was waving at him. It kind of killed him.

He half-smiled. And waved back.

Sophie followed him out as he pushed into the Pearl Street crowd. His smile vanished as Sophie walked next to him.

She's so annoying.

"I'm sorry," she said. "I'm not a mom. I'm not very good at this. I shouldn't have pushed you to take the job. It's just . . . I think what happened with Lilly happened because you were pushed beyond your limit. You need some fun, you know? Some normalcy. I just *so* want you to have a great summer."

She played with the end of her long braid as they walked, and she looked genuinely bummed. Now Oliver felt bad for making her feel bad. On top of making Essa feel bad. Plus, he hated thinking about that last night with Lilly. Hated.

"Am I a horrible person?" he asked.

Sophie looked at him like she was about to deliver the most serious news. "Absolutely not." Her feather earrings swayed in the breeze. She kept her eyes directly on his. "Believe me?"

"No."

"Well, can you believe that I believe you're not horrible?"

Oliver didn't respond.

"Well," she urged. "Can you?"

"I guess so . . ."

"Good. That's a start."

She took his arm and guided him toward the ice cream shop. A girl passed in front of them in a green dress like Essa's. And he thought about Essa's tattoo. That word: *SANCTUARY*. The blade of grass. He thought about how lucky she was to have her little sister following her around at work— happy, grinning, eating lollipops. He was envious. Sick with it, actually.

"I'm going to get two scoops," Sophie announced as they entered the ice cream place. "What do you want?"

Oliver looked at the menu. But he couldn't focus; he couldn't even read the flavors. He looked over his shoulder toward the kite shop. Then he looked back at Sophie, who was waiting for his answer. "I want to work at the kite store," he said.

"Done," Sophie said, pulling out her cell phone. Oliver didn't even know she had one; he hadn't seen her use it even once.

Her fingers pecked out a message on the screen. Then he heard several *bing*s. "Okay. I texted Jan."

Oliver looked at Sophie and wondered if he'd made a huge mistake. If really, he should be on a plane back to Chicago. Back at Lilly's side. Begging forgiveness.

"She says you can start tomorrow."

8

ESSA

"Aren't you going to leave a note?" Puck stared at Essa with her hands on her hips.

"Hang on," Essa said. "I'm counting." Dollar bills flitted through her fingers as she tried to keep track. This was the routine at the end of a shift: counting the money in the register before handing it over to the next person. Puck stood in Essa's peripheral vision like a broken stoplight. Blinking, blinking, blinking. She was going to make it hard for Essa to get through.

"Well?" Puck asked.

"What note? What are you talking about?" Essa slid the register closed with her hip. She loved the sound of the shimmying coins as the drawer moved, how a bell rang when it shut. *Shimmy. Clink. Bing!*

"A note about *him*," Puck groaned. "For Jan. That he wants to work here."

"Uh-oh. Who's *him*?" It was Micah. Who had the next shift. And was late.

"You're late." Essa worried this obvious point would go unnoticed if she didn't point it out. "Which is happening a *lot* lately."

"Sorry." He ran a hand through his super-bushy black hair. He got his perfect complexion from his gorgeous Thai mother and his penchant for weird haircuts from his Swedish father. His mom used to come into the store all time. She had this shiny jet-black hair, cherry-red lipstick, and clothes that always swished when she walked. She was charming, too.

Like mother, like son.

"It's totally and completely different when you're in college. You'll see. It's, like, *real shit* happens," he said.

Or not.

His claim sounded dubious at best. "Like what?" Essa asked. "Give me one example of real . . . things." She nodded her head toward Puck, silently reminding Micah to tone down the language.

"How about the fact that by tomorrow, I have to figure out what the hell *The Allegory of the Cave* is for my summer philosophy class?" He tossed his messenger bag onto the counter.

Essa wrinkled her brow. "The what?"

"The *Allegory of the Cave*. It's in Plato's *Republic*. Don't even get me started." His huge head of hair shook as he spoke; his cheeks flushed a little red. "It's about reality and education and, like, shadows or something. I don't even know. You know what they should sell in college bookstores for Philosophy 1010?"

"No," Essa said. Puck climbed on the stool behind the counter and sat between them. She looked up and seemed excited to hear Micah's answer about college school supplies.

"Sorry, Puckmeister," Micah said. "You can't hear this one." He gently put his hands over her ears. "A fucking helmet," he said over her head. "So you can strap it on and keep your mind from *exploding* with this shit." He gently pulled his hands away from Puck's head. "Sorry, kiddo. Adult concepts. You understand."

Micah's University of Colorado Nalgene bottle rolled out of his bag on the counter and fell to the floor with a loud crack. He bent down to pick it up, the band of his plaid boxers peeking above his jeans. "These bottles are invincible, you know. Can't break 'em." He triumphantly set the bottle on the counter in front of Puck. "And back to the original conversation. Who's *him?*"

"Oliver," Puck said, lighting up again. "He's from Illinois. And he might work here for the summer. He came in today. He's already my friend."

Micah looked at Essa, eyebrows raised. "Why don't they just close the entire state of Illinois and ship everyone here at once? Get it over with."

"Truth," Essa said. She felt like Colorado—or at least Boulder—was getting crowded. Big tech companies and startups kept expanding every year, attracting about a million people from Illinois and California. She felt like everything was starting to get jammed—the streets, the coffee shops, the bike paths. Even the hiking trails. There had actually been a line to get up a mountain trail last weekend in Chautauqua Park.

"But have hope." Essa scooped Puck's pink backpack off the floor. Puck had drawn wheels all over it with multicolored permanent markers. "Oliver didn't sound all that thrilled with the idea. Like he was way too cool for us. We may luck out, and he won't take the job."

Puck huffed and slid off the stool. She took her backpack from Essa. "I *like* him," she said, slipping the straps over her shoulders. "And you should leave a note for Jan. Tell her he was here at least."

"You never like boys. What's up with this one?"

Puck pursed her lips a little and looked thoughtful. She stared at the kites hanging above them, mulling it over. Finally she answered. "He took me seriously." Then she headed toward the door. Essa followed like she was the little sister in tow rather than the other way around.

"Took you seriously? About what?" Essa jumped ahead and pushed against the door, holding it open for Puck to go through. They were hit with a hot breeze off Pearl Street.

"About . . . my favorite dragon," Puck said, pausing. She looked at Essa with her Earnest Face. "He was paying attention."

Essa smiled. She loved the stuff her sister came up with. Puck was always *looking* at people. But not just looking; it was one layer above that. Like she always noticing what they noticed. It was no surprise that Puck was in the gifted program at school. Essa was convinced Puck's brain was already functioning at a college level. *Actually, scratch that,* she thought. If Micah was indicative of a brain functioning at a college level, then Puck was already in graduate school.

"Okay," Essa conceded. "Micah will leave a note for Jan. And tell her that a guy named Oliver stopped by for a job." She looked back at Micah. "Right?"

"Sure," Micah said.

"But Oliver's *my* boyfriend," Puck added. "Not yours. Don't get any ideas." She wagged a finger at her older sister.

"But wait," Micah said. "Is today Wednesday or Thursday?"

His level of distraction was getting worse by the day. Now he wasn't even sure what day it was. Essa was surprised he even made it to college classes, let alone remembered to do stuff like homework. "Thursday."

"Excellent. That makes tomorrow Friday night, a.k.a. Party Night. At the End of the World." His face lit up like he was already standing in the glow of the bonfire they always built at their party spot in the woods. "You in?"

Essa considered. The End of the World was a few miles up Boulder Canyon past an old, burnt-out stretch of forest where everybody from Boulder High partied. Well, everyone except Essa, who had a personal rule against actual "partying." She always took a giant Izze soda and slowly drank it all night. But still, she loved it there. The moonlight. The music. The view of Boulder Valley under the stars. She'd always assumed that once Micah went to college, he'd stop coming to high school parties. That hadn't happened.

"Yeah," she said. "I guess. But you can't get too messed up. I want to do orienteering on Sunday. Anish said he has a great place to drop us."

"Um, it's called 'Mountain Fugitive.' Plain old orienteering sounds so boring. And can we do it next weekend? I have a philosophy test on Monday. Gotta study." Micah's dark eyes glimmered. "And I don't get that messed up. Do I?"

"In the aggregate? Or recently?"

"Both."

"In the aggregate, no. Recently, yes."

"Just don't forget to leave a note for Jan about *Oliver*," Puck whined at Micah.

"You got it, kid." He plopped into the tall chair behind the register and kicked his legs onto the counter. He reached for a notepad. "I'll write her a note right now."

But as Essa ushered Puck out the door, she kept her eyes on Micah and silently mouthed:

Don't.

He nodded and dropped the notepad.

June 9

9

OLIVER

Oliver stood across from Jan, the kite shop owner and his new boss, in the storage room.

Maybe this won't be so bad, he told himself. *Maybe Essa is working today. But she hates me. And she's annoying.*

He looked at the storage room door.

Maybe she'll be here any minute.

Jan stood in front of the storage shelves, explaining stuff. Lots of stuff.

She jabbered on, and Oliver thought she looked pretty old, in that wise kind of way, with her super-short gray hair and deep wrinkles. She wore a long white top and a beaded necklace that seemed to be at least four feet long. Her eyes were a creepy blue, like some of the weird fortune-teller ladies out on Navy Pier in Chicago. He wondered if she was going to turn out to be all-knowing. Like some Yoda figure who talked in questions and blew his mind all the time.

"Goflyakite," she said. She pointed to a Mac on a desk in the corner. "That's the password. No spaces. Just don't look at porn, okay? Save that for your private time."

Okay. Not Yoda.

The Mac looked like a silver bird perched in a nest of empty lollipop wrappers. While Jan turned her back to him and rear-ranged a messy pile of kites, Oliver walked over to the computer, hoping to see where Jan kept the office candy stash. He didn't see any jars of lollipops. But sticking out of the mound of colorful wrappers, a small piece of plain white paper caught his eye. It was a note in a child's handwriting:

Puck + Ayden =

After the equal sign, there were drawings of wheels with spokes.

"These are the Edos," Jan continued by the shelves. She still had her back to him. "Most popular right now." She pointed to the next two piles. "Second bestseller is the Cosmic Dragon. And then the Batkites. But really, our bread and butter is the mail-order business." Jan pulled a kite out of the first stack, and the whole pile started to slide off the shelf. Oliver caught about five in his arms while a million more crashed to the floor.

"Edos?"

"Traditional Japanese kites. Edo's the old name for Tokyo." She held one up. Even though it was flat and in a clear wrapper, Oliver could tell it was awesome. It was a large rectangle kite covered with Japanese warriors and cranes and women in long robes. Everything was painted in reds and golds and purples.

Jan moved on to another shelf. "And this side is all supplies. Spools, winders, line laundry, et cetera, et cetera."

Oliver's eyes went wide.

Jan noticed. "Yes. You're going to have to learn all this." She fiddled with her beaded necklace and reminded Oliver of the horrible math teacher he had back in the ninth grade who got angry every time anyone showed signs of not knowing something she hadn't taught yet. Jan strode over to an open cardboard box and pulled out a large wooden cylinder with handles. "Spools. You wrap the string around these and hold the handle as you fly the kite." She moved on to the next box and pulled out a flat hot pink plastic thing that resembled a comb. "Winder. Does the same thing as the spool. With this one, you kind of wiggle it to let the line out."

Oliver reached into a giant box labeled LINE LAUNDRY. He pulled out several flat plastic packs of colorful nylon.

"They're like wind socks," Jan explained. She took a few from his hands. "This one is a fish. This one's a giant flame." She held up the next one and cracked the first real smile Oliver had seen. "This one's fantastic. Giant squid. He's really great. You attach these to your line and the wind blows them up. They're like kite line decorations. Yeah?"

Her hard edges faded as she talked about line laundry. This kite stuff made her happy. She was so *into* it.

"Yeah," Oliver said. "Okay. Line laundry."

Apparently, he didn't show enough excitement at the line laundry demonstration for Jan's taste. "Trust me," she huffed, "there's *a lot* more to learn. Flying kites is an art form." She looked at Oliver like he was hopeless, like they were standing in a storage room filled with precious jewels that he was mistaking for mere nylon and string. "Just follow Micah today. He's a master. Best employee I have."

"You flatter me." Micah cruised into the storage room, leaving the door swinging in his wake. Oliver peered into the shop behind him to see if he spotted Essa. No luck.

At the sight of Micah, Jan lit up even more than when she was holding the giant line laundry squid. "My dear." She patted his back. "How's the Big Man on Campus?"

"Hungry." Micah walked over to a little wooden cabinet and opened the door. Inside was a giant plastic tub filled with lollipops. The candy stash. He pulled out a handful and shut the door with his hiking boot.

"Whoa," Micah said, as he noticed Oliver. "And who do we have here?"

"This is Oliver," Jan said. But the light kind of drained out of her face when she said his name. Like Micah was an Edo kite that just flew in from the clouds, and Oliver was a plastic bag that just blew in from the King Soopers' parking lot. "He's going to work here for the summer."

"Wait." Micah stepped close and studied him. "Are you from . . . Illinois?"

"Um." Oliver cleared his throat and was totally weirded out. How did Micah know where he was from? "Yeah, Chicago. Lincoln Park."

"Essa told me you came in yesterday—" Micah stopped. "Wait, like Linkin Park, Linkin Park? Like the band?"

"No, no. It's a neighborhood in the city. It's where I live."

"Oh. Right. So you into hiking? Outdoor stuff? That why you came out for the summer?"

Oliver's face burned under the storage room lights, and for a minute he considered lying. But it seemed futile. If Micah asked any questions about the Great Outdoors Oliver's concrete-and-skyscraper soul would be obvious in two seconds flat. "Um, not really."

A know-it-all smile spread across Micah's face. "Yeah, well, Oliver from Lincoln Park, welcome to Boulder." He walked over to one of the overflowing storage shelves and pulled down a thick book. He flopped it against Oliver's chest like it was a giant Lake Michigan fish. "This is a good start."

The title was in large caps: *RIDING HIGH: A BEGINNER'S GUIDE TO KITES.*

Micah reached behind the Mac screen and pulled out another book. A smaller one. "And try this one, too."

Oliver glanced at the title. *Mountain Orienteering: How to Find Your Way in the Wilderness.*

"That's what we do around here. It's badass." Micah winked. "You're gonna love it here."

There was little in life that Oliver hated more than the use of the Ironic Wink. "Yeah," he said. "Sure."

"So it's totally and completely different when you're in college," Micah said. His big, bushy head of curly hair shook a little as he talked. "Totally and completely different. You'll see."

Oliver shifted on his stool behind the front counter. Jan had left long ago, and Oliver was supposed to be watching

Micah run the store and learn how to do it. So far, the job seemed to entail sitting behind the counter, philosophizing about the vast differences between college and high school, and answering customers' questions with an insane amount of exuberance.

The only practical thing he'd learned so far: Micah was the only one who put out a tip jar. Actually, he put out two, stuck dueling labels on each, and changed them daily. Sometimes he used movies. Like Original *Ghostbusters* vs. The Girl Version. Other times, he picked philosophers, like Plato vs. Aristotle. Today Micah had chosen Batman vs. "I'm my own superhero." Actually, Micah explained that it used to say, "I'm my own super-hero, *fucker.*" But he'd scratched out *fucker.*

"I mean, seriously," Micah said, spinning the empty Batman jar. "College makes high school look like one long case study on the Phenomenon of Suffering." He kicked his legs up on the counter. Chunks of brown dirt fell off the soles of his hiking boots onto the glass. A woman in her thirties came through the shop door. "Oh, no," Micah whispered. "Check what she's wearing."

She was pretty. Her long hair was tucked into a messy bun on top of her head, and she was decked out in yoga pants and a loose-fitting tank top. Across her breasts in big black ink the shirt read, *Namaste, Bitches.*

Oliver looked at Micah, confused.

"Namaste is a Sanskrit blessing," Micah said. "It's like . . . sort of sacred."

The woman approached the counter.

"Now watch this," he whispered. "Hey there!" he boomed at the customer. "Welcome to Above the Clouds. Greatest kite store in the universe. How can I help you?"

He oozed charm. And it was working. The effect on the woman was immediate. She smiled, her face suddenly bright and shiny. "My nephew wants a new kite. A three-tiered one? Do you guys carry those?"

Micah was so excited by the mention of three-tiered kites, he nearly lost it. He started talking super fast, and his hair bounced up and down as he jabbered. He went off about string type, reel recommendations, and wind direction.

The woman ended up buying eighty bucks' worth of stuff and left a ten-dollar bill in Micah's tip jar.

Apparently, she was her own superhero.

"Bro," Micah asked, once she was safely out the door, "did you catch that smile she had when I first talked to her?"

Oliver nodded.

"That's a thing. That's a Glory Days Grin."

"Huh?"

"I remind her of her Glory Days, when she was my age. When she was living the dream." He pulled the ten out of the jar and waved it around, snapped it taut. "For that alone, I get ten bucks. Happens all the time."

"Living the dream?"

"College, bro! Partying all night. Meeting Micahs all day."

Oliver looked at Micah and briefly wondered what it would be like to have that much confidence. Even for one day. One hour. Oliver suspected that Micah's reality was a far, far cry from his own.

"Fuck Knuckle!" A short, skinny guy burst into the store.

"Love of my life!" Micah answered. Skinny Guy came over and walked right behind the register, like he owned the place. He was wearing a bright blue T-shirt that said *Boulder High*. Oliver wasn't sure how he knew it, but he could sense that he was on this guy's stool. Oliver immediately slid off, and Skinny Guy took his place.

"Who's this?" He pointed at Oliver like he was kite detritus.

"This is Ollie," Micah answered. "From Illinois. He's working here for the summer."

Even though he'd never been called Ollie in his entire life, Oliver decided to just go with it and managed a weak "Hey."

"Ollie," Micah went on, "meet my pal Anish. A rising senior

stud at the illustrious Boulder High School. Whose family is like Indian royalty."

Anish rolled his eyes. "No," he said. "Not royalty."

"Bro, I've seen the crazy-ass wedding pictures in your living room. There were *elephants*, dude. And those outfits!"

"Grandparents' wedding," Anish said. "I wasn't even born yet. And when I was born, it was in Fort Collins."

"He's modest." Micah winked again.

If Micah was such a college maverick, Oliver wondered why the hell he was still hanging out with high school kids. But of course, he didn't say that. Instead, the worst happened: Oliver stuck his hand out. As in, *he dorkily tried to shake Anish's hand.* Oliver's mom had always taught him to offer a handshake to important adults. Like her friends. Or his grandparents' friends. The manners lesson misfired in Oliver's brain and there he was, extending a hand to a Boulder dude his age.

Anish completely ignored him and his dorky attempt at a handshake. Oliver shoved his hand back in his pocket and miraculously suffered and survived a mild heart attack fueled by self-loathing. Anish continued talking to Micah. "Party at the End of the World tonight! And guess who scored some Everclear?"

"Everclear?" Micah frowned. "Dude, the last time we drank that, you inexplicably ended up passed out in a women's bathroom with a retainer in your mouth . . . that wasn't yours. That's the type of shit that happens when you drink Everclear."

They kept debating which substances were the best to ingest at End of the World parties (wherever and whatever those were), and as each second ticked by, Oliver felt like more and more of a jackass. It was extremely difficult to look cool while standing around listening to people talk about a party he was clearly not invited to.

Thankfully, the bell above the door jangled, and Oliver looked up, wondering if it would be Essa coming in for her shift. It wasn't. It was just a couple of customers. Parents with a ten-year-old boy in tow. Oliver made a beeline for them even though he had no idea what to do once he got there. It wasn't like he was ready to answer kite questions. But still. Anything to get away from Anish and Micah.

The boy milled around the hover racers, fascinated. Maybe Oliver could actually answer questions about those. But just before he reached them, his phone went off in his pocket. He pulled it out and looked at the screen.

Mom.

He thought about sending it to voice mail, texting her that he was busy. But something about it pulled at him. Maybe she was calling with an update about Lilly.

Lilly.

He hadn't thought about her for maybe three hours straight. He couldn't remember when he'd gone that long. The sudden thought of her rushed through him like a bad dream. Like thin air. Like homesickness for a place he didn't even know was still standing. He answered the call.

"How is she?" He skipped a greeting.

"Hi, sweetheart," his mom said. "I just visited. Everything's under control. Really. There are a few new docs on the team. They're great. They're adjusting her meds. How's Boulder?"

They're adjusting her meds. How many times had he heard that? How many times had those words filled a tiny balloon of hope in his chest that rose slowly, higher and higher? How many times had it burst? That's all they ever did, adjust her meds. Most of the time the pills brought her back to reality. Just so she could leave it again a few weeks later and do it all over.

But there it was. In his chest. That little balloon. Rising.

"How bad is she? Are the meds helping?"

"A little. She's still going on about the white cars. But the other stuff seems to be fading. The crossword puzzles. The messages she thinks she's getting from the television . . ."

"Does she remember . . . everything?"

Silence.

Oliver realized that his voice had cracked a little when he

asked the question. And that he was pacing. By the bin of Mini-Unicorns. He dug his hand in and pulled out a wad of them, their tiny rubber horns jutting this way and that. He let them cascade out of his fist, like a unicorn waterfall. "When can I talk to her? I've got to try—"

"I don't know, honey. I'm not sure that's a good idea." His mom paused. Let out a small sigh.

"But she's my sister. I should be allowed to . . ." Oliver trailed off, suddenly too tired to finish his sentence. He glanced at the hover racer display. The customers were long gone. "I don't know what happened that night, Mom. I just—" His voice cracked again, and he stopped talking. He had to.

He saw something out of the corner of his eye.

Micah.

Shit. He's probably pissed that I didn't help the hover racer customers.

"Mom, I gotta go." Oliver straightened the sign on the bin of Mini-Monkeys, trying to look like he was doing something that resembled work.

"Don't go," she said. "Are you okay out there? Tell me you're—"

"Bye." He hung up. And looked at Micah. "Sorry about that. I meant to help those customers, I just—"

"Dude. Totally okay. Seriously." Micah adjusted a few bin labels himself. *Mini-Snakes. Mini-Frogs. Mini-Octopi.* "Um . . . is everything cool?"

He wasn't talking about hover racer sales.

How much did he hear?

Oliver couldn't even remember what he'd said to his mom out loud. How much did he say about Lilly? About what happened that night? About her delusions? He couldn't remember. "Uh, yeah. It was about my sister. Had to take it. Or my mom would be pissed. You know how that goes."

"Totally," Micah said. "See this?" He held up his cell phone. The background of his home screen was a photograph of a beautiful woman on a boat. Her thick jet-black hair was curling in the humidity; her cherry-red lipstick matched the color of her large sunglasses. In the background, angular tree-covered rock formations pushed out of the ocean. Giant seabirds loomed in the sky. She was waving one graceful arm in the air, and a little boy was tucked under the other. He was smiling underneath his mop of black hair.

Oliver raised his eyebrows.

"That's my mom," Micah said. "On a boat off Railay Beach. In Thailand." He looked at the picture again. "If she calls and I don't take it . . . holy shit. She goes all Turbo-Thai on my ass, and I get the matriarch lecture."

"So that's you?" Oliver nodded toward the little boy in the picture.

"Yeah. I was six, I think." Micah's smile was easy enough to read. He adored his mom. He looked down at his ratty hiking boots and ground his toe into the carpet. "So . . . your sister. She sick or something?"

Guess he heard enough.

"Um. Sort of. Yes."

"That sucks. She getting better?"

Oliver didn't say anything at first. He just looked up at the kites hanging from the ceiling. He'd give anything to get out of this conversation. He didn't want to be the kid from Chicago with the messed-up family. With the sob story. With the weirdness that no one could understand. He just wanted to be Oliver. High school kid. Summer kite worker. No big deal.

"Not really. But what are those?" He pointed to a line of kites above them that looked different from the others. These were triangles, but more angular than the rest. They had scalloped edges, racing colors, and clean, hard lines. There were five in a row, and together they looked predatory, like a pack of bats ready to attack.

"Stunt kites," Micah answered, looking up. "Batkite brand. Totally badass. Fast and precise as hell. Also a hundred and fifty bucks."

"Cool." Oliver couldn't think of anything else to say. He knew there must be a million questions one could ask about such a thing as stunt kites, but his mind remained stubbornly blank. "Really cool."

An awkward silence engulfed them.

"Anyway," Micah continued, "you wanna come to a party? Tonight. It's at this really cool spot above Boulder. We call it the End of the World. Anish and I'll pick you up."

Oliver could hear Micah's motive. It was so obvious. As if he'd just been handed an actual party invitation written in a new font: *Times New Pity. Helvetica Charity.*

Oliver looked up at the kites again. The thought of traipsing into the woods at night freaked him out. And sounded kind of boring. And if the rest of Micah's friends were as ice cold as Anish, it would be a miserable night. A miserable night in the woods with people who didn't want him there.

"I'll go," Oliver said.

On the Pathetic/Overeager scale, Oliver's answer was a perfect ten. It came out so fast. So forcefully. He didn't even ask what time or anything. Silently, he chastised himself for sounding so desperate. He wondered why the hell he'd jumped at the chance to go to something that sounded terrible in the first place.

But he knew why. He totally knew why.

The truth made his face burn, and he was grateful Micah couldn't read his mind.

Essa.

Maybe she'll be there.

10

OLIVER

He was in the back of Micah's Jeep, about to throw up. Micah was speeding up the steep, winding roads into Boulder Canyon. They were in the middle of a line of nearly twenty cars, all snaking their way into the mountains, kicking up massive clouds of dust as the road turned from pavement to gravel and finally to dry dirt. The dusty haze around the car was catching the golden light of sunset, and Oliver felt like he was in a movie. Maybe the scene just before the hero's car spins off the road and disappears over the cliff beside them. Oliver peered over the edge at the straight drop. His stomach lurched. It was so far down with nothing to stop them if their car went over. Boulder stretched out below. Beyond the city, the land flattened out and seemed to go on forever.

Micah looked at Oliver in the rearview mirror. "You can see straight to Kansas from here, bro."

"Yeah." Oliver wished Micah would just keep his eyes on the road. As they climbed higher and higher, the altitude made Oliver sick. Waves of nausea rolled over him. He decided he'd made a terrible decision to come up here. But on the very small bright side of the current situation, both Micah and Anish were actually being nice to him. Oliver wondered if Micah had told Anish about his sister, that he'd overheard him talking about some mystery illness on the phone.

"Next up, the Black Forest," Micah called, tapping his hands on the steering wheel.

Anish was rolling a joint in the passenger seat. Micah took a sharp turn around a switchback, the wheels skidded, and the car slid sideways. The rolling paper in Anish's lap floated up and was sucked out the window. "Dammit!" Anish reached for it, but missed. "I wanted to be high before we got there. Slow the hell down and close the windows until I get this rolled."

"Edibles, dude." Micah shook his head. "So much easier."

"They take too long to kick in!" Anish threw his hands up in disgust. "I can't calibrate. I always overshoot the mark. Or undershoot, which is nearly as bad."

Oliver tuned out their conversation as they left the switchbacks and the road entered a high alpine meadow. It was covered with burnt trees. Thousands were still standing, and hundreds more lay still and lifeless on the ground like blackened cadavers. Oliver stared at the upright trees, charred black, with limbs twisting into the sky like they were frozen in their last moments, begging for mercy but denied it.

"What is this place?" Oliver leaned into the front seat.

"Big fire swept through here years ago. How old were we?" Micah glanced sideways at Anish.

Anish couldn't answer because his tongue was otherwise engaged. He had the joint rolled up and was licking the new paper closed. He held up one finger until he was done. "You would've been in sixth grade," he finally said.

"Yeah. Sixth grade. It was massive. Burned this entire area."

Anish pulled a lighter out of his pocket and lit his joint. He took a few shallow inhales until the tip glowed red and then pulled in a long drag. He held it and let go in one slow, smooth exhalation. He didn't even cough once. "Guests next," he said, turning and offering it to Oliver.

Oliver had never smoked before. Or drank. Or done anything, for that matter. He stared at the joint. Maybe now was a good time to trash his sober policy. Was he really the good kid anymore after what happened with Lilly? His mom had to dump him in Boulder for the summer just to get him out of

Chicago. Out of the way. A problem. He was kind of a problem now. Might as well go for it.

But the truth was, it terrified him. Would he be like Lilly? Would he hallucinate? Would he lose all touch with reality? That's why he'd never gotten messed up. Not from alcohol or drugs or anything. How could he knowingly mess up his mind when some people had no choice? When some people were stuck like that for life?

"Maybe later," he said.

"Don't worry, there's plenty where we're headed," Anish said. "We party just at the edge of the burn area. Where the trees are thick again. It's like paradise." He took another drag.

Just ahead, cars were pulling off the road, driving into the woods and crossing the forest floor. Compared to parties in Chicago which always happened in the basement of someone's townhouse or on the roof of an apartment building, there was only one word that captured what was happening right now: *nuts.*

Then he felt like shit for even thinking that word.

"We're here," Micah called. He pulled the Jeep close to a stand of thick, healthy-looking pine trees and parked. He flung open his car door, letting the accumulated weed smoke escape into the woods.

It was nearly dark. The dense forest around them hid the last few rays of sun. Oliver followed Anish and Micah a few hundred yards ahead, to a large clearing in the woods.

"Behold!" Micah said, holding his arms outstretched. "Welcome to the End of the World. Greatest secret party spot in all of Boulder County. And nary a cop has ever busted us up here. It helps that the land belongs to the uncle of the student body president. But still."

Oliver looked around. The place was crawling with people. Some wore BOULDER HIGH T-shirts, some had on hiking stuff, a lot of girls were in yoga pants. In the center of the clearing there was a bonfire, surrounded by a ten-foot circle of bricks laid in the ground. It was like a makeshift patio.

"We built that," Anish said. His eyes had taken on a glassy, foggy look. He seemed kinder, gentler. A little wistful, even. He put a hand on Oliver's shoulder. "Bricks keep any sparks from lighting. This is wildfire country, my new friend. Your ass will go to jail if you start one up here. Doesn't matter how young you are. We're lucky they haven't banned burning yet this season."

"Truth," Micah said. "Starting one in these mountains is, like, worse than murder."

Music started blasting from somewhere. Oliver had never heard the song. It had a lot of guitar. It sounded almost raw, like a concert bootleg. Micah walked over to a keg and filled two red cups full of beer. He thrust one into Oliver's hand. And then held up his own for a toast. "To the End of the World! A most beauteous place."

Anish nearly died laughing. Like, really. Oliver was worried he might die. Which made no sense because all Micah had said was the title of their party spot. And the word *beauteous*.

Mental note: weed makes the unfunny very, very funny.

Oliver took the cup and pretended to take a sip. Micah and Anish were quickly surrounded by other people, so he quietly slipped away from the crowd. He looked at the treetops above him, at all the gnarly, twisting branches. The smell of pine and woodsmoke filled his nose.

He saw the source of the music: someone's portable speakers sitting on top of a car hood. A new song started playing. Another one he hadn't heard, stripped down, just guitar and vocals. It made the woods feel lonely. It made the world feel lonely. Like he was the only one out here in the darkness. Like there was nothing but the looming trees above him, the crunch of pine needles under his feet, the warm glow from the bonfire. Like he needed to go back to Chicago as soon as he possibly—

He saw her.

She was barefoot, standing on the bricks around the fire. Half her hair was pulled into a messy knot, and the rest tumbled down her shoulders, her back. The firelight blinked on her arms, the thin, crisscrossing straps of her black tank top. A skirt was wrapped around her waist and tied at her side.

She was dancing.

She held what looked like some sort of hula hoop wrapped in multicolored tape. She arched her back and let the hoop roll over her chest and then down one arm. She caught it and spun it over her head, stepping through. Her long legs peeked out of her skirt as they moved, as her hips moved, as her whole body slid through the air to the music.

He told himself he couldn't look away because he'd never seen someone dance like that in Chicago. People didn't swirl barefoot next to fires in the woods with hula hoops. People didn't move like she was moving, or wear what she was wearing. He told himself he was watching her because he was bored, because there was nothing else to see out here in these woods, nothing else to do but get stoned or drunk.

But really, he didn't know why.

All he knew was that he couldn't look away.

He had the distinct feeling that he was peering through a window at Essa, at an entire foreign world that was so much better than his own. That it would be impossible to crawl through it. Impossible to be where she was, on the inside, with her. He half-hated himself for it, but all he wanted right then, was for her to look up. To see him.

She did.

The hula hoop stopped moving. So did her feet. She locked eyes with him, recognized who he was.

A look of total and complete disgust swept over her face.

11

ESSA

What on earth is he *doing here?*

Essa wanted to drop the hula hoop and set off in the crowd to find Micah. He had to be at the bottom of this. As far as she knew, Oliver was new in town. He didn't have any Boulder friends. Had he come in the shop again and met Micah somehow? She told Micah not to even tell Jan he wanted to work there. She was so confused.

She wanted to pretend like she hadn't seen him, that she hadn't recognized him. But she'd looked straight at him. It was too late to pretend otherwise. Plus, she hated blanking people. Even arrogant asses from Chicago. She looked in his direction again and gave him an obligatory wave. He smiled and waved back.

Then she bolted.

She dropped the hoop and pushed her way through the various groups. It got harder and harder to see the farther she went from the fire. But finally, she spotted Micah. He was sitting with the hardcore stoners, a.k.a. The Thirty-Minute Parkers. During the school year, just before study hall, they always walked up to the thirty-minute parking lot behind Boulder High to get stoned. Micah was sitting on a broken lawn chair listening to a girl named Skye tell him why it was "pure justice" that Bob Dylan won the Nobel Prize for Literature.

"Micah." Essa knew she was failing to keep the annoyance out of her voice. But Micah didn't even look up.

"So what *is* the difference between poetry and song lyrics?" Skye asked. She was sitting cross-legged at Micah's feet, playing with her braided pigtails. She was wearing a T-shirt that said *Shenanigan Enthusiast.*

"Yeah," Micah said slowly. "And why have I never even asked this question?"

"My granddad always plays Dylan," Skye continued. "And he always goes off about how awesome it is. And I was always, like, 'Whatever, it's *ancient.*' But I really listened to it the other day. And seriously. It's poetry. I could feel it in my arms."

"Micah," Essa said again, more urgently this time. Finally he looked up. Even in the dark, she could see that his eyes were beyond glassy. They were glass-marbles-covered-with-a-layer-of-melted-sugar-covered-with-a-layer-of-varnish glassy. It was nuts. And so unlike him. Well, used to be.

Why is he getting so messed up lately?

"Ess . . . ence," Micah said, dragging out her two-syllable name to one with roughly five. "I can't believe it."

"You can't believe what?"

"That you're here. And I'm here. And we're all here. You know? I mean, it's amazing if you think about it."

"Yes. Amazing." Essa rolled her eyes. "Can you come here? I need to talk to you."

With some effort, Micah got out of his broken lawn chair. Skye looked very upset to see him go. "Come back with more of those weird pineapples?" she asked.

"But of course, madam," Micah said. He bowed to Skye in a show of mock medieval chivalry. Skye burst into a fit of laughter. Micah turned to Essa. "How may I be of service?" He put an arm around Essa's bare shoulders.

"Weird pineapples?" Essa asked. "What does she mean?"

"Nothing. She's out of it . . ."

"Wait." Something was tickling at the edge of Essa's memory.

"My mom almost got in trouble at work the other day for messing up a batch of weed pineapple gummies. You didn't . . ."

"Your mom was throwing them away! I couldn't let that happen."

"Ugh," Essa said. She stared up at the night sky. "I'm going to yell at you about this later. But for now, did you see that guy Oliver? He's here."

"Oliver . . . Oliver . . ."

"The new guy. From Chicago. The one I told you about. He came by the store and wanted to work there. And he's a total arrogant ass. I don't get how he even knew about this party."

"Oh! Oliver. Right." Micah sounded way more excited than he should. "I brought him."

"What? Why?" Essa wiggled out from under Micah's heavy arm and led him toward the fire. "You didn't tell Jan he came by for a job, did you?"

"No, I totally didn't. But he showed up anyway. First day was today." Micah yawned and rubbed his face. "I'm tired all of a sudden. You tired?"

"No. It's nine o'clock." Essa saw an empty log by the campfire and sat down. She scanned the crowd to see if Oliver was still close by. She didn't see him. "So we're stuck with him at the shop for the summer?"

"Go easy." Micah joined her on the log and gently bumped his shoulder against hers. "There's something wrong."

"Yeah, that's obvious. He was standing over there earlier staring at me like a total weirdo."

"No. Not with him. There's something wrong with his sister."

Essa felt a catch in her chest. A small hitch. "What's wrong with her?"

"I don't know exactly," Micah said. "But she's sick or something. I think it might be bad. That's why I invited him. Sounds like his life kind of sucks."

Essa looked at the dancing flames and thought about her own sister. If something ever happened to Puck or she got really sick . . . Essa couldn't even bear thinking about it. "So you have no idea what the deal is?"

Micah nudged her in the side, hard. "Speak of the devil . . ."

Oliver was standing a few feet from them, still sporting an awkward smile. "Hey," he said.

Essa didn't respond. Micah nudged her even harder in the rib cage. "Hey," she blurted out.

"You having a good time, bro?" Micah asked. "There's some killer weed floating around. Watch it, though. Sneaks up on you fast. It's Willie Nelson's new brand. Willie's Reserve. A-mazing."

"I don't really smoke."

Essa felt that tiny hitching sensation again. She wanted to say something to save Oliver from any more of Micah's Weed Trivia. "You want to sit down?" she asked. There was plenty of room on the log for all three of them, but Micah apparently took this as his cue to leave. Which made the whole encounter feel way more awkward than necessary. She reminded herself to add this to the list of things she needed to yell at Micah about.

"Catch you later," Micah said. "I'll be in Thirty-Minute Parking." He smiled and knocked Oliver on the arm. Oliver looked confused.

"Ignore him," Essa said as Micah sauntered off into the darkness.

Oliver sat down on the log, his long legs bumping into her as he tried to find a comfortable position.

"So . . ." Essa searched for something to ask him about. "Boulder. You're here for the whole summer?"

"Yeah." Oliver looked at the leaping flames in front of them. Essa could feel a little sadness wash over him, like a cool breeze had just blown through, refusing to be warmed by the fire. "My mom sent me out. To live with my aunt. To get away from some stuff in Chicago."

"Oh."

Oliver shifted on the log. "And sorry I was a jerk about Boulder when I met you. I just—"

"It's cool," Essa interrupted. The slit of her skirt was on Oliver's side. She crossed her legs, and it fell open, exposing her left thigh in the warm firelight. It felt good on her skin. She wasn't sure whether it was the reds and golds from the flames or if Oliver was blushing.

"So what do you guys do around here? I mean, other than have bonfires." Oliver pulled at a stray thread on the knee of his jeans. "And I don't mean that in a shitty way. Like there's nothing to do or whatever. I mean . . . just, what do you do around here?"

Essa pondered his question for a minute. She wasn't sure she'd ever really thought about it. "My favorite thing would be camping. But it's not really camping. We try to find our way . . ." She paused. "You camp?"

Oliver was seized by the urge to lie. To say that he spent his every weekend back in Chicago in a tent camping at . . . where? He didn't even know if *anyone* camped in Chicago. He didn't know where they would go or what they would even do once they got there.

"Not so much." He gently dug his heel into the soft dirt beneath them. "And by not so much, I mean never. Like, not once."

"Right," Essa said. She searched for a way to explain it. "We do wilderness stuff. We try to find our way off-trail with just a compass and a map. It's called orienteering."

Oliver thought that sounded terrifying. Trying to find your way through the woods.

"And I guess when we're in town, we hang out on the Hill and listen to bands on Pearl Street. We tube down Boulder Creek. Stuff like that, I guess."

"The Hill?"

"It's the hill by CU. The college campus. Mostly full of college kids. There's a great theater where bands play. And lots of restaurants. Cheba Hut."

"The what-hut?"

Essa smiled. "You were serious when you said you don't smoke, weren't you?"

Oliver nodded.

"Cheba's a nickname for weed. They don't actually sell it there or anything. They just serve sandwiches and stuff. But they're all in a stoner theme. Like, there's a toasted sub called Pineapple Kush. Or Shatter Platter." Oliver looked confused again. She could tell he didn't know what kush or shatter were, either. "The pineapple one is just a ham sandwich."

Oliver picked up a pine needle and rolled it between his fingers. "You're into it, then?"

"What, Cheba Hut? It's okay, I guess. I mean, I've had better sandwiches in my life from—"

"No, smoking. You're into it?"

Essa couldn't help but smile. She thought about the stash her mom kept in their kitchen at home. The brownies, the buds, the shatter. How excited her mom was when she got to bring home a sample of newly released weed brands: Willie's Reserve. Snoop's Leafs. Essa had never tried any of it. Ever. "No. Not into it."

Oliver seemed surprised. "Is it weird? Being legal and all out here?"

"Not really." Essa shrugged. "It was easy to get before. It's easy to get now."

"Can I ask why?"

"Why I'm not into it?"

Oliver nodded.

"It's just—" Essa paused. She'd never been asked directly like that before. Her mom made it look like the best thing in the world. Fun. An instant ticket to not caring. Not caring if everything sucked. Not caring if something went wrong. Not caring if the whole world burned down around you. "I'm into Zen. And there's this idea about not getting intoxicated with anything. That you're not mindful. That it causes harm. To you, to society, to life . . ." She drifted off, worried she was boring him. "Plus, it's my sister."

"Puck?"

"She needs me. To be with it, you know? Our mom is . . ." Essa paused. "She just needs me, that's all."

Oliver looked at her. She saw something in his eyes she couldn't quite place. "Same," he said. "I don't get messed up. Because of my sister."

She didn't want to ask him to explain. She tucked her leg back in her skirt and sat on her hands. Waiting.

"It's for her," he said. "It's complicated, but . . . I don't get messed up. For her. It wouldn't be right."

Essa pulled in a deep breath. "Same."

They both looked away and stared at the fire again. Essa felt this tiny tug, a soft shift in her shoulders. A question tumbled out of her mouth before she even had time to think about it. "You want to come out with a bunch of us tomorrow night? We're going hang out on the Hill. Get some food."

The softness in her shoulders disappeared.

Did I just ask him out?

"Yes," Oliver said too quickly. Then he paused. Casually tossed another pine needle into the fire. "I mean, yeah. Sure. Cool."

"It's just a group of us going. It's not like . . ." Essa stalled.

A date. Because I don't date. Ever.

But she couldn't say it. Oliver looked confused.

"Just . . ." Essa continued. "Meet us at seven tomorrow night. Cheba Hut."

12

ESSA

Essa got home around midnight. Not that she had a curfew. She stood at the front door, fumbling for her keys in her bag. She couldn't stop thinking about what Oliver had said. She couldn't stop thinking about the fact that she'd asked him to meet her tomorrow night. She couldn't stop thinking about sitting next to him by the fire.

She let her house key sit in the lock before turning it. She closed her eyes, took a few slow breaths, and tried to follow them, to let the thoughts of Oliver drift by.

Thoughts are clouds drifting by a mountain.

Watch them. Tend to them.

But know

You're the mountain.

She felt solid. Safe. She took one more deep breath and opened her eyes. Puck's window was on the corner of the house. The light was still on.

Why is she still up?

Essa unlocked the door and pushed it open. The house was mostly dark. A dim light filtered into the hallway from the kitchen.

She heard a thump. A shuffling.

"Hello?" she called. She went into the kitchen and saw a clear cellophane bag of gummy watermelon wedges open on the table. She picked it up and read the label.

Edi-Sweets. 500 mg THC. 25 Individually infused 10-mg pieces. Keep from children. No resale.

She opened the bag and sniffed. Mostly the soft pink wedges smelled like melon. But there was a faint swampy odor she knew all too well. Like mown grass that had been left in a trash bag for a week.

Weed.

And only eighteen pieces left. She closed the bag and started down the hallway toward Puck's room. But she heard the thump again. It was definitely coming from the living room. She turned and headed back that way. As she rounded the corner, movement caught her eye.

Her mom. Ronnie. All tangled up on the couch. In a massive makeout session.

Oh my god.

She put a hand over her eyes. "Mom! What the hell are you doing?"

They pulled apart as Essa peered through her split fingers. Ronnie wasn't wearing a shirt, and his gross man-chest hair was in full view. The top of her mom's dress was pulled down around her waist. At least she still had her tie-dyed bra on.

"Hey, sweetie." Her mom pulled her dress up, one arm at a time, but she was moving way too slowly. Ronnie ran a hand through his dirty blond hair. At least he had enough decency to look embarrassed. Essa's mom started to giggle.

"Don't laugh," Essa said. "Puck is home. Can you at least go to your room?"

"She's asleep, honey. It's so late. She's—"

"No, she's not. Her light is on." Essa threw her hands up in the air, disgusted. "Do you even know your own daughter? She's probably in there studying differential-fucking-calculus while you're out here being an idiot."

"Don't you talk to me like that, Essence." Her mom's bloodshot eyes flashed with anger.

Guilt snaked its way up Essa's legs and then her arms. Not

about yelling at her mom. About leaving Puck here while Essa was at that stupid bonfire. She'd left Puck, thinking it would be okay, thinking she was at home and safe. But really, she left her with a bare-chested stoner and her flaky mom. Which was like leaving her with no one at all.

She stared at her mom's baked eyes. "Why can't you just be here when you're here?"

"What is that supposed to mean?"

Essa didn't stick around to explain. She made a beeline for Puck's room and knocked on the door. "Pucky? You up?"

Silence.

Essa knocked again. "Puck? You in there?"

She slowly pushed the door open. Puck was sitting in the middle of the floor surrounded by a crumpled, broken kite. She looked up at Essa, her blonde hair tangled around her shoulders, her blue eyes flat, almost lifeless. Something pink caught Essa's eye. A small pile of candy on Puck's bedside table. Three pieces of gummy watermelon slices.

"Oh my god." Essa raced into the room, reached for the candies. She held them to her nose and recognized the same swampy smell from the Edi-Sweets in the kitchen.

"Puck." Essa knelt beside her, held the candies up. "Did you eat any of these?"

Puck picked up the sad, crumpled kite and shook her head no.

"Puck. Tell me the truth." Essa gently took her sister's face in her hands and peered into her eyes. She sniffed her breath. "It's really, really important."

"I didn't. I promise."

"You feel okay? You don't feel weird? Out of it? Can you breathe okay?" Essa held her ear to her sister's chest, listening for the rhythm of her heartbeat. It was fast, but no faster than usual. Puck's heart always beat like this. Like a tiny bird trying hard to stay in the skies.

"I didn't eat any."

"They're Mom's," Essa said. "They're from her shop. They're

bad, like we talked about. Really, really bad. You *know* what they can do to a kid's brain."

Puck let the kite flutter softly into her lap. "I know."

Puck's eyes looked okay. Her voice sounded okay.

She's okay.

Essa breathed for what felt like the first time in five whole minutes. She wondered why she hadn't passed out already from lack of oxygen, collapsed in the middle of the crumpled kite pile.

But then Puck's words hit her.

"Wait . . ." Essa started. "You knew? You knew these were Mom's candies?"

Puck nodded.

"Then why . . . ?" Essa didn't finish her question. She didn't have to.

She knew what they were. And she was thinking about eating them anyway.

Essa pulled Puck close, gathered her in her arms like limp kite canvas. She rocked her. Back and forth. Back and forth. She thought of her gatha.

Breathing in, I know my breath is the wheel of the ship.

Breathing out, I know the storm will pass.

She knew calm was contagious. She hoped her breath would comfort Puck.

Puck noticed. "Bodhisattva," she whispered. The concept from Mahayana Buddhism about creating peace and harmony in ourselves so that we spread peace and harmony to others.

"I try," Essa said.

"I'm sorry I scared you," Puck said. "That guy has been here all night." She pressed her cheek against Essa's warm shoulder. Essa could feel her sister's tears on her neck. "I didn't want to leave my room. That guy. He looks so gross. And I heard noises."

"The candy can make you so sick, Puck. So, so sick." Essa pulled back and looked at Puck. "They could poison you. You shouldn't ever—"

Puck pulled away.

Essa had been too hard on her little sister. She shouldn't get mad at her, shouldn't let anger seep into her voice. She was just so scared. "What's all this?" Essa asked gently, holding up the broken kite.

"I solved the Puzzle Kite box. The one I told Mom I wanted. But I was wrong; it wasn't the horse. I brought home the wrong one."

"So you broke it?"

Puck nodded, tears filling her eyes again. "I'm sorry," she said.

"You don't have to be sorry. Not at all."

"I shouldn't have stolen it from the store. But Mom never listens. I knew she'd never get it for me. I told her five times I wanted the horse kite. And she kept saying she'd buy it. But I could tell she wasn't even listening. She probably doesn't even know I want one."

Puck put her head back on Essa's shoulder, played with a chunk of Essa's long brown hair. She pulled back again. Knitted her blonde brows together. "You smell like smoke."

"I do?" Essa asked.

"Yeah." She stood up and ran to her bed. Tossed herself down on top of it. "Not you, too," she said into the folds of the comforter.

It hit Essa what Puck was smelling. She sat by her on the bed. Ran a hand along her back. "Pucky, it's woodsmoke. I promise. I was by a bonfire. I wouldn't smoke that stuff. I promise."

"Promise?" Puck's question was muffled, her face still shoved in the blankets. She rolled over and looked at Essa. "Don't ever leave me."

Essa wasn't sure what was more painful. Her heart shattering in her chest, or hearing the delicate sound of Puck's breath as she tried not to cry again.

All kids want, Essa thought, *is for us to be with them when we're with them. Here when we're here.*

"Promise."

June 10

13

OLIVER

Oliver was supposed to meet Essa and her friends outside Cheba Hut at 7 p.m. The shop sign was lit up in bright neon, a cluster of sub sandwich rolls arranged in the shape of a weed leaf. The smell of baking sandwich bread filtered out the doors as customers came and went.

He stood on the sidewalk, hands stuffed in his jeans pockets. As college kids passed him in small groups of twos and threes, he tried to look like he hung out here all the time. He scanned the sidewalks. Still no sign of Essa or any of her friends. Was she messing with him? Did she not really want to hang out tonight? Did she invite him here just to embarrass him?

He felt like an idiot as the minutes passed by. He turned and walked back to the shop window. The menu was taped to the glass:

Big Buddha Cheese: Choice of bread smothered in three-cheese sauce

Pineapple Kush: Smoked ham, Hawaiian pineapple, mozzarella

The Robert Plant: Nothing but plants! Choice of 5 veggies. Guac extra

"Ollie!" Micah boomed. "Welcome to the Hill!" Micah and Anish were strolling toward him.

No Essa.

"My favorite is the Big Buddha Cheese," Anish said. He looked proud to be offering wise counsel. "Best grilled cheese you'll ever have in your life. Seriously. They take it to the next level."

They went into Cheba Hut. The walls were painted a sickening shade of green and covered with bumper stickers and graffiti.

"You should see this place when classes are actually in session," Micah said. He picked at a dried mustard stain on his T-shirt—*Chilltown, Est. 2015, Pop. 1.* "It's crawling. Just summer school people here now. Like yours truly."

"Your turn." Anish pushed Oliver toward the counter. Oliver squinted at the menu above the grill.

"I *highly* recommend the Ghost Train Haze," Micah said. "Pun intended."

They all got their sandwiches and huddled in a booth to eat. The Ghost Train turned out to be a collection of smoked meat, cheese, and a hot sauce that made Oliver's lips feel like they would shrivel and fall off in three to four days' time.

"Dude, what are we doing tomorrow?" Anish looked across the table at Micah. A huge dollop of melted cheese oozed out the side of his large Big Buddha Cheese. "Mountain Fugitive?"

"Next weekend," Micah said, wiping his mouth with a napkin. "Gotta study for a philosophy test tomorrow." Then he balled up the napkin and threw it into the trash can halfway across the room. He nailed the shot. "Essa's in for next weekend, too."

They went on talking about plans that Oliver couldn't follow. Mountain Fugitive sounded like the orienteering stuff Essa had mentioned, but he couldn't be sure. They were talking about past times they'd all played it. They were saying things about shadow stick compasses in a pinch and topo map reading. Landmarks and peaks and gullies. They were talking about getting lost and sitting by the side of a trail for ten hours, waiting for rescue.

"You free next weekend?" Anish bumped Oliver's foot under the table. "We'll just go up for the day."

"I don't know, I—"

The bells above the Cheba Hut door jingled loudly.

Essa walked in.

She was wearing baggy multicolored pants and a tank top that showed her midriff. Her long hair fell over her shoulders as she scanned the restaurant. She ran her hands through her hair and pulled it into a messy bun on top of her head. Oliver sat straight up in the booth.

Micah noticed. "Oh no," he said. "Don't even think it, dude."

"What?" Oliver asked, his voice climbing an octave.

"You're sporting a classic Overeager Stance. Essa doesn't date. I've seen many a man try and fail. And when they fail, they go down in epic, burning flames. She's . . . what would you call it, Anish?"

"Huh?" Anish wasn't paying attention. He was busy deciphering some of the graffiti etched into the tabletop. "What does this say? '*Your existence gives me . . .*' What? I can't read the last word."

Micah leaned over and squinted at the writing someone had scratched into the table with a knife. "'Diarrhea. Your existence gives me diarrhea.'"

"Genius. I want this on a shirt to wear when I'm with you."

"Focus," Micah said. "I'm trying to explain to poor Ollie here why crushing on Essa is the very definition of futility. Am I right?"

"Oh," Anish said, looking troubled. "Dude. Give up on that project stat. Seriously. Essa is super—"

"What? I'm super what?" Essa was standing at their booth. Her choice of a midriff-showing shirt meant that Oliver was perilously close to the smooth skin on her stomach, the swirl of her belly button.

Don't stare.

Don't stare.

Don't stare.

Plus, she smelled like Sophie's incense, a mix of lemongrass and lavender. Which Oliver decided was now officially the greatest scent on earth.

"Awesome," Anish said. "You are super . . . awesome." He reached up and took her hand. He guided her into the booth. Their shoulders were touching. Oliver didn't like it.

"You're full of shit," Essa said. Her eyes were flat. Even after they met Oliver's. He was hoping they'd kind of light up when she saw him. He was hoping they were about to embark on some epic night on the Hill. He was hoping . . .

"I don't even want to be here," Essa said, sighing. "I just want to crash. But Puck's at a friend's sleepover, and Mom is home again with her new boyfriend. I can't even be in the same house with that guy."

"You hungry?" Micah asked. Oliver couldn't tell whether Micah was a douche for not listening to more of what Essa had to say about the drama with her mom, or if he was just really adept at diverting the conversation, at cheering her up. "Oliver here had the Ghost Train Haze."

Oliver shrugged. "I think my lips are about to fall off." He took a drink of soda. Which wasn't helping the burn. He locked eyes with her over the rim of his giant plastic red cup.

Essa cracked a half-smile. "Who let him order that?" She looked at Anish and Micah. They pointed at each other. She looked back at Oliver. "Because your lips will fall off. At least they'll feel like it, anyway. I've only had the vegetarian version, but still. The sauce is the same. Brutal."

Oliver's cheeks burned. Then he lost focus, and a mini chug of soda escaped his third-degree-burnt lips and went down the front of his shirt.

Shit. Shit. Shit.

What the hell was wrong with him? He was losing it. Was it because she said the word *lips*?

That's pathetic.

Micah and Anish exchanged knowing glances. Essa pulled a wad of napkins out of the table dispenser and handed them to Oliver.

"Thanks," he said, smiling. He hoped her eyes might smile back.

They didn't.

"No problem." She turned to Anish. "Now get up. Let's go over to the Fox."

"Who's playing?" Micah groaned. "Can't we just roam? I'm so broke."

"No, you're not. You worked the same hours as me this week. And it's Trout Steak Revival. Come on."

"This bluegrass phase you're in is wearing me out," Anish said. "And I'm still annoyed they started charging two extra bucks for under twenty-one."

Essa ignored their protests. She stood up and headed for the door, leaving Oliver in her lavender wake. He wanted to scramble out of the booth and run after her, catch her, be as close to her as humanly possible. But he stopped himself.

Play it cool.

He hung back. Waited for Micah and Anish to get up and follow her out.

They strolled up College Avenue and then turned on Thirteenth Street. Oliver saw a sushi place, a yoga studio, an ad plastered to the back of a sidewalk bench: *Freaky's Smoke Shop.*

Essa walked ten steps ahead while Oliver was stuck with the guys, who were busy debating the superiority of different methods for boiling water when you're stuck in the woods without a metal pot.

Oliver got the courage to jog ahead and catch up to her. "Hey," he said, a little out of breath. Boulder's altitude was still getting to him.

"Hey." Essa didn't look over.

As they neared the Fox Theater, the sidewalk got more crowded. There was a small throng gathered under the red neon lights. Black letters hung crookedly on the marquee: TROUT STEAK REVIVAL.

"So you into this band?" Oliver asked, pointing up.

"Yeah."

Essa's eyes looked different than they did at the party last night. Maybe it was just the firelight Oliver had seen reflected in them, but Oliver didn't think so. Something was different tonight. She seemed . . . deflated.

"You okay?" He regretted it the moment he asked it. Maybe it was too bold. He hardly knew her, and he instantly felt like he was prying. Whenever Lilly was sick, he hated to be asked if he was okay. Because he wasn't. And he didn't want to talk about it.

"Yeah," Essa said again. But it wasn't convincing. A long strand of her hair had fallen out of her elastic. She reached up and tucked it back in.

Maybe nothing's wrong. Maybe she just doesn't like me.

He tried again. "What's your favorite song of theirs?"

Essa paused as the crowd slowly moved forward. They were under the marquee now. She looked up into red neon lights that bathed her face in a warm glow. "No."

"No? They have a song called 'No'?"

Essa managed a smile. "Sorry, I meant . . . no, I'm not really okay."

Oliver wasn't sure what to say next. He wasn't expecting a real answer like that. When people asked him if he was okay, he always just lied. "Okay if I ask why? I mean, I guess I sort of just did. So I hope it's okay." He gave her a small smile.

The corners of her mouth lifted just a little. "It's okay. It's just my mom. She has this new boyfriend, and when I came home from the bonfire last night, Puck was up, and she'd gotten these candies out . . ."

Essa didn't finish her sentence. Oliver couldn't tell whether she was angry or afraid or worried. Or maybe all of it. Micah and Anish sped past them and made it to the ticket counter.

"Do you really have to do that?" Micah was making a face as the bouncer marked his hand with a giant red ink stamp: UNDER 21. The bouncer didn't respond.

Anish's hand was stamped, making Oliver next in line. He stepped up and fumbled in his back jeans pocket for his wallet. But Essa reached out and stopped him.

"Let's not go in," she said. Oliver thought he could see a little firelight return to her eyes. "You wanna come somewhere with me?"

"Yeah, sure." It didn't even occur to him to ask where, and he nearly dropped his wallet on the pavement as he quickly shoved it back into his pocket.

"But we'll kind of have to hurry. We can't be late. Is that okay?"

Oliver nodded.

Essa reached for her cell and texted Micah and Anish. They'd already disappeared inside the crowded theater. "Uh-oh," she said, looking down at the screen. "They're pissed."

"They can't get a refund and just come back out?" Oliver realized he asked the question in a hopeful sort of way. As if he hadn't asked a question at all, but had made a statement: *please tell me they can't so we can be alone.*

"Nope," Essa said. "They either forfeit the eighteen bucks, or they stay and listen to Trout Steak. I do feel kinda bad. They didn't really want to go in the first place . . ."

"Didn't you say we had to leave soon? If we want to be on time?"

The flicker in her eyes came back again. "Yes. Okay. Let's go. They'll still love me tomorrow."

14

OLIVER

They hurried past shops on the Hill. An art store, a bookstore with lines of poetry painted on the outside, a tiny black brick building called The Sink. Oliver stopped in front and peered in the windows.

"Famous burger and pizza place," Essa explained. "Been there for a hundred years."

Oliver pressed his face against the glass. The Sink's walls were covered from floor to ceiling with graffiti and paintings. He saw images of angels, mermaids, students crammed around a professor with wild-looking hair.

"Puck's elementary school isn't far from here," Essa said, pointing down the street. "See that giant brick building? Kind of looks like it's out of Hogwarts or something? That's it."

"Elementary school on a college campus?"

"Yep. She's a little genius, I'm telling you. It's perfect for her."

They kept walking. Soon the street changed from shops to rows of houses and apartment buildings. Music blasted from open balcony doors. Pizza boxes were piled in trash cans clustered beside entrances. Empty beer cans were tucked at the foot of bushes like shiny bullets of fertilizer.

Oliver wracked his brain, searching for something to talk about as they walked. But nothing came. He wanted it to be like last night, at the fire. He wanted to know everything about Essa, every last detail. But she walked along in silence. She wasn't looking around her. She wasn't looking inside the college parties they passed. Mostly she seemed to just be watching the ground as they walked. She seemed too quiet. Almost . . . somewhere else.

They turned onto Arapahoe Avenue, and the traffic zoomed by them. Outside a large brick building, colorful flags read,

NAROPA UNIVERSITY: DISCOVER THE DIFFERENCE OF CONTEMPLATIVE EDUCATION.

"I think my aunt told me about this place. Is it a . . . ?" Oliver couldn't quite remember what Sophie had called it.

"Buddhist university," Essa said. "I know people that go there. You have to meditate as part of your coursework. And go on retreats and stuff. Pretty badass."

Oliver peered at the front lawns in front of the university's main building. He expected to see monks wrapped in robes shuffling in and out of its doors. Instead, he just saw college kids. Backpacks. Ripped jeans. Yoga pants. The usual.

They continued down the street and the houses got larger, more stately. A few resembled the grand stone homes back in Chicago, up near Evanston. They all had antique-looking windows, large arched doorways, wrought iron railings next to broad front steps.

Essa stopped under the buzz of a streetlight. "We're here."

They were standing in front a large old home. It was red brick with white trim and was surrounded by beautiful wildflower gardens, a pond with a tinkling waterfall, a wide lawn filled with Adirondack chairs. There was a lighted sign that said, BLUE SPRUCE INN.

"A hotel? We're going to a hotel?" Oliver's mouth went completely dry. He froze. Was she taking him to a room? He thought she didn't date, let alone . . . *this*. After they'd just met? Micah had never finished his description of Essa back at Cheba Hut. Did he mean she didn't date but just hooked up? And then bailed? His mind raced in a thousand different directions.

I'm a virgin.

I have no idea what to do.

I HAVE NO IDEA WHAT TO DO.

And I think I'm wearing the same boxers I had on yesterday. The ones with a skunk and the words IT WASN'T ME *on the butt.*

"Not the Inn," Essa said. "*Behind* it."

It was a small, one-story wooden structure with a white door. Next to the entrance was what looked like a half-canoe standing upright, its pointy tip angling toward the sky. Sitting inside the canoe was a stone statue of Buddha, legs folded, eyes closed, an easy smile on his face. A group of people stood next to the half-boat, kicking off shoes and tucking them into a tall wooden cabinet.

"It's a Zendo," Essa said quietly, as if that explained something. She took Oliver's hand again, pulled him through the gardens toward the little building. She kicked off her sandals and left them at the foot of the Buddha boat.

"You're just . . . leaving your shoes out here?" Oliver asked, yanking at his own.

"Yeah, come on." Essa was whispering now and motioned for him to follow her. He noticed all the people gathering outside the building were quiet. And moving a little slowly. They held their hands clasped in front of their hearts as they lined up at the door, bowing before going in.

Oliver grudgingly nestled his shoes next to Essa's. He saw purses and handbags piled around as well. He couldn't believe it. If he left anything outside like this in Chicago, it would be stolen in roughly three minutes.

"But why are we taking off our shoes?" he asked. But Essa was already in line, filing into the building. She clasped her hands together, held them in front of her chest, and bowed as she stepped on the threshold and disappeared inside.

Oliver wanted to bail. He had no idea what to do. When he made it to the door, he didn't bow like the others had. He didn't know how. And the thought of it freaked him out. He just stepped into the room in his socks.

In the dim light, he could see that it was one large room. There was an altar with a giant wooden arch over it. A golden Buddha statue, some bells, a bowl. A few flowers. Burning incense. The walls were white, and the floor was honey-colored wood without a scuff on it, it seemed. Lining the room were square black mats with puffy black round cushions in the center of each one. People sat along the edges of the room, each on one of the cushions, their legs folded like pretzels just like Oliver had seen his aunt do. And they were sitting a few inches from the wall, facing it.

And they weren't moving.

At all.

Oliver felt like they were sitting perfectly, almost inhumanly still. There was something about the stillness he had never seen before. It was like another presence in the room, like these people had somehow commandeered the very air around them and ordered it not to move.

As his eyes adjusted, he saw Essa on one of the cushions, already in pretzel form, already staring at the wall. He wanted to talk to her, to sit close to her, to ask her a million questions. About her life. About Puck. About anything she wanted to tell him. What he distinctly *did not* want to do was sit in a dim room on a cushion and stare at a wall all night.

A guy in the corner struck a few bells. Oliver hurried to an empty cushion and sat facing the wall, his back to the center of the room like everyone else's, his legs barely folded in front of him. The room fell back into the eerie, otherworldly silence. He guessed this was meditation. Just . . . sitting there.

That's when the pain started. Almost immediately. Only a few minutes in, his foot went numb. He tried to move imperceptibly. He tried to shift without alerting the Super Quiet People to his right and to his left. Even the slightest movement sent burning sensations through his legs and up through his butt.

This sucks.

He felt someone watching him. He turned and looked. It

was Essa. She was three cushions down. Smiling. She silently mouthed a few words: *Count your breaths.*

Good thing Oliver could read lips.

How long? he mouthed back.

Forty minutes. She smiled again, like she'd just delivered good news.

I'll never make it, Oliver thought.

His fear and dread about sitting there for an entire forty minutes were broken when he heard someone come in the door. Essa quickly turned her head and looked back at the wall in front of her. Oliver was afraid to turn around to see who came in; he'd make too much noise. So he just listened. Whoever it was walked slowly and made their way around the room. As they passed each person, he or she bowed to the wall. Then Oliver heard the shuffling of fabric. Lots of it. The person was sitting, but it was taking a *long* time. But finally, they settled down. The room was silent again.

Oliver remembered Essa's instruction to count his breaths.

He couldn't even count five. His breaths were like butterflies—no, the ghosts of butterflies—just as soon as he thought about breathing, the thought was gone, a specter that faded into the herd of a million fluttering thoughts.

Is someone outside stealing my shoes?

Did a college kid take off with Essa's purse? Is he already down at the Conoco station buying gas and beer with the money in her wallet?

Can you die from boredom?

Am I really that into this girl that I followed her into this weird room?

The forty minutes seemed to take seven hours, and just as Oliver thought he was going to lose it and run out, the guy in the corner rang the bells again. People turned on their cushions and faced the center of the room. Oliver turned as well, and saw the mystery man who had come into the Zendo. He was sitting on a cushion, his legs folded beneath him, his back perfectly straight. Oliver saw the source of all that shuffling fabric: the man was wrapped in a black robe. It was draped and tucked around his legs, making him look like some sort of statue. *A Zen priest?*

Before Oliver could mouth the question to Essa, people stood, formed a line, and walked slowly around the room. *Very slowly.* Oliver watched Essa, trying to figure out what to do. She peeled a heel off the floor like it was glued down, and she was gently freeing it. Then she peeled the rest of her foot off the floor just as slowly and stepped forward. Over and over again, everyone in the room walked this way and made it around the room in a strange slow-motion march.

Essa looked over at Oliver. *This is kin-hin,* she mouthed.

What?

Walking meditation, Essa replied.

Finally, the walk was over and everyone settled back on their cushions and the priest back on his. He rewrapped his robe around his folded legs and started talking. Oliver could barely follow. The priest talked about the breath. Being the wheel of your ship. The port in the storm. How it was a place of safety. Solidity amidst the groundlessness of life. The constant flux. He talked about turning the wheel of the Dharma. Then he told a story.

"Buddha was surrounded by his students," he said. "He held up a white flower and twirled it, saying nothing. No one understood the meaning of this wordless sermon except Mahākāśyapa." The priest stopped and looked up. "Whose only response was a smile."

Oliver waited for more. For a punch line. A summary. Something that made some sort of sense.

"Buddha responded that Mahākāśyapa understood the Dharma gate, the mind of nirvana that does not depend on words."

Which didn't help at all.

Oliver looked over at Essa, wondering if she was just as confused as he was. But she wasn't. Instead, he saw what he'd been hoping to see all night: Her eyes were lit up, just like at the campfire. Her face looked happy again, like whatever weight had been dragging her down had been lifted. Like whatever happened with her mom and her sister the night before had been forgotten somehow. She was smiling like the priest, this happy, super calm smile. And she was nodding, too.

She caught him looking at her, and he tried to hide the confusion on his face. But all he could think about was how mysterious Essa was. How deep. How she wasn't like anyone he'd ever met or seen or even heard of before.

And how there was no way on earth this hippie, hiking, trekking, mysterious Buddhist girl would ever like him back.

15

OLIVER

Essa lived within walking distance of the Zendo. Oliver had two fears about this. One, he worried that she wouldn't let him walk her home. Two, he worried that she would. If she wanted to say goodbye here, just outside the Zendo, in the stream of calm meditators flooding out of the gardens around them, what would he say?

Nice meditating with you.

No.

Maybe next week we can try the Robert Plant at the Cheba Hut.

No.

I think you may be the most beautiful and fascinating person I've ever met.

NO.

On the other hand, if she let him walk her home, they might get to her front door. The place where everybody always kissed in the movies. He'd never walked a girl home before. He'd kissed two, but barely. There was Cheryl at the sixth grade dance who dared him to kiss her behind the cardboard cutout of their school's mascot—a giant muskrat. Then there was Edie in the tenth grade during a really awkward game of Seven Minutes in Heaven. They were crammed in her dad's closet next to a bunch of shoes that smelled roughly like rotting cottage cheese, and she lifted up her shirt and everything. But he didn't touch anything under there, and when she tried to French-kiss him, she pretty much just ended up licking his teeth.

Plus, the blood still hadn't returned to Oliver's feet after an hour on those tiny cushions in the Zendo. He worried that even if Essa let him walk her home, he might not really be able to walk at all. He tried to shake out his legs without being too obvious.

"What did you think?" Essa asked as they slipped on their shoes beside the Buddha boat.

"It was . . . cool."

Her face fell a little. "It's okay if you don't want to come back. This stuff isn't for everybody, I—"

"I do. I do want to come back. It's just . . . different. That's all."

In the dim garden lights, they walked past the tinkling water-fall and down a stone path that crisscrossed among waist-high wildflowers. A warm, dry breeze began to blow, lifting the scent from the blossoms and sprinkling it all around them.

"That last part. About Buddha twirling the flower," Oliver added. "Was I supposed to get that?"

Essa smiled. "It's a koan. A sort of puzzle that points to prajna, or wisdom. To truth. The idea is that if you think you under-stand it with your rational mind . . . you don't. Truth and reality are beyond all that. Beyond the concepts our minds create."

"But you were smiling. I thought you understood it."

"That one makes me happy," she said. The campfire light was back in her eyes.

"Cool," he said, even though he didn't really understand at all. He looked at her as the breeze kicked up again, at the sanctuary tattoo just below her collarbone. "Is that . . . from a koan, too?"

She nodded. "Case Four. But you've probably got to get—"

"I'm in no rush," he interrupted. Venturing.

Essa looked just beyond him at the group of Adirondack chairs huddled under the giant elm in the middle of the garden.

"Buddha was walking with a group," she began. "He pointed to a place on the ground and said it would be a good spot to build a sanctuary. Indra picked up a blade of grass, stuck it in the ground, and said, 'The sanctuary is built.'"

She stopped and looked at Oliver again.

"And Buddha smiled," she said. She ran a finger over her sanctuary tattoo. Over the blade of grass.

Oliver didn't get that one, either. But he felt something. A little moment of lightness he didn't understand.

"And getting a tattoo of it is ironic," Essa continued. "It's me trying to grasp the story. To hold on to how it makes me feel. Which is antithetical to Zen and part of the whole problem of duhkha—"

"So you must know what that one means?"

"No." She shook her head. "But I know what it feels like."

Oliver raised his eyebrows, asking.

"It feels like . . . home," she said. "Like I'm safe. Exactly where I am. Without having to change anything."

It hit him, what she said. About being home. "Your eyes look so beautiful when you talk about it." He couldn't believe he'd said that. But he had to. He just had to. "Crazy beautiful." This was what Essa did to him. Made him forget things. Forget to think. He felt horrible for saying the word *crazy*.

Essa noticed. "Thanks," she said. "But . . . are you okay? You look a little . . . something." They'd reached the end of the garden and stood at a large wooden gate.

"I just don't like that word. Crazy. I try not to use it." He looked beyond the wide slats of the wooden fence, at the traffic hustling down Arapahoe Avenue. He looked at the flags waving in the lawn of the Buddhist university. At a group of a drunk college guys going the opposite way. Loud. Careening.

"It's okay," Essa said. "I'm not offended. I think I know what you meant. Plus, I tell Puck she's crazy smart all the time. Crazy annoying, too." She grinned.

The mention of Essa's little sister made Oliver sad. It made him miss Lilly. It made him want her to be better. It made him feel lonely. He didn't want to leave Essa. "Can I walk you home?" He couldn't be sure in the dim light, but he thought she blushed. She straightened the butterfly clip in her hair.

Essa looked at the rushing traffic. "It's sort of like . . ." She stopped. Gazed up into the branches of the trees looming over them.

"It's sort of like . . . what?" Oliver dared to step close. He could smell the incense from the Zendo rising from her hair. It mixed with the wildflowers from the garden. He was perilously close to her again—to the smooth skin of her shoulders, to the waves in her hair, to that light in her eyes he wanted to somehow capture and take with him. "You can tell me."

Moonlight glinted in her blue-gray eyes, and heat started to travel up his back. He could hear her breathing. Was she leaning in? He thought she was. Closer and closer. The urge to put his arms around her came suddenly. He wanted nothing else in the world but to hold her. And even though he'd never held a girl before in his entire life, suddenly he felt like he'd know exactly how to do it. He'd know just how to hold her, just how to put his hand next to her cheek, just how to kiss her . . .

She stepped back.

"You see, the thing is . . . I don't date." She took a deep breath. "And I don't want you to get the wrong idea or anything."

Oliver felt like one of the drunk guys from the street had stolen into the garden and given him a swift kick in the gut. Even though Micah had told him that Essa didn't date anyone, he couldn't help but believe it was just because she hadn't found the right guy yet. And obviously, he wasn't going to be it.

"It's not you or anything," she said, as if she'd read his mind. "It's because of Puck."

"Puck?"

"My mom has a different boyfriend every week. And it upsets her—and me—so much. It's so gross, and they're all so creepy, and . . . I just can't have Puck see me take off with guys, either. You know? I'm, like, the stable one in the family. It's my job."

"I get it," Oliver said. "I really do." The ache for his sister Lilly returned. That feeling that he should never have left Chicago. The guilt over what happened the last night he saw her. How she almost . . .

"When Micah told me your sister was sick," Essa went on, "I just thought you could use a friend in Boulder."

So this was a pity date. I knew it.

"Totally cool of you," Oliver lied.

"How is she? Your sister?" Essa looked back into Oliver's eyes. "If it's okay for me to ask."

"Good. She's good."

Actually, he had no idea.

Essa leaned in and gave Oliver a little half-hug. Oliver could tell she wasn't going to press the issue. "See you in the shop," she said. "When do you work next?"

"Not sure," he said. Essa was already through the wooden gate. Oliver followed. "But Anish invited me to go to the mountains next weekend? Some sort of wilderness game?"

A look of worry passed across her face. "I'm not sure you'd like it."

"Oh."

"But I mean, of course you can come." It wasn't convincing.

"No. It's cool. I get it. It's okay."

Essa didn't turn to walk away. She didn't step back. Oliver worried this was his last chance to lean in, to touch her face, to kiss her. The pull was so strong, as if he did it, all the world would right itself. Every problem, every trouble, every bad memory, would slip into the night and be carried away by the dry Boulder mountain breeze.

"Night," she said. And turned to go.

Oliver watched her walk away, wondering if he'd imagined that she'd leaned in before. That it felt like she might kiss him.

But she doesn't date.

Her baggy pants billowed in the breeze as she walked farther and farther away. Her butterfly hair clip blinked under the streetlights. They were only fifty feet apart. It had only been a few minutes since they stood under those tall trees, beside those wildflowers.

He didn't care.

He missed her already.

June 16

16

OLIVER

I have my cell.

That was what the text said. Oliver squinted at his phone. He'd been sound asleep, having a nightmare. He was locked in Micah's Jeep, and it was headed straight for the edge of a cliff. No one was in the driver's seat, but the car was speeding, driving itself somehow. He looked out the window and saw Essa dancing by a bonfire, surrounded by people from Boulder High. They were all watching her, mesmerized by the arch of her back and the curve of her legs as she moved in the firelight. He recognized Anish and that stoner girl Skye in the crowd. No one could see him, though, trapped in the speeding car. Or if they could, they didn't seem to care. The Jeep's tires reached the edge, and the car started to pitch down a thousand-foot drop—

The text had woken him up.

He rubbed his eyes and looked at the screen again. Formulated a response.

Obviously. Bc you're texting me on it, he typed.

I stole it back from Fitzy.

Oliver sighed, his brain kicking into gear, his thumbs flying across the cell screen. You're not supposed to have your phone.

Not supposed to talk to you, either.

True.

Oliver's thumbs stopped. He didn't have an answer to that one.

He looked out his bedroom window at the Flatiron Mountains. They were coated in a soft pink glow as the sun rose, chasing away a low-hanging fog from the jagged granite. Alpenglow. That's what Sophie called it. The way the mountains lit up in the sunrise. It was only six in the morning.

His phone jingled again, and he looked back at the screen. It wasn't a text this time. Now she was inviting him to a FaceTime call. He didn't know if he should take it. He didn't think about it very long. He answered. A little wheel spun at the top of the screen.

Connecting . . .

There she was. Her face filling his phone. Her long brown hair tangled and tumbling down to her waist. Her blue eyes bright and smoky, her skin pale and perfect, almost as white as the wall behind her. He thought she looked like some sort of fairy. Like her giant glittery wings were tucked just behind her, out of sight. That they might unfurl at any moment and beat their magic into the air. Sometimes it was so clear to him that she wasn't from earth, that she'd come from some other mythical world and desperately needed to get out of this dull, cold real one. She was dying here.

Lilly.

"They think I'm ready to get out of here," she said.

He wanted it to be true. He peered at the screen, into her eyes. Sometimes he could tell just by looking. They seemed flat, calm. Like maybe the medicine was working. Like maybe it had closed the door to whatever world she'd been in the last time he saw her. Like maybe it had brought her to this one.

"They said I shouldn't even be here in the first place," she added.

The little bit of hope that had risen in his throat turned sour. Of course she should've been hospitalized. After what happened last time, no doctor would tell her she shouldn't be. She was lying. Or delusional.

"Tell me," Oliver said. It's what he always said. It was code between brother and sister. A request for her to let her guard down, to open up, to tell him what was actually going through her mind instead of the song and dance she always gave their parents and her psychiatrists. He hoped she didn't ask him any questions, that her mind was moving too fast to think about how life was going in Boulder. He wondered what he'd say if she did ask. He'd tell her it had been almost a week since he'd seen Essa. That their shifts hadn't overlapped in the kite store. That she hadn't invited him to any more bonfire parties or Cheba Hut meals or meditation sessions in the Zendo. He would tell her he hated being out here, that he wanted to come home, that Boulder was turning out to be super boring.

He'd be lying, too.

"Why would I be thinking anything special?" Lilly opened her eyes wide, faking shock. He saw a hint of resentment scurry across her face.

It reminded him of her Angry Pirate Face. Their Chicago townhouse had large stone walls on either side of the driveway. When they were kids, one side was Lilly's pirate ship and the other was Oliver's. Of course she took the side that had the better stones; Oliver's ship was crumbling and moss-covered. They would march up and down the walls for hours, barking orders at imaginary crew members, staving off invented mutinies. He could still see Lilly's long hair flying behind her as she marched a sailor off the gangplank. He could still hear her voice as she called over to his ship for more supplies. They'd made up the entire world, but at least they were afloat on the same ocean, at sail on the same sea.

When her delusions started in her teens, all that changed. They weren't on the same anything.

"I can't believe what you did to me," she said now, her face still dim on Oliver's iPhone. She recoiled a little when she said it, looked away from the screen. Like an animal suddenly afraid, trying to make herself smaller so she wouldn't get hurt. Again.

"I'm sorry, Lil. I lost it that night."

"Whatever. Did you see all that blood?"

The scene from the last night with Lilly back in Chicago flashed in his mind. Like a horror film. Flickering. The way his head had pounded with rage. The way he'd clenched his fists. The screaming. "I'll believe you, Lilly. I will. Just tell me what you're thinking."

"You won't believe me." Tears pooled in her eyes. "I just wish I'd died that night. Next to you." Oliver imagined her glittering fairy wings turning dull, drying out, cracking and falling to dust.

There is no torture like mental torture. And I can't help her.

"Don't say that. It'll get better. It will." He knew he didn't sound convincing. "Just tell me what you're thinking."

"He's coming—" A door behind Lilly opened and flooded her room with light. Except it wasn't her room at all. It was a closet. Now Oliver could see brooms and cleaning supplies stacked on the wall to the right.

"Found you." It was Fitzy, the hulking night guard at the psych hospital who Lilly knew all too well. "Time to go."

"Five more minutes," Lilly pleaded.

"Nope."

Oliver saw Fitzy's large hand come down over the screen as he took her phone back. He could hear Lilly's voice in a hiss close to the receiver.

"The crossword answer in the *Trib.* Twenty-four down," she said. She was frantically trying to get a message to Oliver before Fitzy ended the call. "*Felony.* I'm right, Oliver—"

The call went dead. His screen went black.

He held the phone in his hand for a few minutes more. He stared at it as if she might appear again at any moment. Sane. Fixed. The Lilly he knew as a kid. An old familiar ache saturated his chest, an urge to find an answer, a cure. But they'd been to the best psychiatric hospitals in the country, talked to psychologists of every stripe, tried every medicine twice over.

Schizophrenia.

It would be better sometimes. And then it would be worse.

And it would tumble over and over itself like that most likely for the rest of her life. It was a thing to be managed, to be suffered, to be endured. There would be bright spots; there would be life for her. But it would never be constant; it would never stand still.

He thought of the word the Zen priest used.

Groundless.

He tapped the screen of his phone and knew who he wanted to text.

Essa.

He had this feeling that maybe somehow she had an answer he hadn't thought of. Or that maybe one of those people in the Zendo would know what to do. Maybe the Zen priest. Maybe he'd understand somehow.

It was only six-thirty.

Essa would probably want nothing to do with him if she knew how messed up his life really was. How messed up his family was. How messed up he was. She already hadn't texted him in a week. He should probably give up and just go back to Chicago.

He looked back at his phone.

He'd text her after noon.

17

ESSA

"There are a hundred and eight beads on a mala." Puck tugged on her mother's shirt. "Do you know what those are? Malas?"

"Yeah, honey." Her mom was staring in the window of a llama wool shop. "Do you think that vest is cool?" She looked over at Essa. "Or no?"

"A wool vest?" Essa asked. She eyed the burnt orange llama wool and the large wooden buttons. "Not cool."

Not that they could afford anything made of llama wool, anyway. But it was a Friday. Essa's mom didn't have to work at Pure Buds; Essa didn't have a shift at Above the Clouds. So they'd decided to go "shopping" on Pearl Street. They did this every now and then, walking past the shops, acting like they could buy anything they wanted. Getting in heated debates about which clothes to buy, which pieces of art to acquire. It was a crunchy town, but not a cheap one. These shopping trips were pure conjecture.

"Maybe if it was in a different color? Like maroon? And it was fall?" her mom asked.

Essa eyed it again. Cocked her head to the side. "Nope. Not even in maroon. Not even in November."

"*Moooom.*" Puck tugged at her mother's shirt again. "I want a mala. From over there." Puck pointed at a store on the other side of Pearl Street. Above the large shop window was the store's name, painted in thick golden letters:

OLD TIBET

SPIRITUAL GIFT SHOP

The shelves in the store's front window were slightly bowed and sagging from the weight of everything they held. There were golden singing bowls of all shapes and sizes, each sitting on a multicolored pillow. Wooden racks held countless malas with fluffy tassels at their ends. The beaded necklaces gleamed in the sunlight. Some beads were wooden, like honey-colored sandalwood or a dark chocolate rosewood. Others were made of gemstones: jungle green jade, turquoise amazonite, rich blue lapis lazuli. There were intricately carved boxes of incense, brass lamps, embroidered wall hangings. Dotted throughout were small Buddha statues in all positions. Sitting Buddhas, laughing Buddhas, reclining Buddhas. Buddha with his hands in different mudras, or positions. Dhyana mudra, hands resting on one another, thumbs gently touching. Bhumisparsha mudra, a hand pointing toward the earth. A teaching mudra, Vitarka, with the tips of thumbs and index fingers lightly touching.

Puck took her mother's hand in hers and pulled her in front of the Tibetan shop. "There," she said, pointing to a mala with teal-and-white beads and a brown tassel. "I want those. They're amazonite."

"Amazonite? Did you make that up?" Her mother squinted at the string of beads. "Is that a real stone?"

"Yep. See how the turquoise is kind of swirled with white and yellow? So awesome."

Her mother wrinkled her brow and looked for a price tag. "*Seventy dollars?* What are mala beads again? They better be magic for that price."

Puck looked at Essa and rolled her eyes. "See, Essa? She never *listens.* Plus, we're supposed to be pretend shopping anyway."

"Go easy," Essa said. "Just tell her what they are."

"I've told her three times," Puck whined. She turned to her mom. "They're used by several religions. In Buddhism, some sects use them to count mantras, to meditate. In others, they're not as important. It depends. Zen is different from Tibetan Buddhism. Anyway, there are a hundred and eight beads because—"

"Ooh, I love that embroidery of the tree. We could hang that in the living room. Behind the couch?" Her mother looked at Essa for confirmation.

"Um, no," Essa said. "These aren't really decorations; they have meaning. Like, religious significance. That's the bodhi tree. Where Buddha attained enlightenment."

"*Ficus religiosa*, to be precise." Puck held one finger in the air to make her point. Essa smiled; her sister looked like a little professor badly in need of a hairbrush.

"I grew up in Boulder, remember?" their mother said. "It's practically a Buddhist town. I've seen all this stuff for years. I know about it. Sort of . . ."

"So there are lots of explanations for the hundred and eight beads," Puck said, more urgently now. "See?" She pointed to a yellowed piece of paper that was taped inside the store window. It listed the many meanings of the number 108, everything from its significance in Vedic mathematics, to Tantric systems of physiology, to the claim that there are 108 human feelings.

Essa's mom squinted to read it. "The first manned spaceflight lasted a hundred and eight minutes? And there are a hundred and eight stitches in a baseball? What the hell does that have to do with Buddhism?"

Essa stared at the amazonite beads. Each one was exactly the same size; they looped around the display, on and on, bead after bead, seemingly endless.

"My favorite explanation is that the beads represent our desires," Essa said, still gazing at a string of them. "They remind us that if you fulfill one desire, another is right behind it to take its place. We always think if we get what we want, we'll be happy. But they're inexhaustible, the things we want. And we know it. At some level we know that it will never be enough."

Experience is unsatisfactory.

"That's duhkha," Puck chimed in. "And the way to make it stop is to follow Buddha's Eightfold Path."

"What if we put this Buddha in the garden?" Their mother was pointing at a small stone statue. It was a laughing Buddha with a generous belly. "I've seen these in people's yards. They look cool. Or maybe this wheel?"

"That's the wheel of the Dharma, Mom. Each spoke represents a step on the Eightfold Path. Steps like Right Effort, Right Mindfulness . . ." Puck didn't finish. It was obvious their mother wasn't listening and Puck was giving up. She shook her head in apparent disgust. "I don't even want to go in anymore." She jogged ahead of Essa and her mom.

"Stay close!" Essa called. Puck was already ducking and weaving through the crowd, in and out of the dappled sunshine coming through the trees on Pearl. Essa's eyes locked on her sister's blonde hair, tracking the flashes of gold like a swimmer watching a coin tumble through the water on its way to being lost in the depths.

"Just let her sulk," her mother said as she wrapped her dreadlocks in a loose rubber band. Her ponytail was as thick as Essa's forearm. "I just said I liked the tree stitchery. What's she so pissed about?"

Essa kept her eyes on her sister and contemplated a response to her mother's question. "Most likely? Cultural appropriation and the commodification of a religion. But that's just a guess."

"Huh?"

Essa wanted to explain. How Zen centers started cropping up in California in the 1960s and 70s, popularized by Beat poets and a countercultural "hippie" fascination with meditation and Eastern religions. How some people said Buddhism had been Americanized and segregated by race in many communities. Or commodified and obscured by the mindfulness movement. But she couldn't say any of that because she had to go. Puck had disappeared in the crowd outside the Boulder Cafe.

"Gotta catch Puck," Essa said as she took off after her sister.

The Boulder Cafe sat in the grand curved corner of a large building on Pearl Street. It resembled a large slice of yellow cake with fluffy white icing on top. It was three stories of yellow brick, and at the very top just under the eaves, a giant white wooden mural of flowers and garlands wrapped around the entire structure. Above the antique wooden door hung a glass lantern that gently creaked in the nearly constant Boulder summer breeze. The line to get in to the café stretched around the corner and spilled onto the brick plaza of Pearl. It had been a popular city landmark for over twenty years.

Puck wriggled her way through the snaking line and disappeared inside. Essa tried to follow her, but being considerably larger than her tiny, elflike little sister, she had a much harder time getting past the crowd. She bumped into a tall tourist dressed completely in black who was holding a cup of Starbucks coffee.

"*Quelle folie!*" the woman shouted as her coffee spilled on her shirt. Essa had no idea what the woman had said, but guessed it was French and not a compliment.

"Sorry," Essa said. "Just trying to find my sister. She's inside."

The French woman did not look amused. Essa kept moving, pushing past several couples, a few more tourist types, and then found herself snagged in a large group of girls her age who were dressed in matching Western wear. They all wore white cowboy hats with sparkly bands, purple vests, and bolo ties. Essa knew immediately who they were.

Westernaires.

It was a horse riding group up in Jefferson County that was for girls only. They did stuff like barrel racing at rodeos, trick riding and jumping. It was sort of like Girl Scouts. On steroids. On horseback. Essa could feel the confidence oozing out of the girls' pores. They all stood so rock steady, their hands stuffed in the pockets of their dusty jeans, their arms strong from wrangling two-ton beasts every day after school.

Chicks who ride horses = badasses.

Badasses, and not big fans of crunchy Boulder girls.

Essa gathered her courage and tapped the shoulder of one of the girls' shiny purple vests. "Hey," she said. "Did you happen to see a little girl go past here? Blonde hair?"

"Sorry." The Westernaire shrugged. Her face was covered with a smattering of freckles brought out by the Colorado sun. "Didn't see her."

"Okay, thanks anyway. I—"

"A little girl about this tall?" A middle-aged guy in a straw hat interrupted and held his hand up, indicating Puck's height. Essa nodded. "Yep, she ran right past me. Headed down there." He pointed toward a darkened staircase behind a glass door next to the Boulder Cafe. A weathered metal sign hung crooked from the doorknob: PUBLIC RESTROOMS.

Below it there was a large cartoon hand pointing down. Essa had never been down there; she always used the restrooms that were inside the café.

"Thanks," Essa said. She pushed her way through the glass door and headed down the wooden stairs. They creaked under her sandals. The hallway was dim and filled with the rotting, fermented smell of stale beer. A lone fluorescent light buzzed overhead at the bottom, casting a pale white glow over the graffiti on the wall. There was a drawing of a yellow-and-black shield with a badger in the center. He had a joint hanging out of his mouth. Underneath, it read, HOUSE OF HUFFLEPUFF.

Essa rolled her eyes and pushed open the door to the women's restroom. The floor was covered in thousands of tiny black and white tiles and littered with wet paper towels and tissues. The beer smell was still pungent. "Puck?"

Silence.

All Essa could hear was the dripping of water from a leaky sink faucet. She leaned down and looked under all the gray bathroom doors, hoping to see her sister's tiny feet. She didn't. "Puck? You in here?"

The bathroom stayed quiet. Essa looked in one of the wavy mirrors over a sink and noticed the paleness of her skin. A knot of worry twisted tighter and tighter in her throat; she worried she might vomit. There wasn't anything else down here but these restrooms. Where could Puck be? And why did she even come down here in the first place? There was a perfectly nice bathroom on the first floor of the restaurant. The only other place to check down here was the men's room. But why would she be in there?

A sound echoed through the bathroom, bouncing off the cool plaster walls and the hollows of the dirty porcelain sinks. Essa felt cold, like a late Colorado spring snow had just blanketed every limb and branch of her veins. She realized what it was.

Just her phone.

A text message.

She took a deep breath and pulled out her phone. The message was short: Hey.

Her eyes widened as she realized who it was.

Oliver.

She didn't think he'd message her again, not after their conversation outside the Zendo. Since then, she'd made sure not to schedule a shift at the store that overlapped with his. Didn't he get it? She had to work and take care of Puck. And right now she had to *find* Puck. She ignored him and put her phone away. She had to search the rest of this awful basement.

She put her hand on the bathroom door to leave, but heard a sound. Coming from the middle stall. Just a little movement.

Essa tiptoed toward the stall door and gently pushed. It creaked as it swung wide open and there, standing on top of the toilet in her ratty sneakers . . .

Puck.

"Seriously, you need to wipe that grin off your face ASAP," Essa said. "This is so not funny. I almost threw up, I was so freaked out."

Puck's smile remained squarely in place. "Great hiding spot, huh?"

"No. No, it is not. It's totally creepy down here, and you shouldn't be here alone. You could—"

"Watch out!" Puck sprang off the toilet and launched herself high in the air. She landed about a foot outside the stall door, nearly on top of Essa. "Toilet Vault. Perfect ten!"

Her stubborn smile was even larger.

"You know what I should get?" Essa asked. "One of those obnoxious kid leashes. You know, where I strap it to you and walk you around like a little puppy. It would make my life so much easier." Puck wasn't listening. She'd jumped up on the counter next to the sinks and was swinging her legs back and forth over the edge. "And wash your hands," Essa added.

"Why? I didn't go!"

"If you vault off a public toilet, you wash your hands. That's just how it is."

Puck rolled her eyes, but acquiesced. She leaned over the sink to her right and turned on the water. Essa grabbed a wad of paper towels from the stainless steel dispenser on the wall and held them out for her sister to dry her hands.

Puck turned up her nose. "Don't you see the sticker?" She pointed at the towel dispenser. Someone had stuck a large round sticker on the side that read, THESE ARE MADE OF TREES. "Use the electric hand dryer, Ess. Everybody knows that." Puck popped off the counter and positioned herself under the dryer. She knocked the START button with her elbow, and the machine roared to life.

"Whatever, you're using a ton of electricity. It's probably just as bad," Essa countered.

"CAN'T HEAR YOU," Puck shouted.

Essa knew she could. Puck just wanted to make Essa shout. She was the love of Essa's life, but also a giant pain in the ass. Essa gave in anyway. "ELECTRICITY. JUST AS BAD."

"NOPE. LOOK IT UP. DRYERS USE LESS ENERGY OVERALL COMPARED TO MAKING PAPER TOWELS. PLUS, THEY AREN'T PAPER TOWELS. THEY'RE PLANTS."

Essa pursed her lips, annoyed.

Puck. The littlest Zen master.

Essa felt like trying to understand Zen with her mind was like trying to organize the ocean, jumping in and separating it into individual drops with her hands. But she suspected she knew what Puck was getting at. The idea that our minds try to grasp reality by creating fixed symbols, static ideas and concepts of things. It makes us feel safe, stable, grounded amidst a world in constant flux. Recurring discomfort. Duhkha. Was the towel a towel, a piece of paper, a tree, the water that fed the tree, the sun that filled its leaves with green? Weren't all those things interdependent, one unable to exist without the other?

She could hear the Zen priest: *Words are useful to navigate the world. But not useful to really know it.*

It was mindfulness, too. Being aware of what the towels were. In awe of all the conditions that came together to create one. All the life.

Or maybe Puck was just trying to sound deep.

Before the dryer had finished its cycle, Puck wiped her hands on her shirt and started practicing dance moves in the mirror. She spun to the left and then to the right. As she moved on to karate kicks, flicking each leg as high and as hard as it would go, Essa's phone went off again. Another text message. What's up?

Oliver again. He obviously didn't understand. She couldn't date. She couldn't flirt. She couldn't have some summer romance with Chicago Boy. She couldn't even try to have a new friend. Not one that leaned in like he did behind the Zendo. Not one that looked at her that way. She couldn't answer his text.

She answered his text.

The usual. Just chasing my sister into creepy underground bathrooms.

?

Long story.

Tomorrow is Saturday, he typed. You going back to Zendo? Can I come?

Essa stared at her phone; her thumbs stayed still. Finally, they started to move across the screen. No.

She saw three little dots, the ellipses on the screen that meant Oliver was typing a response. But then they disappeared.

Essa hadn't meant that she was going to the Zendo and that Oliver couldn't come. She wasn't going tomorrow. She was headed out with Micah and Anish to the mountains to practice orienteering. But she didn't want him coming to the Zendo even if she planned to go. And she didn't want him to come along to the mountains. She didn't have time for boy drama like her mom had all the time. She didn't want Puck to see her arm in arm with some guy who would be gone in a few months anyway. She didn't want to invite Oliver to do anything.

Come with us, she typed. We're going to the mountains. Games. Mountain Fugitive.

Essa gaped at the screen, barely believing her response. But what was more unbelievable was the heat traveling up her back and down her arms, melting the hard chill that had been there just minutes before.

Sweet. Pick me up? I have no car. He inserted a sad-face emoji.

Essa hated emojis.

Yes, she typed. Pick you up at 7 a.m. Gotta beat the summer storms. She inserted an emoji. A smiling face wearing a safari hat.

What the hell am I doing?

Awesome, Oliver typed. My aunt's house is at 426 Vulture Peak Rd.

She inserted another one. A thumbs-up.

A thumbs-up? I HAVE NEVER USED THE THUMBS-UP IN MY ENTIRE LIFE.

She put the phone away and sighed. She looked down at the wad of paper towels still in her hand, walked to the garbage can, and almost let them go. But as Puck continued to dance and kick in the mirror, Essa could hear Puck's voice in her head telling her that the towels weren't towels; they were plants. All Essa could see now were a handful of tiny trees, the water that fed them, the sun they reached for as they grew. She couldn't bear to watch them tumbling into a black plastic garbage bag. They didn't belong there. She couldn't throw away the sun.

She rolled her eyes. "Know-it-all," she whispered.

"Huh?" Puck paused, out of breath.

Essa didn't respond. She walked to the dispenser and gently put the paper towels back in, one by one.

June 17

18

OLIVER

The last time Oliver had been blindfolded, he had been six years old. His mom had thrown him a birthday party on the rooftop of their townhouse, and they'd played a rousing game of Pin the Tail on the Donkey. The donkey poster was hung from an easel in the center of the rooftop deck, but when it was his turn, Oliver had missed entirely and dropped the paper tail over the railing. He'd yanked his blindfold off and watched the donkey tail float and flutter down a four-story drop.

Now, blindfolded in the back of Micah's Jeep, racing to who-knew-where, Oliver questioned why his mother had thought it was a good idea to blindfold a bunch of six-year-olds and set them loose on the roof of a building. Especially when the parents were all gathered around a rolling tray of mimosas. But then again, he was currently questioning his own judgment, wondering why on earth he'd agreed to play Mountain Fugitive, which apparently involved being blindfolded, driven into the wilderness, and dropped.

Essa was blindfolded next to him in the backseat, and as her hand accidentally brushed his . . . he remembered why he agreed to play.

"How does this game work again?" he asked, hoping his voice hadn't climbed several octaves due to the excitement of the Hand Brush.

"Anish will drive us somewhere, lead us into the woods, and

then give us a compass and a topo map. We have to figure out how to get to a point on the map that he picks," Essa said. "You use orienteering skills."

"Orienteering?"

"And you've got to be able to get to your location with sufficient precision, or your getaway van shall *not* appear," Anish said.

Oliver turned his face toward the window and felt the early morning sun on his blindfold. It was a red bandana wrapped so tightly his eyes were starting to throb. "But why are we blindfolded?"

"Just makes it a little harder," Essa said. "This way we don't have time to scout where we're going as we drive. Sometimes we do it, sometimes we don't. Just adds a twist."

"And the feeling that you could puke any second," Oliver added, adjusting his bandana.

"You guys need to toughen up," Anish said. Oliver could feel the car leaning as Anish sped around another curve. "I'm not driving *that* fast."

"Think about the sounds you can hear," Essa said. "That helps. When you can't see, it's a little easier to focus on noises."

She was right. Without his eyesight, the rest of his body was on high alert, like his skin had stopped off at Starbucks on the way. It was hypersensitive, buzzing at every sensation. When her hand had brushed against his for just a moment, he had felt so much. The slope of her knuckle, the smooth surface of the wooden ring on her thumb.

"Dude, slow down," Micah said, blindfolded in the front passenger seat. "Or at least hit the brakes around the curves. Ollie and I are about to hurl. And if I do, I'm aiming at you."

"No way," Anish said. "I never get to drive the Jeep! I'm testing its limits. And if you get carsick, forget listening to sounds. Try a weed lozenge. Works like a charm. I think I have one . . ."

Oliver could hear Anish digging in his pockets and the subsequent squeal of the tires as they rounded another curve. Oliver was tossed to the right, but purposefully leaned a little farther, hoping to "accidentally" bump shoulders, knees, hands—anything—with Essa.

It didn't work. All he touched was stale Jeep air.

"So what do you mean? Listen to sounds?" he asked her.

"So instead of focusing on your discomfort, focus on sounds. Like right now. What can you hear?"

Oliver tightly pressed his throbbing eyes under the blindfold and listened. He couldn't even think about sounds; all he could think about was Essa. He pictured her dancing by the bonfire with a hula hoop. Her legs peeking out of her skirt when they sat on the log side by side. He thought about her tattoo, the gentle angle of her collarbone, the swirl of her belly button.

"So?" Essa asked. "Hear anything?"

"Um." Oliver tried to force his brain away from thoughts of her. At first, all he could hear was the whine of the car engine as Anish gunned the gas. They were definitely climbing into the mountains; his ears popped from the pressure change. He realized that was a sound. The pop of his ears. He'd never paid attention to it before. "The car engine," he said. "And my ears popping. Does that count?"

"Cool. Yes," Essa said. "What else?"

Oliver tried again, and a whole world of sounds sprouted around him. He could hear a gentle hum coming from the middle console up front—he guessed it was Anish's canned energy drink vibrating in the cup holder. He could hear a rhythmic whipping sound—one of the car windows wasn't closed all the way. The crunch of tires as they hit a gravelly patch of road, the thrum of Anish's fingertips on the steering wheel, the tapping of Micah's hand on his leg as he drummed to the beat of a song. A song. The radio was on. Oliver hadn't even noticed.

Smaller and smaller sounds rose up around him. The delicate whisper of the seat belt rubbing against his shoulder. The tiny clack of Essa's beaded earrings as the Jeep passed over a small pothole. A *whoosh* as Essa crossed her legs and the fabric of her hiking pants rubbed against itself. A puff of breath as she exhaled.

You. I hear you.

But he didn't say that. Because it would be way too creepy.

"I hear lots of stuff," he said.

"Like what?"

"The engine. And the window's down a little, I think."

"I can hear the whistle of the bike rack on top," Essa said, tilting her head toward the roof. "Hear that? And did you catch the sound of that bug hitting the windshield?"

"No, missed it."

Essa shifted in her seat. They were quiet among the sounds for a while. "That's mindfulness, you know," she said. "That's really all it is. It's waking up. Paying attention. It changes your brain. Calms you down. All sorts of—"

"Are we going to RMNP?" Micah asked in the front seat. "My ears are going nuts."

"RMNP?" Oliver asked.

"Rocky Mountain National Park," Essa answered. "It's west of Boulder."

"Think what you want, fugitives," Anish said. "Soon your asses are going to be dropped in the wilderness, and I guarantee you're going to have a hard time finding a decent route out of there. I've outdone myself this time."

A spray of gravel kicked up underneath the tires, clattering against the underside of the car like someone was taking a machine gun to it.

"And why is it called Mountain Fugitive?" Oliver asked.

"Just you wait, Ollie," Micah said. "If you're ever in a rough spot and need to rob a bank and become a fugitive in the woods with the loot, you're going to be happy as hell that we introduced you to this game."

"Excellent point," Anish said.

"Thank you, I—" Micah stopped talking midsentence. "That's it. I'm going to boot."

"Dude," Anish said. "You took your blindfold off. Not fair."

"I'm out," Micah said. "Looks like a good day to chill in the back of the Jeep with a weed lozenge while Essa and Ollie pick their way through the woods."

"What?" Essa asked. Oliver could feel the warmth of her body as she leaned closer to him, closer to the front seat. "We can't go alone. If I get hurt, Oliver won't know how to find his way out to get help. The first rule of survival is to take a buddy. Who knows what he's doing."

There was an awkward pause. Oliver heard four bugs splatter against the windshield.

"I mean," Essa continued, "no offense or anything."

"So . . . game off or on?" Anish asked.

Oliver waited for Essa to say it was called off. That she couldn't trek into the woods alone with a city kid who couldn't even put up a tent, let alone find his way through the wilderness with a compass.

"You okay to play with just me?" she whispered.

He thought about it. For one-eighth of a nanosecond. "Yes."

"You'll have to do what I say to do, okay? It's pretty serious. We could get lost."

"No problem."

Essa paused again.

Oliver shifted in his seat, and his leg rested against hers. He thought she'd pull it away. He thought she'd move over.

She didn't.

"Anish," she said. "Keep driving."

"Can I take this off now?" Oliver asked as the sounds of Micah's and Anish's footsteps faded away.

"Yes," Essa said.

Oliver blinked in the bright sunlight. They were surrounded by tall pines and waist-high boulders. The ground was dry and covered with wiry sagebrush and pockets of wildflowers and buffalo grass. He turned in a circle, looking for . . . he didn't know what. When Essa had said they'd be dropped off in the woods, he'd imagined a big park or a golf course, somewhere with signs pointing the way. Bathrooms. A snack bar.

Outdoors, Chicago style.

But this?

He looked out over the meadow in front of them, a field of emptiness. Beyond that, he could see across a wide, wild valley to mountaintops in the distance. Mountain after mountain surrounded them, tree covered and hunched together like the nubby green backs of turtle shells. There were no man-made structures in sight.

He heard something above him. A rustling. He looked up and saw a large black bird high on a pine branch, adjusting his feathers and looking back at him. It cocked its head to one side and then the other, like it recognized Oliver and Essa, like it had been waiting for them. Something about the sheen of his feathers, the inky blackness of his curious eyes, the way his talons dug into the branch, convinced Oliver the bird was a bad omen. Like it had a message for them and it wasn't good.

"First things first," Essa said. She pulled her long braid over her shoulder and fiddled with her backpack. "We drink."

She wants to get wasted? Up here? Plus I thought she didn't . . .

Oliver could tell Essa read the expression on his face. "Ease up there, Chicago," she said. "I meant *water*. We need to drink some water before we start. First rule of survival . . . stay hydrated." Essa whipped a long plastic tube out of her backpack and stuck one end in her mouth and took a long drink. Then she held it out for Oliver. "Here. Take a drink." Oliver looked confused. "It's attached to a bladder full of water in my pack. You *really* have never done any outside stuff, huh?"

"Zero," Oliver said. He took the tube and pulled in a long swallow of lukewarm water. The fact that they were sharing, that her lips had just been wrapped around the water spout before his, made him feel like there might be hope for the two of them after all.

"We always take one bladder for every two people. At least," she explained. "You can get so dehydrated up here."

Or maybe this is just what you do. Share water tubes.

Essa picked her way around a stand of pines to a place with a better view. "See that peak," she asked, pointing. "The one way off, with the square top? That's Long's Peak. People die on that thing every year. It's in the national park. We're miles from there. We're in the foothills, but where, exactly, I'm not sure yet."

Oliver thought she'd know right away where they were. He looked up in the trees again, searching for that big black crow. It was gone. Silently flown off when Oliver wasn't paying attention. He wondered if the bird had seen a bear or a pack of coyotes nearby, if it had flown to safety. He wanted to ask Essa about the animals up here, about the chances of them getting attacked and eaten. Or just lost and starving to death.

"Cool. We'll find our way. No worries," he lied.

Essa smiled. "Don't be scared." She looked him in the eye. Held it a little too long.

"How could you tell?"

"I just can." She held out the water tube again, and he took it.

"Staying hydrated, right?"

"Right," she said.

"So how do we find our way out of here?"

Essa adjusted her backpack and squinted into the sun. "Well, even if we didn't have a map, we could start to figure out where we are. Start with the mountains we can see. The big ones." She walked farther away from the stand of pines and sat on a large boulder. Oliver followed close behind. There was just enough room on the rock for him to sit next to her. "See those two peaks close together?"

"Yeah," Oliver lied, looking in the direction she was pointing. He thought all the peaks looked close together.

"Those are in the Indian Peaks Wilderness. That's Kiowa Peak and Apache Peak."

He looked harder, but they still all looked the same to him. Just a long, bumpy ridge of indistinguishable, choppy granite peaks. One after the other under a blistering blue sky. The mountain range reminded him of the stegosaurus skeleton at the Field Museum in Chicago, each peak like one of the bony plates that lined the dinosaur's spine. He couldn't believe she could tell them apart.

"Yeah," he said, nodding. "I totally see that."

"Then go way over to your right. That next big peak is Mount Audubon. It's big and sloped. See it?"

Oliver nodded. Essa turned and studied his face. "You're full of shit," she said, smiling.

Oliver squinted again at the horizon. "You are correct. I have absolutely no idea what you're talking about."

Essa pointed again. "Lean this way. Now look directly where my finger is pointing." He leaned into her shoulder. She put an arm around him and pulled him close, still pointing at the ridgeline. "See now? Look. Audubon is *right there.*"

Even if there had been an airplane flying over the mountain dragging a gigantic neon sign behind it that read, DUDE, THIS IS MT. AUDUBON, Oliver wouldn't have known where it was. All he could focus on was the sun-kissed glow of Essa's arm, the freckles on her shoulder, the wooden beads on her wrist.

She hopped off the boulder and started looking around at the ground.

"What are you doing now?" Oliver asked.

"Help me find two rocks about this big." She pointed at her open palm. "We generally know the mountains are west of here, and we could also get that from the sun's position. But it's always good to be precise. And for that, we need a compass. Which we have. But if we were lost without one, I could make one. With two rocks and a stick."

She wasn't kidding. She found two palm-sized rocks and a

stick about a foot long. She jammed the stick into the ground and placed one of the rocks at the end of the stick's shadow. She looked at him and smiled triumphantly.

"That's a compass?" he asked, raising one eyebrow.

"That's a compass."

"Seriously?"

"As time passes, the shadow will start to move," Essa explained. "After about twenty minutes, we put the second rock at the end of the shadow's new position. The line between the two rocks is your east-west line. The first rock marks west, because the sun moves from east to west during the day. Get it?"

"Wow. Yeah. I actually do. So now we . . . wait?"

"Yep. And we'll have an accurate compass reading. From the looks of where we are in relation to Kiowa, Apache, and Audubon, we must be in the foothills near Sunshine Canyon or Lefthand Canyon." Essa pulled out her topographic map. Anish had marked their drop spot. "Yep. We're up Lefthand Canyon. Looks like he wants us to find the quickest route to Gold Hill from here."

"Gold Hill?"

"Old-school gold rush town. It looks like a movie set, honestly. Population two hundred something."

Essa studied the map, showing Oliver how to read a topo. How each skinny curved line represented an elevation. How to avoid climbing too much or hiking to the edge of a ridge. How to take a compass bearing and plot the fastest way there.

She sat down and held the map in her lap. She looked so at home on the hard, dry ground. Like she was made to live outside, like the sage and the sun and the granite were family, siblings who were so happy to have her up here for the day.

"You're a badass," Oliver said, sitting next to her and peering over her shoulder at the map.

Essa's face lit up at the compliment.

That's when Oliver noticed it. The same feeling he'd had in the wildflower garden outside the Zendo. The dry mountain breeze around them, the trees looming overhead. The air feeling alive and moving and electric, but still at the same time. He looked at her lips.

Essa ran a finger along a crack in the dry dirt next to her. "Can I ask you a question?"

"Sure."

She looked up, her eyes soft. "What's wrong with your sister?"

This. Always this. Always Lilly.

He looked at the compass. The shadow had started to move. Soon they'd know what direction to head in. He didn't want to talk about this. He didn't want to go into the whole tragic ordeal. He wanted to turn to Essa, to wrap his arms around her waist, pull her next to him and kiss her. And kiss her and kiss her and kiss her. Until the sun went down. Until the wind grew cold. He wasn't scared anymore; he didn't care if they had to sleep out here all night.

"You don't have to tell me if you don't—"

"She has schizophrenia," he said. "She's sort of in and out of reality all the time. When it gets really bad, she has to live in a hospital. That's where she is now."

Essa stopped running her finger along the ground. She was still and didn't say anything for what felt like a long, long time. Oliver watched the stick's shadow silently slide across the ground, the sun whispering a clue about how to get them home. Oliver knew what was coming next, what Essa would say after learning about his sister's illness. Most people had the same response: *I'm so sorry.*

Or, *That must be so tough.*

Or, *How awful.*

As if his sister had died. Or she was a bad day, bad luck, a bad hand.

"Are you ever in the same one?" Essa looked right at him, the sun glinting off the butterfly clip at the end of her braid. "The same reality, I mean."

A smile slipped across Oliver's face. No one had ever asked

him anything even close to that. He thought about all the wild things Lilly thought were real: messages hidden in the bricks of buildings, secret codes in crossword puzzles, newscasts asking for her help with unsolved murders.

"No," he said finally. "I just lie and pretend I'm in hers. That I believe all her conspiracy theories and paranoia."

He thought back to her first real delusion. It wasn't about anything glamorous, like a secret code or a hidden treasure. It was about the tumble dryer.

"Put your hand on it," she'd said, pressing her palm to the top of the cold, lifeless dryer. They were in the basement of their Chicago townhouse. "Feel it vibrating?"

She was seventeen at the time; Oliver was fifteen. They'd taken her to different counselors and doctors. They knew something wasn't right, but she'd never hallucinated. Not like this.

"Um . . ." Oliver touched the dryer and stalled, trying to figure out what to say.

"They've put a device in it," Lilly whispered. Her eyes were so intense, fiery, sharp. "They're listening to us. They're going to pump poisonous gas in through the dryer any minute."

"Lilly, I don't think . . ." He stopped when he saw the rage. The distrust. She was testing him by telling him her theory. Testing his loyalty. A chill went down his back. For the first time in his life, he was afraid of his own sister. He didn't know this new person standing in front of him. He had no idea what reality she was in, what she might think next.

"I think our parents have enemies." She nodded slowly, as if that would clear everything up. "There. It's vibrating again. Feel it? They're recording us."

Oliver wasn't sure he had a choice. "Yeah," he said, resting his hand on the cool white metal. "I do."

From then on, that's what he always did. Acted like he believed her. Like they were pirates on the same ocean again.

Now Oliver looked down at the dry cracked ground. "It's the reason I'm the only one she trusts. It's the reason we're close."

He picked up a small stone and tossed it, watching it arc into the sky and make its way down again. "Or were."

Essa paused. Raised her eyebrows, silently asking for more of an explanation. Oliver didn't offer one.

"It's sort of the same with my mom," she said, looking at the mountains in the distance. The sun was shining on their granite faces, making gray look like a cheery, graceful color able to compete with the optimistic blue of the sky. "She's not really here when she's here. Or at least, you can never be sure."

Oliver followed Essa's gaze and thought he could identify Mount Audubon this time. The gentle slope Essa had described, the ridgeline between it and the peaks of Kiowa and Apache. He wondered if mountains were like a language. Maybe he had to study them and listen to them, be around people who knew them well, until suddenly they started to make sense. Word by word, peak by peak.

"It sucks," he said. "Feeling lonely beside someone you love." Oliver worried the second he said it. He worried it was too much. Too sappy. Too emo. Too much of a downer.

"Exactly," Essa said.

Essa looked at the stick's shadow, and Oliver thought he saw tears pooling in her eyes. She blinked them away. The shadow had moved almost an inch. "There," she said, placing the second rock at the end of the new shadow. "That's our east-west line. Which makes that way north. And that way south."

Oliver looked in the directions Essa was pointing. Any second she would get up and they'd start walking. This little moment without any direction, without a fixed way to go was about to end. He looked at her sanctuary tattoo and wondered if she was like a language, too. Like the mountains, like the mysterious koan story he'd heard in the Zendo. That maybe if he studied Essa long enough, he'd learn how to know her, how to make an inroad, to make her open up and let him in, if only for one brief summer.

"I don't have to explain things to you," he said. "It's like you've known everything I'm going to say all along." It tumbled out of Oliver's mouth before he could edit his thoughts, before he was even sure what he was saying.

Essa had pulled the sun stick out of the ground and was getting ready to stand up. She stopped. He worried that he'd fumbled the words, that what he said hadn't made sense. That he'd actually have to explain to her what he meant by saying that he—didn't have to explain things to her.

Essa put the stick back on the dry ground and stayed next to him. She didn't ask him to explain; she didn't have to. "It's like we can just . . . be," she said.

Oliver smiled. *Exactly.*

He stood and held out his hand. She took it and let him pull her up. A swirl of dust blew against their legs, a gust of wind that moved the pines. Just behind her, Oliver saw the crow again. It had alighted in the tree, this time on a lower branch. The bird had the same knowing look in its eye, the same other-worldly presence, but Oliver decided that it wasn't a bad omen after all. It was a good one.

A few weeks in Boulder, and I'm already reading omens and kissing hippie girls.

And he was. His hand gently slid around the nape of her neck, just under her thick braid. She leaned so close he could feel the curve of her breasts, the hill of her hip. He kissed her. Again and again. It was all the things: Tingly and warm and addictive. A little awkward and clunky and rushed. He was worried he had too much spit in his mouth. He was worried he was a bad kisser.

But the way she was kissing back, he suspected he wasn't.

Essa finally pulled away, smiling. "So . . . north?" she asked.

"I'll go wherever you point me."

19

ESSA

Essa was right. They were in the foothills, not far from Sunshine Canyon. They headed north and used the topo map to find the easiest route to Sunshine Canyon Road.

Essa smiled, still flushed from the kiss. "Okay, then we should go west," Essa said, pointing. The road was dry and dusty, and looked like a worn and weathered leather belt stretching into the distance. Essa pulled two granola bars out of her pack as they started walking. "Don't let yourself get too hungry."

Essa couldn't believe how easy it felt to be with Oliver, how natural. Like they'd been hiking these hills together since they were kids. Like they'd been stealing kisses in the shadows of stick compasses for years. Which made her feel like she suddenly had a boyfriend. Which made her feel guilty. Which made her think of Puck. Before she zipped up her backpack, she reached for her cell phone. She was sure she wouldn't have service until they got closer to Gold Hill, but she wanted to check anyway. Puck was at a friend's house all day, a friend with a very dependable mom. She would be well taken care of, but Essa hated being out of reach all the same. That was the biggest downside to her love of the wilderness.

Her screen lit up. No bars.

"Checking on Puck?" Oliver asked.

Essa nodded. She loved that he knew that right away. "No service up here."

"Do you always feel guilty? Being away from her?"

"Pretty much." Essa gently kicked at a piece of gravel on the road and sent it flying into the tall, dry grass beside her.

Oliver forced the last brittle bite of granola bar down his throat. "Same here. Being away from Chicago and all. Leaving Lilly." He tucked the wrapper in his pocket. "My aunt keeps telling me to have fun this summer. But half the time I feel so bad . . . You're lucky that your sister gets to hang out with you so much."

"I am," Essa said. But at the mention of Puck, a new worry pierced her mind. Not about being up in the mountains and out of cell range, but about going back down. With Oliver. "So about Puck."

"Yeah?"

"We can't tell her. About . . . this."

"About what?" Oliver grinned.

"About whatever is happening here." Essa motioned between the two of them.

"My lips are sealed."

Finally they saw the buildings of Gold Hill around a bend in the road. They walked down Main Street, past an old inn, a dilapidated post office, a leaning wooden structure with canned goods in the windows and a sign: GOLD HILL GENERAL STORE.

Next to the shop was a small clapboard schoolhouse with a weathered plaque nailed to the side: GOLD HILL ELEMENTARY. BUILT IN 1873 TO SERVE THE GOLD HILL MINE COMMUNITY. OLDEST CONTINUOUSLY OPERATING SCHOOL IN COLORADO.

Oliver stopped. "Is this place for real?"

"Yep. Told you it looked like a movie set." Essa looked up the hillside behind the elementary school at a smattering of one-story log cabin houses. They all looked like they were built in the 1870s. They had mismatched windows, cloudy and hanging crooked. Chimneys leaned and jutted into the sky like straws reaching out of ratty paper cups. A donkey tugged at a patch of grass in a front yard. She looked down a side dirt road that branched off Main Street.

"There they are," she said as she pointed. Micah's Jeep was idling beside a large cherry-red barn. She pulled on Oliver's arm and led him down the road.

"So there's not a Gold Hill mine anymore, but people still live here, right?"

Essa didn't get a chance to answer. She was cut off by the sound of a long, low whistle.

"You found your way in record time, Ess." It was Micah, apparently so impressed with Essa's navigation skills that he let out a second whistle. "Did you even take one wrong turn?"

Essa pulled the water tube from her pack and took a drink. She rubbed a hand on the back of her neck where a thin layer of dust clung to her damp skin. "The view helped. I triangulated our position relative to Apache, Kiowa, and Audubon. Guessed we were near either Sunshine Canyon or Lefthand Canyon Drive before I even looked at the map."

"Impressive." Micah's smile disappeared. He studied Essa's face. "Are you okay?"

"Totally. It didn't take us that long, and we had plenty of water—"

"No, I mean, you look kind of . . . weird." Micah raised an eyebrow and took a swig of water from his Nalgene bottle.

Essa tried to control her face, to will any evidence of blush out of her cheeks, to erase any trace of joy from her lips. Was their kiss that obvious? Had Essa and Oliver come out of the woods different than when they went in?

Essa avoided Micah's stare and climbed into the backseat of the Jeep. Oliver stood next to Micah with this satisfied grin on his face. She shot Oliver a look that she hoped was clear: *Cut it out.*

She reached for the door to pull it closed, but Micah stopped her. Leaned in.

"Something's up," he said softly, his face close to hers. "He's cool, right?" He glanced in Oliver's direction. Oliver was making his way around the front of the car. "He didn't try anything or—"

"No." Essa cut him off. "No way. Chill out."

Micah paused. "Then why won't you look me in the eye?" He fixed his deep brown eyes on Essa.

She looked at him for a moment, but then glanced away. She focused on the side of the cherry-red barn and the rusty horseshoe tacked above its gaping door. She wondered when someone had hung it, if it had been up there since the 1800s, if it had brought the family any luck. She thought about Oliver's family and her own. Maybe they both needed horseshoes above their front doors.

She looked back at Micah. "Everything's good."

"If he's a creep and tries to get with—"

"That was awesome," Oliver said eagerly as he climbed into the backseat from the other side. "How often do you guys play this?"

Essa just looked at her lap as Micah glared at Oliver, sizing him up. Neither of them answered his question. Her phone pinged from the depths of her pack. "Must have service here," she said, pulling it out. "Got a voice mail."

Anish came barreling out of the general store looking ridiculously pleased with himself. He jogged toward the Jeep and got into the front passenger seat. "Check this out," he said, holding up a yellow-and-green glass bottle with a picture of Bob Marley on it. "You guys heard of Marley's Mellow Mood? It's, like, a drink with some sort of herb in it that chills you out. Cashier says to watch out. He's passed out a few times after drinking it." Anish smiled and looked for a reaction, but Oliver was staring out the window, Micah was staring at Essa, and Essa was trying to hear her voice mail.

"And look." Anish tried again. He held up a small wooden llama about the size of a grapefruit. It was a little rough around the edges, obviously carved by hand. Its legs were all different lengths, and its head was unnaturally crooked at the end of its long neck. But the llama's eyes had a warm, sweet depth to them. "So this off-the-grid-looking woman was in there carving these. Wild. Says she has ten real llamas at home. Always takes one hiking with her because they calm her down and make her take it slow through the woods. So she takes in all the scenery, you know? Called them her therapy llamas. Says her carvings have, like, won wood carving awards. Were you all aware of a wood-carving subculture in Colorado? Man, I love subcultures."

Everyone was still ignoring him.

"Um," Anish began. "Is something up?"

"Guess not," Micah said, sighing. He slid into the front seat and started the car.

"Yes," Essa said, leaning forward. "There is. Get me home." She tapped on Micah's shoulder. "Fast."

"I knew it," Micah said, turning. "Is Oliver creeping you—"

"No," Essa interrupted. "It's Puck."

20

ESSA

The message wasn't clear. All Essa could hear was Puck sobbing, punctuated with a few words Essa could barely understand. Something about their mom. Something about a map. And a photograph.

Essa tried to call her back, but the call wouldn't go through. As soon as they pulled out of Gold Hill, her service dropped. She sent text after text, but a red exclamation point popped up beside each one: *Failed to send.*

The drive home felt like it took hours. Even when Essa's cell service came back, Puck wasn't answering. By the time they pulled up to the house, Essa was frantic. She raced to the front door and started fumbling with her keys. Her hands were shaking so badly, she couldn't get her house key lined up with the lock.

"Here." A hand reached in and steadied hers.

Oliver.

She didn't realize he'd followed her out of the Jeep and up to the porch.

"I want to come with you," he said. "You shouldn't be by yourself. If something really bad—"

The sound of Essa's phone cut him off; she had the volume turned up all the way so she could be sure not to miss a message from Puck. It was a text from Micah: Gotta drive Anish home. You okay with Chicago?

Essa looked over Oliver's shoulder and saw the Jeep still idling at the curb. Micah and Anish waved and flashed weak smiles. They looked worried, like Essa was venturing up a poorly marked mountain trail and they feared she might not come back in one piece. She waved at them to go ahead.

"Ready?" Oliver had turned the key in the lock. He held his hand against the door and raised an eyebrow, silently asking for permission to open it.

Essa didn't know how she felt about him seeing her family, such as it was, or witnessing whatever crisis was unfolding at her house. But she didn't have time to send him away; she barely had time to realize she didn't want to.

She nodded, and Oliver pushed open the door.

"Puck?" Essa walked into the living room, the kitchen, and then glanced out the backyard. No one was there. She ran down the hall, hoping to see Puck's door shut; she always closed it when she was inside.

It was open.

Essa ran past Puck's room and into her mother's and, for the first time in her life, hoped her mom was in there making out with somebody. Essa wanted Puck to be upset about something usual, something Essa could handle, familiar emotional territory that she could Big Sister her way through. Essa had comforted Puck a million times when her mom brought home dates. Essa and Puck would hole up in Puck's room and play with a bag of runes from Above the Clouds or assemble a new kite or just lie on the floor and stare up at the ones hanging from the ceiling.

Her mother's room was empty.

The purple velvet bedspread was crumpled in a ball in the center of the bed. A multicolored glass pipe lay on the bedside table, her mother's favorite bowl. It was filled with dark black resin, the leftovers from a smoke. The room always smelled bitter and swampy. She couldn't tell if her mother had recently been here or if this was just the usual scent.

Essa glanced in the direction of her mother's bathroom, the setting sun blaring through the window inside it. She didn't squint fast enough as she walked in, and the strong western sun got in her eyes. All she could see for a moment were spots.

"Mom?" Essa called, half blind. She hoped that she would find her mother soaking in the bathtub, a book of poetry in her hand. Or maybe with her earbuds in, jamming to a Dead album. Instead, as Essa blinked the sun spots out of her eyes, she saw that no one was there. The tub was bone dry. So was the sink. A lone, ratty towel sat crumpled beside her mother's toothbrush. Essa picked it up and placed it on the towel rack beside the toilet.

When she looked back at the sink, she saw what was underneath the towel: a mala. Essa took the necklace in her hands. They weren't the expensive amazonite beads that Puck wanted; they were a much cheaper wooden version. Essa hoped her mom had gone into Old Tibet while Essa was chasing Puck into the public bathroom and bought them for Puck as a gift. Puck would be so happy; she wouldn't care that they weren't the exact ones she wanted.

Another thought came to mind.

Mom wouldn't have gone into Old Tibet and bought these for herself . . . would she? After Puck asked for them?

Maybe that's what the fight was over. Puck's mom was just insensitive enough that Essa could actually picture it: Puck pointed out a gift she wanted and their mom decided to buy it for herself. A sad attempt to stay cool and wear the things that her younger daughters liked.

Essa felt her stomach ease a little. As bad as it would be if Puck had called her about a fight over a necklace, Essa could definitely repair that.

"She's in here."

It was Oliver calling from down the hall. His voice sounded tight, tense. The mala clattered to the tile floor as Essa dropped it and ran.

She followed Oliver's voice to Puck's darkened room. She

stepped inside, let her eyes adjust. Puck had duct-taped several of her mom's tapestries to the windows; barely any light was getting through.

Essa heard a sniffle. It was coming from a small mound in the center of the twin bed.

Puck.

She was under the covers, crying.

"What took you so long?" Puck asked, her voice muffled.

Essa sat on the bed and slowly lifted the blanket. Puck yanked it back down, but not before Essa caught a glimpse of her little sister wadded up in a ball, a pile of used tissues tucked around her. "I'm sorry," Essa said. "We were up near Gold Hill playing—"

"Gold Hill?"

"It's this old town," Oliver explained. "An old gold mine. We were—"

"It's *not* an old gold mine." Puck's voice was still muffled by the covers, but the fact that she was beyond annoyed came through loud and clear. "There wasn't an actual mine in Gold Hill. They panned for gold in streams."

Essa sat down on the bed. "Why are you so mad about—"

"Thanks for inviting me," Puck snapped. "You said I could go on one of your day trips. But I guess you wanted to be alone up there . . . with *him.*"

Essa closed her eyes as a strong wind of regret blew through her. She suddenly felt horrible for letting Oliver kiss her; she should have known better. Micah could tell, and now she felt like Puck could tell, even from her fortress under the covers. It must be obvious; the air around Essa and Oliver must have changed, their connection charging the space around them. Some small part of Essa had held onto the hope that Puck wouldn't be upset if she dated Oliver; he was the first boy Puck had ever been nice to.

"Is that all you're mad about?" Essa asked. Another sniffle was Puck's only response. "That we went without you? Or did Mom do something? I'll fix it. I'll—"

Essa stopped midsentence when she saw several pieces of paper sliding out from under the covers. Puck was shoving them toward her. "Here," Puck said.

There was a bumper sticker. *Keep Portland Weird.* The words were printed against a backdrop of a Portland city map. Every street was named "Weird Ave." Underneath the bumper sticker was a page ripped out of a magazine and folded into a square. Essa picked it up and slowly smoothed it out. It was an advertisement for a mobile home.

Only $50,000. Zero deposit. Low monthly park fee. Most affordable mobile home community in Oregon! Call now.

This was what Puck had meant in her voice mail. A map and a photograph. She'd meant this bumper sticker map of Portland and this photo of a mobile home.

"I don't get it," Essa said slowly. "What are these?"

"We're moving there. Into a trailer." Puck blew her nose.

Essa looked back down at the advertisement. She could see Puck sitting on the porch of their new mobile abode, miserable, heading off to a new school, her talents getting overlooked and wasted with new teachers. Puck and Essa both friendless. Their mother jobless, trying to make ends meet in a new city and failing every other month.

But why?

"Mom wants to move there?" Essa asked, her eyes still wide as she stared at the Portland bumper sticker.

Puck slowly lifted the comforter and peered at Essa with her red-rimmed eyes. "No," she said. "Ronnie does. They're getting married."

Puck broke into a fresh round of tears. Essa felt her chest cracking open, her arms and legs going weak like she'd just finished a ten-mile hike straight up a mountainside. She'd never seen this particular look on Puck's face, like she was three years old again, like she'd skinned her knee and no one had responded to her cries for hours.

Essa swiftly reached under the covers and pulled Puck into

her arms. She rocked her sister back and forth while Puck's tears kept coming.

"It's going to be okay," Essa said again and again. She had to work to keep her voice soft and reassuring; rage was starting to shake her from the inside out. How could their mother do this? She'd claimed to be in love more times than Essa could count, but she'd never gotten engaged. She'd never actually made plans to marry anyone. And she'd definitely never threatened to leave Boulder. Mom was to Boulder what water was to a swimming pool. The town shaped her, molded her. She fit so well inside it that Essa was sure her mother would fall apart on the outside, disperse like someone had opened the drain.

"I hear something," Oliver said. He leaned out of Puck's bedroom door and looked down the hall. "It's a guy. What does Ronnie look like?"

"Like a jackass. In Birkenstocks," Essa said, still holding Puck tightly in her arms.

Oliver looked again. "Yep," he whispered. "I'd say that's him. And he's coming this way."

"Hey, Ess." Ronnie came into the room, running a hand through his windblown hair. He looked like he'd been in the sun all day, warm and glowing and happy. Making plans to take his bride to Oregon.

His bride.

Essa wished that she'd stopped by Cheba Hut on the way home, that she'd ordered a Big Buddha Cheese and eaten every last bite of it . . . so she could throw it up all over Ronnie's bare toes.

"Don't call me *Ess*," she said. "Don't call me anything."

Ronnie glanced at the Portland bumper sticker, "I know we hardly know each other, but it's going to be great. You'll see. Portland is awesome. Am I right?" Ronnie looked at Oliver, as if the other guy in the room would provide some backup, some camaraderie. Oliver just glared at him.

"Come on," Oliver said, crossing the room to Essa and Puck. "Let's go."

"Stay a minute?" It was Essa's mom. Standing in the doorway. She was in her favorite ripped jeans and a tank top that didn't have a back. It just tied around her neck and waist with spaghetti strings.

Puck lifted her head when she heard her mother's voice. She pushed away from Essa and ran toward the door. Ronnie reached out and tried to stop her, but Puck was too quick. She sidestepped his grasp and disappeared down the hall.

"Don't touch her," Essa said, looking at Ronnie. Her veins felt tight, like taut ropes twisting around her heart, thrumming with tension at her temples.

"You want me to—?" Oliver pointed at the door.

"Yes," Essa said. "Make sure she stays here."

Oliver took off down the hallway, calling Puck's name. Essa leveled her eyes at her mother. "How could you do this?"

Essa's mom sat next to her on the bed and reached for the butterfly clip at the bottom of Essa's braid. Essa pulled away. "Guess you're not going to introduce me to your boyfriend?"

"He's not my boyfriend," Essa said. "I can't have boyfriends. Because of you."

"What? That's ridiculous. You know I don't care if you date." *So. Oblivious.*

Essa didn't have the energy to explain what she meant.

"Puck wasn't supposed to find out about this," her mom continued. "Neither were you. Not yet."

"When were you going to tell us?"

"Soon," her mom said. "I was going to get you both together. Talk it through. Puck was spying on us. You know how she is. She was crouched outside the living room when Ronnie and I were talking. Ronnie brought the ad over for the mobile home and—"

"I got her that bumper sticker as her first Portland keepsake," Ronnie said, smiling. As if Essa would think he was clever for giving his mother such a great gift. "It's funny because see," he continued, "Portland has been changing over the years with all these rich folks moving in. It's losing its roots. It's always been a super chill town. One of the chillest. So that's why people say keep it weird and all because—"

"Ronnie," Essa's mom cut him off. She shook her head and turned back to Essa. "I was going to see what you thought of all this. I really was. I was going to explain how I feel about him, how I think we could have such a fantastic time in Portland. It's just like Boulder, you'll see. And we'll make sure to find the right school for Puck. And for you. And I know that might be rough for you, to spend your senior year away, but I thought you might like it. The adventure and everything. I have a girlfriend there who can get me a great job. That pays more than Pure Buds. I could provide more for you girls."

For a moment, Essa softened. Her mom was sounding semi-thoughtful. Aware. She'd actually considered Puck's schooling, Essa's senior year, finances. The sound of a new town and a new start sounded good all of a sudden. More money for Puck. Maybe she could actually take the tap lessons she wanted. Or take real drama classes instead of being a pity case at the Boulder summer drama camp. Maybe—

As Essa's shoulders softened, she leaned a little closer to her mom.

She smelled liquor.

"Are you—" Essa sniffed. She was sure of it; her mother reeked of booze. The smell reminded Essa of the stairwell that led to the basement bathrooms below the Boulder Cafe. The odor emanated from her mom's breath, an invisible cloud of dank, sour air.

"I'll make this move awesome, I promise."

Essa noticed it then, how her mom was blinking too slowly and leaning a little to the left on the bed. Her mom tried to sit up straight but looked too fluid, unmoored like her joints weren't quite knit together and they might slide apart at any moment. Like she'd literally come apart at the seams. "You're drunk."

"No, I'm not." Her mother looked shocked, offended. She waved a hand in the air, and three wooden bracelets jiggled down her arm. "We just had a little. To celebrate." She looked at Ronnie. Smitten. Happy.

Happy.

Essa took a long look at her mom. She was overwhelmed with the feeling that something was breaking. Irreparably. That Essa was finally giving up on connecting with her, on knowing her, on having any clue who she really was or how she really felt. Essa looked at her mother's eyes, at her hair, at her thin frame perched on the side of the bed. She thought about what it must be like to be her, what it was like to think the things she did, to choose what she chose. Essa wanted to say something. Something right. Because she couldn't shake the feeling that it might be the last honest thing she'd ever say to her mother. She wasn't sure she'd be able to care enough to ever try it again.

Essa looked at the floor and thought of the Zendo. She imagined her round cushion in the center of the room. She saw herself on it, legs folded, watching her breath.

Sitting zazen, noticing her thoughts. Not with any sort of goal, really, and not to control them, but just to notice them. To witness what a storm they were, what a chaotic swirl of likes and dislikes, judgments and approvals, memories and predictions, desires and disappointments. Trying to arrive in reality, in the moment, breath by breath.

Essa looked at her mom again. She thought she would ask her mother something profound: If her mom ever paid attention to her mind. To its constant chatter. If her mom was in control of her attention, or if it was in control of her. Maybe Essa would say something about how hard it was to be present, to stay in the moment, and that if you were messed up, it must be impossible. Maybe she'd say something snappy, something that would cut.

I can't read your mind. But I know when it's gone. And it's the loneliest feeling in the world.

She didn't say it.

She considered trying to explain. How Essa and Puck never knew if their mother meant what she said or if she'd even remember it. How they were never sure if their mother was listening, registering, witnessing their lives in any dependable way.

She didn't say any of that, either.

Instead, Essa stood up and headed for the door. She had to say something. But what tumbled out of her mouth wasn't particularly profound, and it wasn't an explanation. "Maybe you're right," she said.

Her mother's face brightened. "Really? Seriously, you might love Portland. It's wonderful. I mean, I've never been there myself, but Ronnie says—"

"No. Not about Portland." Essa paused and looked up at Puck's ceiling. At the kites hanging there. Bright, colorful . . . happiest when high. "About everything else."

Her mother raised her eyebrows, confused.

Essa was always freaked out, too afraid to date, too scared about all the things that could happen to Puck, too obsessed about trying to be the perfect role model, the glue that held the family together. And it was falling apart anyway. Essa tried so hard to be in reality, to face things as they were, to sit on cushions in Zendos and be aware of life, moment by moment.

Escape doesn't work. It doesn't cure duhkha.

Stay in this moment. Present moment.

Maybe Zen was wrong.

Essa looked at her mother again. Engaged. Making plans. Smiling at her new love. Always loose and easy like her life was trouble free. Forgetting what time to be at work. Forgetting to worry. About anything.

"You always say I'm the oldest teenager you know," Essa said. "Maybe you're right. Maybe that's the problem." Essa looked at the ceiling again, and this time she focused on the owl kite, the one she always thought looked scared, like it had seen something shocking, something that had silenced its hoot.

Maybe it wasn't scared at all. Maybe it was just numb, checked out. Free from feeling sad, or worried, or cautious. Free from feeling anything.

Essa left the room; she didn't have the energy to explain.

But it was simple, really.

Maybe I just need to get high as a kite.

She tried to shake away the thought, let it drift by like a stormy cloud passing over a mountain, not quite full enough to rain.

I couldn't do that to Puck.

I wouldn't.

But the thought felt sticky, stubborn, like the burnt black residue in her mom's pipe.

Oliver was at the kitchen window, watching Puck throw rocks at the wide-slatted wooden fence in the backyard. Hard. "I tried to talk to her," he said. "It didn't go so well."

One of Puck's rocks missed the fence entirely and sailed over the top into the neighbor's yard.

"What did she say?"

Oliver hesitated. "It's embarrassing."

Essa raised her eyebrows. "Embarrassing? Did she tell you a story about Mom or—"

"She asked if I was in love with you."

Essa kept her eyes on Puck. On one of her sister's long, skinny arms pulling back just before a throw, arcing like a green branch in the wind.

And what did you say?

She didn't ask the question, hoping Oliver would offer his response.

He didn't.

"You hang out with a guy for one day and everybody assumes . . ." Essa trailed off, thinking back to their kiss. "People are crazy. I mean . . . stupid. Not crazy." She instantly felt horrible for using that word.

"It's okay," Oliver said, jamming a hand in his jeans pocket. He looked down at his sneakers.

Essa wanted to go back in the woods near Gold Hill. She wanted to be sitting next to Oliver, watching the shadow of her rock-and-stick compass slowly sliding across the ground. She wanted him to hold her as the shadow grew long and thin and finally melted into the dusk. She didn't want to be here, failing. Essa had always been able to take care of Puck, to make things better when their mom screwed up. She watched Puck shove her golden hair away from her sweaty forehead.

Puck, I don't know if I can fix this one.

"She say anything else?"

Oliver leaned against the sink. "Yeah. She asked me when you were going to the mountains next. She wanted me to ask you if she could come. She's pretty pissed that we didn't invite her on the Gold Hill trek."

Essa sighed and shook her head. "I've explained to her a thousand times that she can't come on one of the long trips. It's too dangerous. She probably thinks I'll bend because of how upset she is. But I can't let her come. It would be—"

"So when *are* you going next?"

"Next weekend. At least, that was the plan last I talked to Micah. We planned to do a three-day trip . . ."

"You still going? Or do you want to cancel because of . . . all this stuff?"

"And by 'all this stuff,' you mean my mother's epic shittiness?" Oliver nodded. "Pretty much."

"No way," Essa said. "We're not canceling the trip. Because if I don't get out of here, I just might smoke my brains out."

Oliver didn't look shocked, just sad. Sad for Essa, sad for Puck, sad about the whole situation. Essa leaned against the counter next to him. He slid close, and she put her head on his shoulder.

"Can I come with? On the trip? Keep you company?" Oliver asked.

Essa didn't answer. She gently pulled away and turned to look out the window. "Shit," Essa whispered. "She's gone."

Essa raced out the open kitchen door to the backyard. She looked left and then right. No Puck.

"Down here." Puck was sitting on the ground, leaning against the house. Her legs were tucked underneath her.

Essa studied her face. Had Puck heard what Essa said? About needing to get out of here? About smoking her brains out? Had she seen Essa put her head on Oliver's shoulder?

"What are you doing?" Essa sat down beside her, shoulder to shoulder.

"Throwing rocks," Puck said. "Hating Mom."

Essa half-smiled. "Me, too. I mean, the hating Mom part." She racked her brain for what to say. She thought of their Zen teacher. What he would say, even though she wasn't sure she believed any of it anymore. "You holding onto your breath? It's the wheel, you know. The anchor."

"I forgot."

Essa smiled again. They looked straight ahead at the backyard with its patchy grass and crooked fence. They looked at the giant elm in the center, the breeze moving its leaves this way and that. Essa lifted her arm to put it around her little sister.

But Puck popped up and avoided her. "Gonna go ride my bike to the shop," she said. "I feel like looking at kites."

Essa tried to sift through the look in Puck's eyes, trying to see if she could spot anything hidden there. "Listen, about what I said in the kitchen," Essa began. "I didn't mean—"

"Wasn't listening," Puck said, cutting her off. She reached down and picked up a long stick. She swung it at her side like a trusty sword, as if her mother's plan to move had put Puck in battle mode. Like she wanted to be prepared for attack at any moment, a monster around every corner. She swatted it this way and that, slicing the tops of the overgrown blades of grass.

That wasn't like Puck. She never liked to hurt living things. Even grass.

She made her away around the house and out of sight.

Essa shifted on the ground, not sure what Puck had seen or heard when Essa was in the kitchen with Oliver. She wasn't sure what she was going to do about their mother. She wasn't sure what she was going to do about Oliver. Essa looked into the sky and thought about meditating, about listening for sounds, about counting her breaths, about being in the moment instead of trapped in the storm of her thoughts. But it sounded hollow somehow. Like it wouldn't help.

Five more days until they set off for the mountains.

Five more days.

June 19

21

OLIVER

"Why does a kite shop have to open at eight A.M. on a Monday morning in the summer?" Oliver rubbed his eyes and stared at Micah, who seemed to be unbelievably awake at this hour. Which was probably a good thing, considering he was standing on the very top step of a rickety ladder.

"Early bird gets the worm, my friend." One earbud was jammed in Micah's right ear, and the other dangled loosely in front of his T-shirt. He was simultaneously bobbing his head to whatever he was listening to and attempting to hang the latest product arrival: giant kites that looked like paragliders. There were six to be hung, each larger than the last. Each one was a multicolored, double-layered canvas wing that looked like a large slice of a soft down comforter. Oliver decided they were beautiful. He'd seen people attached to real paragliders, swirling above the Flatirons in the early morning hours; these were the smaller kite versions.

"What's that one called?" He gestured to the paraglider kite that Micah was currently wrestling with.

"It's the Lykos, baby," Micah said. "Responsive without being touchy. Built for speed. Catalogue says it's been clocked at a hundred twenty miles per hour. That's like a cheetah. Not a lykos."

"Lykos?"

Micah tapped his foot on the top step of the ladder. "You ever take a philosophy class?"

"No. I'm in high school. We don't have philosophy classes. And you're going to fall, man," Oliver warned. He held on to the bottom of the ladder and steadied it. "And I am totally not catching you."

"Lykos. It means 'wolf' in Greek. And there's this book—" Micah stopped talking; one of the paraglider's lines came loose from the ceiling. He leaned perilously to the left and caught it before the whole thing came gliding down on top of him. He successfully attached the last polyester line to the ceiling and let go. The Lykos billowed open and filled out in the cool breeze coming from the air-conditioning vent.

"Wow," Oliver said, staring up.

"What a beaut!" Micah spread his arms wide and beheld the kite. Fully opened, it was over six feet long. "Essa's gonna love this." Micah glanced down at Oliver. At the mention of Essa's name, Micah's expression changed from one of Kite Awe to worry. "Speaking of Essa . . . you stay long at her house the other night? She told me what her mom did. She's going to marry this new guy and run off to Portland?"

Oliver stepped out of the way as Micah climbed down the ladder. "Um, yeah. I stayed a little while." Oliver looked back up at the lofted cells of the Lykos. "Wait. What does Lykos have to do with taking a philosophy class?"

Micah looked like he was about to answer the question, but then got distracted as he walked to the counter and picked up the next kite to be hung. It was the largest paraglider in the series. "I don't get the names of these things," he said as he pulled the kite out of its large plastic sleeve. "I mean, they name one after the Greek word for wolf, and then the apex of the series is called *The Mighty Bug*? What gives? Shouldn't this one be *The Plato*? Maybe *The Professor.*"

Oliver moved the ladder a few feet to the left, readying it for Micah's next ascent. Micah hoisted The Mighty Bug over his shoulder and mounted the steps. He looked like a hunter returning from a successful hunt with some sort of primary-colored big game hanging limp in his arms. As if he was off to skin his prize and sell its canvas coat for a hefty price.

"So . . . lykos? Philosophy?" This was the thing with Micah. You had to gently keep him on course.

"Right. One of the most-read philosophy books of all time . . . *Zen and the Art of Motorcycle Maintenance.* Character was supposed to be like a wolf, so the author named him Phaedrus thinking that meant 'wolf' in Greek. It doesn't. He should've named him Lykos. Classic philosophy trivia. You read it?"

"No." Oliver shook his head.

"Chicks dig philosophy, bro. Better bone up on the topic. The writer is lucky Phaedrus means 'brilliance.' What if it had meant 'cucumber'? Or 'shoe'? It could've changed the *entire* meaning of the thing."

"Move a little to the left," Oliver instructed as Micah prepared to poke a hanging wire into one of the foam ceiling tiles. "So what's it about?"

Micah looked down as he took another hanging wire out of his pocket. His thick black hair was particularly full. Oliver decided it looked a little like one of the puffy kites. "What's what about?"

Again. The focus issue.

"The book. *Zen and the Art of Motorcycle Maintenance.* It's about Zen?"

"Oh, right. Well, the author's note says it has nothing to do with Zen." Micah huffed. "But that's such a Zen thing to say."

"Is *everybody* Zen around here?"

Micah plunged the wire into the ceiling and fastened it tightly. "Hell no! I'm half-Thai. My mom's Theraveda, man. Zennies sit too much! My ass couldn't handle it." Micah let go of the kite, and it unfurled, tugging tight on its polyester hanging lines.

"Theraveda?"

"Different school of Buddhism. Ask Puck. She can tell you all about it." Micah climbed down the ladder, his work finished.

"Don't you mean Essa?"

Micah gathered up the empty kite bags and threw them in the trash. "Nope. Meant Puck. She's, like, a genius. You know that, right? She's so into the Buddhism stuff. Knows everything. Gotta love that girl." Micah eyed Oliver. "How was Puck doing when you left the other night?"

"I don't know, I—"

"You don't know?" Micah raised his eyebrows.

"She was hanging out in the backyard, and she wouldn't really talk to me. I tried," Oliver said. "The only thing she asked me about was the trek to Gold Hill. And then she accused me of . . ."

Being in love with Essa.

Micah looked at him, apparently waiting for him to finish the sentence.

Oliver didn't.

Micah furrowed his brow, a too-intense look filling his eyes. "She accused you of what?"

"Nothing," Oliver said. "Never mind."

Micah seemed to soften. As if he realized he was being too harsh and was trying to backtrack. "Sorry," he mumbled. The bell over the shop's front door jingled as a few customers came in and headed for the bin of mini animals. "I'm an only."

"Only?"

"Only child. Puck's like my little sister. We hang. She helps me memorize all the dragon figurines we sell; I help her with computer stuff. I'm protective, I guess." Micah flashed an awkward smile.

"Yeah," Oliver said. "Sure." He just wanted the conversation to end. There was something about Micah's response that didn't feel right. He sounded envious that Oliver had been at Essa's house. But why? Micah had never seemed into her, but maybe Oliver had missed it. Or maybe it was about Puck. Micah got way too intense at the mention of her name, like the subject of Essa's little sister had hit a nerve he didn't want to talk about. Oliver wasn't sure he bought the only-child/surrogate-brother explanation.

"I better go make sure they don't try to pocket any of the mini animals," Micah said, gesturing toward the customers. "We're missing, like, fifteen of the new ones."

"The new ones?"

"Hippie Mini-Ducks. They're wearing flower headbands. Peace necklaces. The whole nine yards. People eat 'em up." Micah smiled another unconvincing smile and headed for the customers.

Oliver watched him go.

Boulder:

Hot Zen girls.

Jealous Theraveda guys.

Pot-themed sub sandwiches.

And now . . .

Hippie Mini-Ducks.

Micah stopped before he reached the animal bins. He turned back to Oliver. "Did she invite you?"

"Huh?"

"Essa. Did she invite you on the trek? It's going to be three days. Really brutal. We have to find our way through the backcountry. And Anish can't even come, either. Realized it's his grandmother's birthday this weekend. And she's making her famous chicken korma. Anish misses chicken korma for no man. Or woman. Or hike in the—"

"Yeah," Oliver cut him off. "I'm going."

Micah looked at the floor and slowly nodded. "Great. We're going to the Comanche Peak Wilderness. Should be fun." He smiled and headed for the customers but looked like he was trying to hide his disappointment.

It didn't work.

June 22

22

ESSA

"I'll carry the tent," Micah said, opening the back of his rusty Jeep. "And don't say I never do anything nice for you."

"If you're going to whine, I'll carry it." Essa adjusted the butterfly clip in her hair and looked up in the sky, squinting in the bright Colorado sun. In the distance, patches of glimmering snow dotted the gray peaks and ridges of the Mummy Range. Snow hung around in the high elevations until midsummer. But they were well below the tree line at eighty-five hundred feet. It had already melted. "And why'd you bring a kite?" Essa asked, pointing to the limp canvas next to her pack.

"I didn't," Micah said. He eyed the red-blue-and-yellow pattern. "That's the new Lykos. Anish must have stashed it in here. He keeps saying he wants to try it. I hope he didn't take down the one that I hung. That thing was a pain in the ass."

Essa took one last look at the sky over the meadows and thick forest beyond them. Dark clouds threatened from the west.

But it's only 7 A.M. It's not supposed to storm until after noon.

She'd checked the forecast over and over before they left Boulder in the wee hours of the morning. It called for clear skies until 1 P.M. and then a brief shower, typical for summer afternoons in the mountains. The clouds to west looked worse than that. Much worse.

"So how does this work again?" Oliver was in the front seat, studying a map he'd pulled out of a Colorado guidebook. He was holding the map upside down. He looked back at Essa. "We're trying to get where?"

Micah raised his eyebrows at Essa, making it obvious that he thought it was a horrible idea to have invited Oliver.

"I thought you liked him?" Essa whispered. "You're the one who invited him to the bonfire that night—"

"And where the *hell* are we?" Oliver looked back down at his map.

Essa looked at Micah. "He won't hold us up," she whispered. "He'll be fine . . . I think."

"You just better not be into him," Micah said way too loudly. "Puck will go apeshit."

"I'm not into him, okay?" Essa lied. "What's your problem, anyway?" She walked toward the front of the car and to Oliver's open passenger's-side window. "Your map's upside down," she said, gently turning it around in his hands. The tip of her long brown hair brushed against his leg as she leaned in.

"Oh." Oliver smiled. "Thanks." She caught him glancing at her tattoo.

Sanctuary.

He looked at it like he was still puzzling over its meaning. Like he was thinking about the koan it came from. Or maybe he was just thinking about her. She couldn't tell, but it made her skin feel a little tingly, a little touchy. Like it was being watched. Admired.

Essa crossed her arms on the window frame and rested her chin on her forearms. "We use our topo map and compass to find the quickest backcountry route . . ." Essa paused, studying the map on Oliver's knees. "To there." She pointed to a small circle of blue. "Brown's Lake."

Oliver's hazel eyes burned with a question. "But why?" He smiled.

She knew he was giving her a hard time, but she also knew he didn't get it. Not really. He said he'd liked their little trek to Gold Hill, but now they were much higher and going much farther. Essa loved it up here; she loved leaving her messed-up life below. Especially now, with the Portland plan looming. But she always felt it as they climbed into the mountains, like every thousand feet of elevation took her farther and farther from reality. Like height was a door she walked through, a portal to a better world. Nearer to the sky. Simplified under the sun's close glare. She and Puck survived on so little down in Boulder. But down there, it was painful. Up here, it made her feel alive.

"It's a game," she said. "Sort of. If you were camping or hiking and you'd lost your way, you'd need to know the best way to get out. It's like practice."

"Right . . . practice." Oliver shifted his long legs, his knees poking out of his ripped jeans and shoved up against the Jeep's glove box. He looked back at the map. The worry about inviting him started to grow.

You kiss a guy one time, and you're already making bad decisions.

"And are we here?" Oliver pointed to his newly righted map. "Comanche Peak Wilderness? Because my book says it's full of coyote, mountain lion, mule deer, elk, marmot, and black bears. I mean, mountain lions and bears? Holy shit. And what the hell is a marmot?"

"Yes, we're in Comanche," Essa said. "And I'll explain what a marmot is on the way. They're chill. Don't worry about it."

She conveniently avoided addressing the mountain lion and bear issue as Micah came around from the back of the car.

"I hate to break up this moving wilderness date, but look up." He pointed into the sky at the approaching dark clouds. "We need to get going."

With their packs jostling against their backs, they struck out across the broad alpine meadow. The plan was to head northeast on the Comanche Peak trail and then break off into the backcountry from there.

The first three hours of the hike was on a well-marked trail. It wound through a forest and then climbed to a ridge with views of the looming Mummy range. Essa kept an eye on Oliver, and surprisingly, he was doing well. Despite the altitude, he wasn't too out of breath. And he didn't complain or seem all that worried about being in the wilderness.

Until they left the trail.

"So how do you know which way we're going?" Oliver jammed his hands in his jeans pockets and looked over the open, unmarked field ahead of them. "Don't we need one of those rock-and-stick compasses?"

"You know what I have in here?" Micah patted the side pocket of his backpack. "A topo map. And a real compass. Amazing inventions."

"Don't be a smartass," Essa said. She turned to Oliver. "Gold Hill was easy. We didn't really need to take a bearing. But here, we're using the real deal. A real compass."

Oliver nodded, and they all walked on in silence. Birds twittered around them, and the breeze suddenly picked up. Essa eyed the clouds. They looked thick and endless; she couldn't see the back edge of the storm. That was always the thing in Colorado—the big sky. Usually, if there was a storm, you could see where it began and where it ended. Which made a storm a beautiful thing, the visible impermanence of it.

But not this storm. The front edge of it was racing to blot out the sun, and the mountains were shielding wherever it ended.

"Wait. Did you hear that?" Oliver stopped and turned. He scanned the rolling field behind them and the random mounds of giant rocks and sporadic clumps of trees sprinkled across it.

"There," Micah pointed to a rock pile ten feet away. "Just a pica, dude." Essa and Oliver turned in time to see the mouselike animal scurry between boulders and dive into a hole.

"No, that wasn't it," Oliver said, still scanning the field. "It was louder than that. Too loud for a mouse. Are bears out already?"

"Chill," Micah came over and put a hand on one of Oliver's broad shoulders. "It's going to be a long three days if you freak at every noise. This is the great outdoors! It talks if you listen."

"Talks?"

Essa flanked Oliver's other side. "We're in a meadow. We'd see a bear easily out here. Just try not to panic. Okay?"

"Yeah, but we're heading in there, right?" Oliver pointed ahead at the dense forest.

"Just trust us," Micah said. "The first rule of wilderness survival: panic makes everything worse."

"I feel like you guys have at least five different 'first rules of survival,'" Oliver said. Micah glared at him. "Just sayin'."

A peal of thunder sliced the thin air. They still had at least another thirty minutes until they could make it to the tree cover of the forest, and the last thing a hiker wanted was to be the tallest object in an exposed meadow when a lightning storm moved in. Dozens of Colorado hikers were killed by strikes each year. Essa didn't want to be one of them.

"We need to speed up," she said. A stiff mountain breeze swept around them, tinged with cold as the sun was doused behind a cloud. "We need to get under tree cover."

She walked ahead, her trusty battered hiking boots crunching the stiff alpine grass. Micah followed, his pack now bouncing against his back in rhythm with his bushy hair. He pulled out a red bandana and wrapped it around his forehead.

"Wait," Oliver said. He stopped. Again.

"What now?" Micah mumbled.

"I saw something." Oliver was standing ten feet behind them, his eyes fixed on a point in the distance.

"There's nothing back there," Micah huffed. "That's a field of big rocks and a few tree stands. Seriously, we need to keep going."

But Essa saw it, too. Movement. A flash of something. In a clump of large boulders and a few twisted runt pines. It was too big to just be a raccoon or a marmot. A small bear? A mountain lion? She tried to shake it off, but adrenaline moved through her veins, an icy feeling oozing from her chest down into her arms.

Whatever it is, it'll leave us alone.

"Just make noise as we go," Essa said. "Talk louder than usual. It's like bear and mountain lion repellent. They don't want to mess with us any more than we want to mess with them."

Another loud clap of thunder rumbled through the sky.

"Shit," Micah said. "Rain will be here any minute. Let's go."

A bolt of lightning flashed to their left. And again to their right. A brilliant arc of white struck a mountain top.

"Run," Essa said.

Just as the rain burst out of the sky, they reached the trees. They ran another two hundred yards, pounding across the darkened forest floor. Dead and broken tree limbs littered the ground like the craggy broken bones of people no one cared about enough to bury. Brown pine needles crunched underfoot. Thick raindrops made their way through the tree cover overhead, but it was better than being exposed in the meadow. Hopefully, if lightning struck again, it would strike a treetop and not one of them. They stopped to catch their breath.

Snap.

They all heard it.

Their heavy breathing immediately stopped, and they all turned toward the noise at the same time. There was something in the woods with them. Something shifting behind a tree. Then it made a sound. Not a roar. Or an animal grunt.

A giggle.

"Hello?" Essa stepped forward. "Is somebody there?"

Twenty feet away, like a ghost, like a vision, she emerged from behind a tree. Her blue eyes shone bright in the misty gray light like two robin's eggs that had fallen out of a nest. Her stringy hair dripped down her unicorn T-shirt. She wore the pink back-pack that was much too big for her shoulders; the wheels she'd drawn on it with a permanent marker were still clear and round, refusing to smear in the rain. A tiny smile spread across her candy-stained red lips.

Essa dropped her pack.

"Puck?"

23

ESSA

Essa knelt on the ground beside Puck and pushed a few strands of her sister's wet hair away from her face. Puck's cheeks were bright pink, flushed from running in the rain. Essa held her like she was a wounded bird Essa had found in the woods, broken wings, crooked feathers.

Then Essa got pissed.

"Why on earth are you here?" Essa still knelt on the ground, her pants soaking up rain from the ground. "Wait . . . *how* are you even here?"

Puck smiled. "I was hiding under the kite."

"What kite?" Essa asked.

Micah knelt beside them. "You mean the kite in the back of my Jeep? The paraglider?"

Puck nodded. "Yep. I was so scared! I thought you guys were going to lift it up and bust me." She beamed, proud of her deception. "I've been trailing you guys for hours. Yay."

"Don't say 'yay,'" Essa said, glowering. "This is not smart. Not funny. Not cool in any way, shape, or form."

"I mean, it's pretty smart," Micah said smiling. He put his hand on top of Puck's wet head and ruffled her matted hair. "You gotta give her that."

"So you're a stowaway?" Oliver asked, his face lighting up. "I mean, that's pretty badass. I've always wanted to be a stowaway."

Puck kept her lips pursed and glared at Oliver, making it

clear to everyone that she was still not happy about whatever was going on with him and Essa. But her face softened like she couldn't keep it up any longer. She reached into her pink backpack.

"I *am* a badass," she said with a grin. "And I *brought* Badass." She held up Badass the Dragon like she was a trophy awarded to the Best Stowaway of the Year. "She had to come."

"Right on," Oliver said, gently laughing. Micah started, too.

"Do *not* laugh, people." Essa stood up, the rain dripping down her braid and back, her pants sagging with the weight of rainwater. "This is so not funny. We have to go home. Immediately." She grabbed Puck's hand and started hiking back the way they came.

"Hold up, Ess," Micah said. "You can't go back now. In case you haven't noticed, there's a storm? Lightning?"

"I don't care," Essa called back. "We're going."

She made it another ten feet, yanking Puck by the arm.

"Ow," Puck whined. "You're *pulling*."

"Why did you stow away?" Essa asked, still marching through the woods.

"Because I wanted to come. *Duh.*" Puck yanked her hand out of Essa's, but still stormed along behind her older sister. "I've only been asking to come on one of these trips for a million years."

Thunder crackled above them. The loudest yet.

Essa froze.

Of course they couldn't go back now. She couldn't take Puck into an exposed alpine meadow with lightning striking all around them. They couldn't hike for three hours soaking wet in a storm at over eight thousand feet elevation. Essa looked back at Micah, her eyes wide. "What are we going to do?" she called.

Micah yanked his bandana off his head and wrung out the water. "You know what we're going to do. Think."

But she couldn't. She realized that maybe for the first time in all her mountain hiking days, she was in a complete and total panic. Thoughts skipped in her mind like tiny stones across a lake, bouncing along the surface and disappearing beneath the water.

Thought. Thought. Gone.

Thought. Thought. Gone.

Essa walked back toward Micah and Oliver. She grabbed Puck's hand again. "I can't . . . think," Essa said, shaking her head.

"Okay, I'll walk you through it," Micah said. "What's the protocol if you're exposed in a storm?"

"Um . . ." Essa closed her eyes. "Shelter. Find shelter."

"Right," Micah said. "We're under tree cover, but that lightning is close. So we'd be better off under an outcropping of rock if we can find one. Then what?"

Essa's breath was coming way too fast.

Shelter. Shelter. Shelter. What comes after shelter?

"Heat," Micah said. "If we were going to be stuck here a long time, we'd need heat. To dry off once this passes. So we should . . . ?"

"Gather any dry wood we can find. Get it into our shelter so it stays dry."

The sky broke open again with thunder; it rumbled in her chest.

"Right, and look for pine sap," Micah surveyed the trees around him. "Which shouldn't be hard here. Now let's go."

"Pine sap?" Oliver looked confused.

"It's a fire starter," Micah said. "One of the best there is. Great in wet conditions." Micah looked up the hill in front of them. "Let's head this way."

"Wait," Essa said. "Let's just wait out the storm and then hike back. There's no need to go through all this like we're staying on the trek."

Micah looked up at the raindrops and groaned. The sky had darkened to a thick, opaque gray. "The beginning," he said slowly, "is the most important part of the work."

"You better not be—"

"Quoting Plato?" Micah asked, looking back at Essa. "Indeed I am. What if this storm lasts all night? What if we can't hike out of here? The decisions we make right now, in the beginning, will determine what kind of night we have."

"Storms never last all night up here," Essa moaned. "It's Colorado. It's summer. It'll be over by three or four."

Micah raised his eyebrows. "That sounds like the shit people say in movies right before they get killed in some epic storm," he said. "We should follow protocol. Find shelter, get a heat source. It's good practice. Plus, what else are we going to do? Sit here in the rain and sing campfire songs?" He turned and began hiking up the hill.

"Fine. You win. But why don't we head back toward the trail? That way we're at least heading in the right direction."

"Better shelter up this way," Micah called back. He didn't turn around. He just kept trudging, determined. Which was unlike him. Usually he conferred with Essa about decisions they made out here.

Essa rolled her eyes and took Puck's hand. "We'll follow Micah," she said. "But as soon as humanly possible, we are going *home.*"

She squeezed Puck's hand, so relieved that her little sister didn't get lost or hurt following them in the woods. Puck smiled, looking so pleased with herself. So impressed with the feat of getting to go on one of these treks.

"Don't get any ideas," Essa said, trying to look stern. "I still love you. But I am still totally pissed."

The storm didn't stop. The rain just kept coming. They searched the mountainside for shelter for at least an hour and couldn't find one; the sides of the hill were smooth, the boulders were all too small. There was nothing to crawl under or in.

"So let's put up the tent," Micah said, pointing to a slightly sheltered spot against a rock face. He motioned for Essa to turn around so he could get it out of her pack.

"I don't have it," Essa said. "You have it."

Micah raised his eyebrows. "Incorrect. You said that if I was going to whine about it, you'd carry it. I was totally planning on whining about it."

"*Great.*" Essa closed her eyes and tilted her face toward the raining sky. She felt the cold raindrops hit her cheeks and run down her neck, soaking the collar of her shirt. She looked at the wet ground. "Looks like we'll be spending the night in a brush shelter. A very wet brush shelter."

"Oh, shit," Micah said.

"It's okay." Essa sighed. "We're good at building these—"

"It wasn't just the tent in the tent bag." Micah's eyes were wide with guilt. "It also had the flashlight. And the lighters. And the emergency flint."

"Oh, shit."

"A brush shelter will be awesome!" Puck said. "I read all about it. We need a support log. And root rope. And *tons* of pine branches." Puck ran to the nearest tree and started gathering boughs that had fallen to the forest floor.

Micah smiled as he watched her. "So . . . let's get stoked? And build a brush shelter." He looked back at Essa. "And sorry. Totally my bad."

"You're forgiven, I guess," Essa said. There was no sense in getting pissed. They needed shelter; she had to make sure Puck would be dry tonight. Essa eyed a fallen tree limb, about as wide as her leg. "There's a decent support beam. You guys get some roots, and I'll do the knot."

The process for building a brush shelter was always the same. Find a fallen limb strong enough to use as the main support beam. Find a bush or other small plant and pull up a handful of live roots to use as rope. Tie the support beam to a tree and layer pine limbs and other brush over it until a cavelike shelter started to take shape.

Oliver helped dig up roots until his hands looked muddy and raw. Essa tied the support beam to the tree because she was the best at bowline knots. Puck was fifty yards off, collecting pine branches for the walls. She was standing on her tip-toes, trying to reach a broken limb.

"Here," Essa said, jogging to Puck's side. "Let me help." Essa reached up and pulled the branch down and handed it to Puck. "Good find."

"I'm only collecting stuff that's already broken or fallen. Those are the wilderness rules. And we totally shouldn't be digging up roots. Leave no trace and all. But this is an emergency."

"You studied the rules, didn't you?" Essa wiped her hands on her pants. The pine sap stuck to her palms despite how wet they were.

"I told you I'd be a good partner for this. Did I tell you I learned how to make a Band-Aid out of pine bark?"

"You did," Essa said. "And I'm impressed."

"So if you get cut, just tell me."

"I will. But let's hope that doesn't happen."

They walked another twenty yards to the left, where several pine branches had fallen. The only sounds Essa could hear were the patter of the heavy raindrops on the trees and an occasional bird tweeting in spite of the storm.

Until she heard whistling.

She looked back in the direction of Micah and Oliver. Oliver was bent over the ground, digging up the roots of a small plant. His hands were covered in dirt and mud as he scratched at the earth. Micah was busy lacing branches together over the shelter. Essa couldn't tell which one was whistling.

"Who's the songbird?" she called.

"What?" Oliver called back.

"Who's whistling? And what's that song?"

The rain came even harder, and Puck started to giggle. She twirled and held her arms wide, as if the droplets were falling on her giant make-believe wings, sliding off her colorful feathers.

"Not me," Oliver said. "Can't whistle. Never been able to."

"Not me," Micah called over his shoulder, threading some root rope around a pine bough. "Must be Puck."

Essa looked over at Puck, still dancing in the storm.

Puck wasn't whistling, either.

Then who . . . ?

"You know where you are?"

Essa spun around. It was a man wearing a straw fedora. The rain was collecting in the hat's slightly upturned brim and cascading off to the side, a tiny waterfall that arced to the ground. Puck stopped dancing.

"Yeah," Essa said. "We do." She looked back at Oliver. He wasn't paying attention; he was too focused on yanking a small root out of the ground. Micah was busy messing with the shelter.

"My grandfather's plane went down somewhere around here. Had a lot of Japanese antiques on board. So valuable." The man looked around the woods, as if there might be a plane lodged in the soft forest floor just behind Essa. "I've been looking for what was onboard for years. Think a lot of it was scattered throughout these woods."

The little hairs on the back of Essa's neck stood up, her skin tingling. *Great. A nut job.* She knew there was a trail in the Comanche Wilderness that led to the site of an old WWII plane crash, but still. What were the odds that it was his grandfather's plane? Or that there were antiques that survived the crash?

"Haven't seen it," she said. She turned and managed to catch Micah's eye. He dropped the large pine bough in his hand and came over.

"I was just passing this way and heard you folks talking," the man said. "Wanted to make sure you knew where you were. You're way off trail up the—"

"We're good." Essa cut him off. "We've backpacked up here a lot. But thanks."

She looked at the ground and saw that the man was wearing soft rubber clogs with holes in them. Black cotton pants. Not what you'd wear backcountry hiking. He looked so out of place—almost like an illusion, something from a surrealist painting.

Essa walked closer to Puck, instantly feeling protective. Sometimes hikers ran into creeps in the woods. It didn't happen often, but it had happened before. Essa guessed he was a sketchy person who was trying to live in the wilderness or was running from something or was just plain out of it.

"Everything okay?" Oliver joined them, a tangle of roots in his hands.

"Yeah," Essa said. "Let's go." She steered Puck in the direction of the shelter.

"Have a good hike," the man said. He started whistling again as he turned and slowly walked away, his white straw fedora like a freak summertime snowflake bobbing through the woods, refusing to melt.

"*Creeper,*" Oliver said. "I thought you guys didn't have those out here. I thought you only ran into dudes like that in the city."

"He was weird," Puck said, wrinkling her brow. "Who wears clogs like that in the woods?"

"You know what they say," Micah said, still watching the guy walk away. "Fear is the anticipation of . . . creepers."

Essa leveled her eyes at Micah. "Let me guess," she said. "Plato again?"

"Nope. Aristotle. Bet you didn't know he was fond of the word *creepers.*" Micah smiled. "Okay. So I slightly modified the quote."

Essa rolled her eyes and draped an arm around her sister's tiny shoulders. In a way, Essa was suddenly glad Puck was here instead of back down in Boulder. She thought about how there were so many creeps in the world. So many dangers. And maybe Essa would rather have Puck with her up here, even in the cold and the storm.

As long as you're with me, you're safe.

"So, who wants to hear the real Aristotle quote?" Micah asked as they walked back toward the shelter. No one responded.

"Excellent. The real quote is 'Fear is pain arising from the anticipation of evil.' But 'creeper' is a fair substitution."

"I'm sure that's what Aristotle was referring to," Essa said.

Micah turned to Oliver and Puck. "You guys want to collect some pine sap off that tree?" he asked, pointing. "I'll start a fire in a little bit. Could use some fuel."

Puck didn't look thrilled, but agreed to go with Oliver. The two headed off to scrape the dripping sap off a nearby tree.

As soon as they were out of earshot, Micah turned to Essa. "Question for you."

"Go for it." Essa pulled the elastic off the end of her wet braid and slowly undid the overlapping strands. She bent over and shook out her hair; the damp braid had crimped it into hundreds of tiny waves.

"That guy," Micah said, looking back in the direction where they'd seen him. "He say anything before I got there?"

"Not really," Essa said. "Something freaky about looking for his grandfather's plane? Antiques? I think he means the trail to the B17 site. I don't know. Totally wacko."

"Did he tell you where we are?"

Essa's eyes widened. "No," she said slowly. "He started to, but I cut him off. Why?"

"Just wondering."

Essa stared at Micah, noticing that he seemed a little jittery, a little on edge. "Micah. Do you not know where we are?"

"Well . . . we walked for almost an hour in the storm, and I thought I knew exactly where we were going when I led us up that ridge. But when I went to look for pine boughs, I didn't recognize any of the landmarks I'd noted to get us back. And it was so dark with the storm, I didn't really . . ." Micah trailed off. Essa looked around her at the dripping trees and realized the worst:

She hadn't been paying attention.

After Puck had shown up, her mind had gone into panic mode; all her survival skills had flown out the window. Micah had convinced her they needed to set off to look for shelter and firewood, and she'd just blindly followed him. She hadn't looked for landmarks; she hadn't even tried to figure out if they were walking north, south, east, or west. Now, everything looked the same.

"When we dry out, we'll take a bearing with the compass," Essa said, trying desperately to stop the panic pooling in her chest like the rainwater in her hiking boots. "We'll hike to a high point. Get a good view. We're *not* lost."

"No," Micah said, shaking his head. "Hell, no. Definitely not lost."

Essa smiled thinly, and Micah headed back to work on the shelter. She needed to stay calm, to follow her breath, to be in the moment. She needed to call on all her orienteering skills, her survival skills, her gut instincts. She needed to keep Puck safe and get her home as fast as possible. She needed the thought that was racing through her mind to go away.

We're lost.

24

ESSA

The rain didn't stop until dusk. If they set off for the car, they would have to spend several hours hiking in the dark. With no flashlight.

There was only one option—stay the night.

Micah put together a small nest of cedar bark and pine sap. He used leftover roots, a curved live branch, a thick stick, and the driest slab of wood he could find to build a bow and drill: a fire-starting tool. The roots wrapped around the branch and were tied to either end to create the bow; he used it to work the thick stick back and forth against the dry wood slab, smoking and finally creating an ember he could dump on the nest. Once the fire was crackling, he put Essa in charge of watching it and promptly crawled into the finished shelter and fell asleep. Essa and Oliver sat by the flames and stuck their wet, sock-covered feet as close to the heat as they could without burning them. Puck was close by, bent over the ground playing with sticks.

Oliver wiggled his toes. Essa eyed the deadfall trap Micah had set nearby.

"You guys really going to eat a mouse if you catch one?" Oliver asked. "Did we not bring enough food?" He looked at the deadfall, which consisted of a large rock perched on top of two sticks rigged to fall if they were triggered. The rock was supposed to squash whatever animal was below.

She knew why Micah had set it. Oliver was right; they'd brought plenty of food on the trip. To last three days. A few extra if necessary. But if they were lost, none of them knew how long their stores would need to last. Micah was preparing for the worst.

"Micah's just practicing," Essa lied. "Good wilderness skill."

"But I thought you were a vegetarian?"

"Yeah, I am. Puck is too. But we'd eat meat in a true emergency." Essa looked at Oliver. "Not that we're in one or anything. An emergency." She said it a little too quickly, and hoped Oliver didn't pick up on her nerves. She shivered and scooted closer to the fire. The storm had brought much cooler air than usual for June. There was a chill that was making her cold to her core. It didn't help that everything she had was soaked. Essa picked up the small pot they'd brought with them and held it over the fire. It was filled with rainwater. "Check this out. Pull some pine needles off that branch and hand them to me."

"Huh?"

"We'll make pine needle tea," Essa said. "You just dump a bunch of needles into hot water and let them steep. And voilà— tea. It's actually pretty high in vitamin C, so it's a good way to get some nutrition." She gently moved the pot, adjusting it over the fire.

"Look what I made! It's stick art." Puck sat up and leaned against the white bark of an aspen tree. She pointed at the ground. "You're gonna love it."

The flames of the campfire leaped in the air as a stiff breeze blew from the east. The fire curled around the small pot Essa was holding and singed the side of her finger. She nearly dropped the pot from the pain. "Damn Colorado wind."

"Seriously, come here." Puck stood up and brushed away the little twigs and stones that were stuck to the backside of her pants. She pointed at the ground. "I made a forest stick mural. I think it's beautiful."

"Not now, Puck," Essa said, still concentrating on the

throbbing pain in her swelling finger. "In a little bit, okay? I'm making tea."

"We haven't even been hungry that long, and you're getting cranky. Don't forget to look at my art." Puck wagged a finger at Essa and then ran over to the shelter. "I'm going to see if Micah wants to go star hunting with me. I can't see any from here." She craned her neck to get a view of the sky. It was too dark to see the outlines of clouds, but Essa knew they were there by the absence of starlight.

"Fine, but don't go far," she said. The water began to boil.

"Do I put the needles in now?" Oliver asked, ready with a handful.

"Yep," Essa said. Oliver dropped the thin green spikes into the water, and Puck disappeared inside the shelter.

Darkness thickened around them. Essa and Oliver finished off the pine needle tea as the fire pip-popped. Essa slid off the log she was sitting on and spread out on a spot close to the flames.

"Dry over there?" Oliver asked.

"Close enough," Essa said, stretching her arms above her head.

Oliver stoked the fire with a stick, sending a spray of embers into the night sky. "We should get some sleep."

"I don't think I can. Not until I get Puck out of here. I won't be able to sleep a wink."

"You guys are pros," Oliver said. "As soon as the sun comes up, we'll just hike back to the car and be out of here."

Essa didn't respond. She stared into the flames.

"Right?" he asked.

"Yeah," Essa lied. "As soon as the sun comes up, we'll head back." She watched the fire dance in his eyes. He eased off the log and sat down next to her. She couldn't believe they were up here like this. Stuck, maybe lost. "I bet you never imagined you'd be in the mountains like this when you were planning your summer out here."

206 🍂 Emily France

Oliver grinned, but it faded quickly. "I didn't exactly plan my summer. It was sort of . . . planned for me."

Far off, an owl pierced the night with a lonely hoot. It made Essa feel melancholy, inexplicably homesick for a home that was in total disarray. A home that was being invaded by a wannabe medicine man. A home that was being moved to Portland.

"What do you mean?" Essa could feel a change come over Oliver. He seemed smaller, quieter, like he'd retreated inside a memory he didn't want to have. "Tell me." She whispered it.

"The last time I was with Lilly in Chicago," Oliver said, keeping his gaze at the fire. "She was just out of control, you know? In a delusion. Something about our dad being involved in a crime. A felony. My parents were in the kitchen arguing about the divorce, and I was back in Lilly's room, trying to keep her calm. She said she'd been getting clues in the crossword puzzles from the *Chicago Tribune* about Dad's crimes. That she was putting it all together. That's how her mind works. She starts seeing clues everywhere. Like her whole life is a mystery novel."

The fire hissed loudly and spit a hot ember at Essa's legs. She pulled them back just in time. A sound came from behind them in the woods. A *crack*. A *snap*. She looked over her shoulder but didn't see anything in the darkness.

Probably a raccoon.

"Normally I just go with it," Oliver continued. "I just act like I believe whatever Lilly is saying. Just to be wherever she is." He stopped and stared up at the dark sky. He shook his head. "I should've just asked her to show me the crossword clues, to tell me what felony she thought Dad had committed. I should've acted like I was going to call the police on him, get to the bottom of it, take care of it . . ."

Oliver stopped talking. He slumped like the memory was a heavy wet wool coat someone had just draped over his shoulders. Essa waited for him to continue. He didn't.

She looked at him, hoping he wouldn't stop. "What did you say instead?"

Oliver took a deep breath. "I said what our family therapists have always told us to say. You're not supposed to tell a person with schizophrenia that their reality is wrong. But you're not supposed to tell them it's right, either. That just feeds the delusions. You're supposed to say that you understand what they are thinking or seeing, but that you don't see things the same way." He worried a wet thread of his jeans between his thumb and forefinger. "You're supposed to acknowledge that you're in two different worlds. She has hers. And you have yours. Both valid."

"And that's what you said?"

He paused and stared into the flames. "Sort of. I said I understood that she thought Dad had committed some horrible crime, but that I didn't."

Essa could tell Oliver was close to tears. "That's not so bad," she said. She sat up and scooted closer to him. She rubbed his back. "That's what the doctors told you to do. You were just being honest—"

"That's not the end of it," Oliver said. "She got so upset. So mad at me. I'd always been her advocate, you know? The one who got her. Who understood. She started screaming about how I'd betrayed her. And then I just lost it. I told her she was crazy. Completely nuts. And then I . . ." Oliver trailed off again. "I can't really talk about it anymore. Hurts too much."

Essa didn't give any thought about what to do next. She didn't run through her options.

She wrapped her arms around him.

She meant to just breathe. In and out. To just be with him. To be with what was really happening. The crackle of the fire. The curling heat from the flames. The cool wind sliding through the trees. The animals they couldn't see. The heartache nested in Oliver's chest like a handful of baby birds squawking for attention.

Memories are like clouds drifting by mountains.
Watch them. Tend to them.
But know

You're the mountain.

"That must hurt," Essa whispered. "So much. That she's so sick." As she held him, his warm cheek brushed against hers. The smell of his skin blocked out the scent of pine and wet leaves. Her eyes closed. She didn't know if she reached for him or if he reached for her, but they found each other. She felt like she disappeared in his arms, like there was nothing left of her except the sensation of his lips, his arms around her waist, the gentle pressure of his chest against hers. The understanding between the two of that word: sister.

A loud *thud* sounded near the shelter. Then she heard the mad rustling and footsteps.

"Hell, yes!" It was Micah. Who had apparently raced out of the shelter. Essa pulled away from Oliver and squinted in the darkness. Micah started dancing. "Who's eating mouse tonight?" He swung his hips to the left. Then the right. "This guy!"

"The deadfall," Essa said, smiling in the darkness. "It worked."

PART II

THE SECOND NOBLE TRUTH:

The Arising of Duhkha

I want.
I want her.
I want to feel.
I want to have fun.
I don't want to miss out.
I want to hear a good story.
I want things to be different.
I want to be different.
I want the good to stay good.
I want the bad to stay gone.
I want to live.
But sometimes, I want to die.

These desires. They're inexhaustible. Unquenchable.

The arising of duhkha.

June 23

3 A.M.

25

ESSA

It was her job to keep Puck safe.

It was Essa's job to keep an ear out, an eye out, to be aware of any danger. It always had been. But it was especially true up here. Especially true tonight.

She'd awakened, searched inside the shelter and out; Puck was gone. And so was Oliver. Micah was groggy and useless.

"Puck! Oliver!" she called again into the dark woods. "If you're hiding, come out. This isn't funny!"

Off to her right, she heard something. Footsteps. She was sure of it. Out of the blackness, she could barely make out a shadowy figure coming toward her. Tall. Long legs. Broad shoulders.

"Hey."

It was Oliver. He put a cold hand on her arm.

"Where were you?" Essa was nearly screaming. "Where's Puck?"

"I was taking a leak. Away from camp like you said, so we don't attract bears. She's not with you?"

"No," she said. "You didn't see her? Did she come out after you?"

"I don't think so," Oliver said. "I mean, not that I know of. I didn't see her, I—"

"Puck!" Essa called again into the nothingness, pulling away from Oliver's cold grasp. She looked at his face, wanting to see his eyes, his expression. It was too dark. Then, like tripping over a tree root in the woods, seeing it snake out of the ground too late, like tumbling face first into the loam, something hit her:

She'd fallen in love with him.

And she hadn't even known him a month.

She stared at his face again, hidden by the night.

Is he telling me the truth?

She turned toward the gaping blackness of the woods behind her. "Puck! Where are you?"

She pulled in a breath and held it as she waited to hear Puck's tiny voice call back to her. She didn't dare exhale, afraid her own breathing would obscure a sound. Her chest squeezed tight and then tighter still. She closed her eyes and willed her ears to hear better than they ever had before. She forced all her energy into them and for a moment felt like she could hear at superhuman levels. Like she could hear the tiny tinkling of insect footsteps as they crawled along the cold, dead leaves at her feet. Like she could somehow hear the silent flight of bats overhead, the turning of an owl's head.

She heard a rustling. Twenty yards off.

She didn't care if it was a bear. She didn't care if it was a mountain lion. She didn't care if it was the creepy guy from the woods standing in the darkness with an ax. She took off into the black, straight for the sound, holding her hands out in front of her, begging them to land on her little sister's soft shoulders.

"Puck!" Her feet hit the cold forest floor. Faster and faster. "Are you there?"

She didn't run into Puck. She ran into Micah. He was out of the shelter now, scraping for an ember that might have survived the night in the fire pan.

"We need a light," he said. She could barely make out his hands; they were digging in the remnant of last night's fire with a stick. "Shit. It's just ashes."

Oliver sidled up to them. "Don't we have a lighter?"

"Don't have one, remember?" Micah said. "Which was my fault. We started it with the bow and drill."

"Right," Oliver said. "Yeah. Bow and drill." It was obvious from the sound of his voice that he hadn't been watching and had no idea how a bow and drill worked.

"Just make the bird's nest," Micah said.

"The what?"

"Dude, did you not see anything we did? The bird's nest. That bunch of kindling I made to catch on fire."

"Right, right. Bird's nest."

"Just grab dead pine needles. Feel around for the plank of cedar bark we had. Shred it into tiny pieces and put it all in a pile, like a nest." Micah was already using the wooden bow and drill. Essa could hear him twisting the spindle against a block of wood as fast as he could, trying to get the friction to create a glowing ember. Starting a fire this way could take a long time.

Oliver and Essa searched the ground for the chunk of cedar bark. They swept the ground all around them, first to the left, then the right. All they felt were prickly pine needles, leaves, roots. Then Essa felt something else. In the dim starlight, she could just make out a collection of sticks, put together in the shape of two mountains. A small circle made of stones was above them. Puck was hunched over here last night, playing with their kindling, making forest artwork. A mountain range with a stone sun.

Essa felt a pang in her chest as she thought of her sister's tiny frame hunched over this very spot just last night. Puck had been here. And she'd asked Essa to come look at her art project. Which Essa had failed to do. Essa had said she was busy getting the camp ready or the fire started or . . .

What was I doing? Why didn't I stop and look? That might have been the last of Puck's art I'll ever see.

Essa tried to push the darkness of that last thought out of her mind. She went back to her gatha.

Fears are like clouds drifting past a mountain.
Watch them. Tend to them.
But know
You're the mountain.

She grabbed a handful of pine needles to take to Micah and stood up. "Puck!" she called into the darkness again. "If you can hear me, we're making a light! We're coming to find you!"

"I think I've got it," Oliver said. He handed Essa the small plank of cedar bark.

"We have to shred it," she said. "Small pieces."

Oliver started making a pile of needles and tiny bits of bark. The moon briefly peeked out from behind a cloud, and she could see Micah working the bow harder and harder, the spindle twisting like mad. The smell of the friction smoke from the drill snaked up her nose. Finally, she saw a tiny glow.

"Dude," Micah said, "hand me the nest! I've got an ember."

Oliver picked up his small nest of kindling, crouched next to Micah, and held it near the bow. Micah dumped the tiniest glowing spark on the pile. Essa dropped to all fours and blew on the ember. Luckily, enough of the kindling had dried out from the storm. The fire caught.

"It's starting," Oliver said. "What now?"

"Feed it," Micah said. "Just tiny stuff. Don't suffocate it."

Oliver and Micah worked over the tiny pile, and as the flames grew, Essa took off for the shelter. She crawled in, searching in the dark for her small backpack. Her hands hit the cold canvas and zippers, and she ripped open the bag, blindly feeling inside until she found what she was looking for: a small white candle. She always carried one.

She scrambled out of the shelter and ran toward the fire. She knelt on the ground and pushed the candlewick against the flames. Oliver hunched next to her and blew on the fire to help the candle catch. The firelight tinged his chestnut eyes with a red-and-orange glow.

"You *sure* you didn't see Puck when you left the shelter?" Essa asked him as she pressed the candle closer to the flames. It wasn't catching. The wick was so tiny. It had nearly broken off in her bag. "Did you hear anything in the woods when you were out there?"

Oliver leaned back, took a deep breath, and then blew on the fire again. It jumped a few inches higher. "No," he said. "I really didn't hear anything."

Essa's monkey mind took off again, and images flooded her brain. Puck being dragged off by a bear or a mountain lion. Puck getting turned around and walking for miles and miles in circles looking for camp. Then the scenes got worse: Puck being hurt. Puck being dragged along the ground, shoved off a nearby cliff. Puck buried under a nearby pile of pine needles and leaves.

Essa looked again at Oliver's beautiful face, his dark hair and eyes, lit by the flames. His long legs bent on the ground by the fire pan.

Are you hiding something?

He'd never finished the story of what happened with his sister in Chicago right before he came to Boulder. He'd said he'd lost it. He could barely talk about it. Did he . . . do something to her? It hadn't occurred to Essa that maybe he'd hurt his own sister. Maybe he'd lost his temper. She just thought he'd meant . . .

"There! It caught," Oliver said.

She heard a faint *whoosh*ing sound as the candle lit. She stood up, holding the tiny light in the darkness.

Essa held it high and could see their brush shelter clearly now, the unruly pile of pine and bark and leaves sadly hanging on a pole tied to a tree. She swept the candle to her right, seeing nothing but the skinny white trunks of aspen in the flickering light, standing together like dried, cracked leg bones stuck in the dirt. She swept her arm to the left and saw nothing but the forest floor and the gaping blackness beyond.

She ran ahead, first in one direction and then another,

guarding the light with a cupped hand, desperately looking for a flash of blonde hair, straining to hear the sound of a little-girl giggle, squinting in hopes of seeing her sister's bright eyes peering at her from the darkness. Essa wanted a million lights, a million hands, the magical ability to grasp for miles around her all at once, to pull Puck in from wherever she was, even if it was at some far end of the earth.

Essa's smallness came to her then. A desperate, powerless ache.

"Puck! Are you there?"

She saw no movement. She heard no sound. She turned in a circle, sweeping the light around her, a dizzying array of trees and shrubs and nothingness swirling past. A cold breeze surrounded her and snuffed the candle out.

Essa was plunged back into unrelenting blackness. And in this new darkness, she knew one thing. She hadn't kept Puck safe. She had failed.

26

ESSA

All they could do was wait for dawn.

They'd searched as far as they could in the darkness, fanning out in all directions from the fire, never venturing so far that it was out of sight. To light their way, they'd fashioned torches out of large sticks, root cord, and dead pine.

They hadn't found Puck.

Essa sat on the ground near the fire, her eyes trained straight ahead, watching the darkness like it was a solid and separate thing, a slumbering animal that would wake any moment, shake off the sleep, and move out of her way so she could see the woods around her.

"We'll find her," she whispered over and over again as she hugged her knees to her chest and glared at the stubborn blackness. "We'll find her."

And silently, her gatha:

Breathing in, I know my breath is the wheel of the ship.

Breathing out, I know the storm will pass.

Out loud, to the vanishing night:

"But maybe this one won't."

Oliver sat on the ground next to her and reached an arm around her trembling shoulders.

"Don't," she said sharply, shifting away.

Oliver sighed. "Sorry. I don't know what to do . . ."

Essa didn't respond.

"The sun should be up any minute now," Micah said, tossing another stick onto the flames. The sky was starting to turn a milky gray, like someone was adding drops of cream to the night. "We'll set a compass bearing. Essa, you take east. I'll take west. Oliver will take—"

"Puck!" Essa shouted. The darkness had thinned just enough; Essa could start to see. She hopped off the ground and shouted for her sister. "Where are you?"

There was no response.

"I'm going to go this way," Essa said, pointing.

"Is that east?" Oliver asked Micah. "So I'm supposed to go—"

"That's . . ." Micah looked into the brightening sky. "Generally eastward, but hang on. I'll get the map, and we'll take a bearing . . ."

"I'm not waiting," Essa said. She looked at Oliver. "And Oliver can go with you."

"Okay, but—"

Essa didn't stay to hear the end of Micah's sentence. She headed into the woods, her boots churning the dead leaves underfoot like a boat's propeller making waves of water in her wake. She looked left and right as she ran, hoping to see a new brush shelter leaning against the side of a tree with Puck's small sneakers sticking out. Her sister, a little hungry and cold, but happily asleep. Essa looked up in the trees, hoping to see Puck perched in one of them like a baby owl, silent and studying the ground below. Playing some cruel game of hide-and-seek, just waiting to be found.

Essa didn't see that.

She didn't see anything but dense stands of pine trees, the slope of the forest floor, the occasional clearing with a view of the knobs of Comanche Peak.

"Puck!" she called into the emptiness. "Puck, where are you?"

She stopped looking for brush shelters or for Puck's hiding spot in a tree. She started looking for ominous things. A tuft of blonde hair peeking out from a mound of leaves. A lone sneaker, muddy and mauled, dropped in the woods like a last word. The curve of Puck's shoulders, lifeless and cold as the boulder she leaned against.

She didn't see any of that, either.

"Puck!"

The faraway screech of a hawk circling in the sky was the only response.

Come back.

She searched for another two hours, trying to keep her eye on the sky, on her direction, on her relation to the peaks in the distance. She saw nothing but wilderness, humming along as usual. Chipmunks scurrying between rocks, marmots calling with their usual squeaks, wildflowers carefully opening, reaching for the rising sun. She begged the forest to talk to her, to show her something, anything that would point to her sister.

It didn't.

She began to circle back toward camp, making a wide arc to cover more ground. As she got closer, she heard something.

Her name.

"Essa!"

It was faint, but snaked through the woods loud and clear.

It was Micah's voice.

He was calling her back to camp. Maybe they'd found Puck, maybe she'd be sitting by the campfire, drinking a cup of pine needle tea. Maybe she'd be telling of her adventure, getting lost last night when she tried to go the bathroom, getting turned around, spending the night in the woods completely alone. Essa ran, faster and faster, toward the sound of Micah's voice. With each footfall, she felt higher and higher on hope.

She'll be there. She'll be standing next to Micah. They'll be laughing.

Essa ran up a small rise, and their campsite came into view.

She saw Micah.

She saw Oliver.

By the time she reached them, she felt like a newcomer to

high altitudes. Light-headed. Out of breath. Lungs aching, trying to pull enough oxygen out of the thin air.

"Did you find her?" Essa panted the question, bent over, hands on knees.

Micah shook his head no. "And you know what we have to do," he said.

He was right. She knew exactly what they had to do. She was trained in wilderness survival. She knew the protocol for losing a member of your party. Especially if that member was a child. But the answer made Essa want to crawl onto the forest floor, to bury herself deep in the loam, to die right there, to rest until the soil reclaimed her, until all evidence of this trip was lost to time.

We have to go get help.

We have to leave here without her.

May 16
Chicago

27

OLIVER

"Do you think he has a girlfriend?" Oliver was on Lilly's bed, his feet kicked up against the wall. He was tossing a wiffle ball. He watched it sail up toward the ceiling of his sister's room and fall back again into his hands. He wondered why it had holes in it. A wiffle ball. Who thought it was a good idea to take something solid like a ball and slow it down like that? Let all the air in. All the resistance. "I mean, he's always flirted with waitresses and shit."

Lilly was on the floor, hunched over her toenails. She was slowly painting a triangle on her big toe. "No," she said, leaning back to eye her work, checking to see if the sides of the triangle were even. "No way. That's so plebian."

The sounds of their parents' argument grew louder. Their mother's voice was shrill. Their father's, low. Angry. They'd been at it for almost an hour.

Oliver glanced at his sister. He knew why Dad had filed for divorce. Partly it was the stress of his work schedule. The stress of their mom's. But that was just the icing on the cake. The long hours, the missed dinners, the canceled vacations might have all been doable if it weren't for . . .

"It's not because of me," Lilly said.

"No, of course not."

But it was. It was Lilly's hospitalizations. Her episodes. The stress had eaten away at their family, bite by bite. Oliver tossed the wiffle ball again.

Up.

Down.

Up.

Down.

He eyed Lilly, trying to figure out where her mind was. He couldn't tell if she was lying, if she knew her parents were constantly fighting about her. About her illness. Sometimes she wasn't even clear that she had one.

"I know what it is," she said. Her eyes narrowed as she carefully filled the triangle with thick pink polish.

"Oh yeah?" Oliver tossed the ball against the wall this time. It ricocheted at an angle. Oliver lunged sideways, but couldn't catch it. He watched it roll under Lilly's bookshelf. He let his head hang over the side of the bed, stared at his sister upside down. The blood ran to his face, and he could feel it getting tighter and tighter, his heartbeat thrumming in his ears.

"He's a criminal." She said it casually. Like that was a typical thing to call your father.

"You mean, like criminally neglectful? Criminally rigid? Or criminally patronizing?" Oliver cracked a smile, hoping she'd laugh. Hoping that's what she was thinking. Something normal. Average. Real.

"No." She slipped the nail polish brush back into its tiny jar. She looked at his almost-purple face. "Sit up. It's serious."

No, no, no.

Oliver pulled himself up too fast, and the room spun around him. He tried to stare at the wall to get oriented, to make the moment stop. He looked at the place where Lilly used to have pirate posters taped up. At the spots where the tape had yellowed the wall paint, left rectangular sticky marks. After she started to get sick, she'd taken them all down and drawn on the walls with marker. She loved shapes. Triangles. Circles. Squares.

"He's hiding something, Oliver."

"Who, Dad?" He feigned shock. Stalling.

"I found this." Lilly scooted across the floor to her bookshelf.

She pulled out her favorite book, *The History of Fairy Folklore*. It had a misty green cover, sea-blue typeface. At least fifty pages were dog-eared. Well worn. Studied. She pulled out a folded piece of paper that had been tucked inside.

"Lilly. . ." Oliver stopped. An iciness started down his neck.

"Look." She handed him a crossword puzzle pulled from the *Chicago Tribune*. The answer to four down was circled.

"H-I-T-C-H-C-O-C-K," Oliver read out loud. Then he read the clue. "Director of *Rope*, 1948."

"Know anything about that movie?" Lilly asked. The conspiratorial look was in her eye. The look of a treasure hunter who'd just found the secret key to the prize. The look of a sister, gone. Totally and completely gone.

"No," Oliver said, coaching himself to keep a neutral face, to not let on that he feared she'd come unhinged again. That a delusion had built up fast enough, strong enough, that it was going to finally spill out of her mouth. That she was going to let him in.

"Two guys murder a friend just for the fun of it. They put the body in a trunk. Have a dinner party to see if anyone knows what they did." She smiled. "Get it?"

No.

"Oh," Oliver said slowly. "So you think that . . ." He stopped, baiting her to finish her sentence.

"Mom and Dad's fight about that dinner party. The one Mom canceled because of her deposition? And Dad had already put the tray of drinks on the trunk in the living room." Her eyes flashed fairy blue. Fiery. Alive.

Mad.

"So you think that Dad . . ."

"He's going to kill someone, Oliver. Or he already has. And Mom knows it. She's uncovered his plan." She pulled another piece of paper out of her book. It had notes scribbled all over it. "I think he's—"

"Lilly, don't." Oliver couldn't believe he'd said it. He was usually so good at playing along. If he let on, even just a little, that he didn't believe her . . .

"Don't what?"

"Just . . . don't." Maybe it was the fact that he thought his dad might move out of state after the divorce. Maybe it was that feeling of the bottom falling out. That his sister was gone. That his dad was about to be. Oliver suddenly felt so alone. His dad had his world. His mother had hers. Lilly flew with fairies and theories and schemes only she would ever see. And Oliver had . . . what? Who? He eyed the wiffle ball under the bookshelf. "Dad's not a criminal."

Lilly's face went flat. Like the lid of a trunk, closing and locking.

Click.

"You don't believe me," she said slowly.

"No," Oliver said. "I don't."

Her rage was instant. She separated the world into two groups: The ones who didn't believe her and the one who did. The second group was empty now.

"Or maybe they're splitting up because of you," Lilly practically spat her response. "Because all you do is play video games and get Cs and have no friends and—"

That was it.

Something cracked.

"It's you, Lilly. It's you. You're sick. You're so, so sick."

She looked like she'd been slapped. Kicked. Hit. Like deep down, she knew it was true. Just for a moment. In some space in her heart, a chamber that was locked behind door after door, a dark pool filled with algae and dying cattails and lit by fireflies that were swirling and swirling in the dank, stagnant air.

It was true.

And she knew it.

But just as fast, she didn't.

"You're with them? You're in on it? You?"

He didn't remember much after that. Just flashes. Flickers. He told her she was crazy. Schizophrenic. A maniac. Unhinged. Unreal. He was sure he was screaming. That she was screaming back. That she ran into the bathroom. That he followed her.

That the next words he said:

"Call an ambulance."

June 23

11:30 A.M.

28

ESSA

"You were playing what?" The ranger eyed the three of them, looked over their muddy, sweat-soaked clothes, their exhausted faces. For a moment, Essa feared he wouldn't believe them. He seemed suspicious, looking at them like they were a bunch of teens who'd been getting wasted in the woods, rolling in with an unbelievable story just to mess with him. But she couldn't be the one to convince him. She'd tried as soon as they'd arrived at the ranger station, and she'd been able to say only one word: *Help.*

She'd lost it after that.

"Mountain Fugitive," Micah said. "It's really just orienteering. Doing multi-day treks. Less for speed and more for efficiency. We weren't timing it or anything. We were just trying to find the quickest backcountry route west of the Comanche Trail over to Brown's Lake."

The ranger raised his eyebrows, and his stiff camel-colored hat tipped a bit to the front. He used one finger to push it back into place. "That's extremely dangerous," he said as he scribbled on a notepad. "There are already recommended backcountry trails." He sighed. "Okay, so you were playing . . . a game. And why did you have a nine-year-old with you?"

"She stowed away," Micah said. "We had no idea that she—"

"A stowaway?" The ranger's auburn mustache twitched a little to the right as he smirked. "How did she accomplish that? Did you arrive in the Comanche Peak Wilderness by ship?"

"He doesn't believe us," Essa whispered. She wanted to say it louder. She wanted her voice to boom through the station: *HELP US. MY SISTER IS GONE.*

But all that would come out was a whisper.

"He doesn't believe us," she said again.

"She was under a kite." Micah said it like it was the most obvious method of stowing away in the world: kite riding.

The ranger put down his pen. "This is a really sick prank," he said. "Really sick." He ripped his notes out of his pad and crumpled them slowly. "You can go to jail for falsifying a missing persons report, you know."

"Falsifying?" Micah threw his hands up in the air. "She was under the Lykos. It's a huge kite. It's been clocked at a hundred twenty miles per hour. Responsive without being—"

"He doesn't mean that Puck *rode* the kite," Oliver explained. His voice sounded commanding, steady. "Or that she hid under one in a pack or anything. She was hiding under a kite in the back of his Jeep. We didn't see her before we set off. She exited the vehicle when we weren't looking and followed us into the woods. By the time we realized she was trailing us, we were caught in a storm and it was too late to turn back."

Exited the vehicle?

Essa had forgotten that Oliver's mom was an attorney. That must be where he got his ability to speak like this to authority figures. He seemed so credible, believable. She watched as the ranger picked up his notepad again.

Oliver must be telling me the truth. He couldn't have . . .

"Under a kite," the ranger repeated, scribbling down the words.

"She just wanted to come along with the older kids. With her older sister," Oliver said, eyeing Essa. "Whom she adores."

Essa knew Oliver was right. Puck adored her; she always had. Essa thought about the feel of Puck's small, warm hand, the smell of candy on her breath.

Essa found her voice.

"You have to believe us," she said, stepping forward. The ranger was behind a counter that was loaded with maps and guidebooks. Essa spotted a safety poster hanging on the wall.

Be Prepared!

Never hike alone!

This is Mountain Lion Country!

"My sister is out there. Alone. Lost. We need a search team. Immediately. She's already been gone since three A.M. Or maybe even earlier than that. That's just when I woke up, and she wasn't there, and we saw this guy in the woods—"

"A guy?"

"Yeah, a total creep. Said he was looking for antiques that had fallen out of his grandfather's plane."

"Okay," the ranger said, finally looking concerned. He unfolded a large color map of the Comanche Peak Wilderness. "The best you can, pinpoint where you last saw her. And where you parked your car. Write down a description of everything. What she was wearing, what she had with her. And describe the man you saw before she went missing." He pressed the map flat on the countertop. "We'll mount an SAR."

Essa ran her hand over the curved topo lines indicating elevation. She looked at the slopes, the mountainsides, the steep drops. *Which line are you on, Puck? Which line?*

"SAR?" Oliver asked. The ranger was already on his walkie-talkie.

"Search and Rescue," Micah explained.

"Here." Essa plunked a trembling finger down on the map. "Here's the Comanche Peak Trail. We followed this northeast and broke off somewhere around here." Her finger ran slowly across the map. "This is the high meadow we crossed. Where Oliver first thought he heard something. See how it's broad and flat here? All the same elevation."

"Then it climbs on the eastern edge," Micah said, following Essa's finger.

"We skirted the mountainside, looking for shelter and dry wood. We walked for . . . how long?"

"An hour," Oliver said. "At least."

"We were going slow," Micah said. "Maybe we made it two miles? Three?"

"Which would put us here," Essa said, pointing to a ridge-line on the map. "This has got to be close." She waved at the ranger, who was still busy barking things into his walkie-talkie. She pointed at the map.

"They've pinpointed the approximate location. Backcountry. West of Comanche Trail. Hold for the coordinates," he said. He held the walkie-talkie away from his mouth. "They're sending the search helicopter. Think hard. Tell me everything you can remember."

Essa described everything. Her sister's unicorn T-shirt, her jeans, her bright pink sneakers. The man's straw fedora, his rubber clogs.

"A crew is on its way," the ranger said. "We'll find your sister, okay? Most missing people are found within the first twenty-four hours. Just give us a day."

Essa nodded, holding on to his words, deciding to believe them.

She had to.

June 24

29

OLIVER

Puck had been gone for almost two days.

"I'm so glad you're home." Aunt Sophie clutched him like he'd been the one missing and was now found. It was already nine o'clock at night; he'd been gone all day in the mountains. He and Micah had stayed at the ranger station, handing out cups of water and snacks to the search volunteers. Dogs had picked up Puck's scent about a mile from camp, but lost it again at a creek.

Now, in Sophie's living room, he let himself be held, thankful to be out of the mountains, away from the frenzy of the search, back into thicker air that didn't make his lungs ache.

Finally he pulled away, peeled off his shoes, and dropped them by the door. He dragged one of the giant Dinner Pillows into the middle of the living room floor and crawled onto the carpet. Sophie gave him a bowl of soup and a giant cup of water. The soup was full of things he never ate: tofu, chickpeas, lemongrass. It smelled like a car air freshener.

And it was the best thing he'd ever eaten.

He drained the bowl and rested his head on the pillow. Closed his eyes. Sophie crawled onto the floor beside him. "Still no news?" she asked softly. He shook his head.

"They lost her scent by a creek. That's all they have." Oliver took a deep breath. Remembering. "We woke up, and she was just . . . gone."

Sophie slid another pillow into the center of the room and rested her head next to his. "How terrifying to be lost up there. Alone."

Oliver kept his eyes closed, but he could feel Sophie watching him. He could feel her fear.

"So how are you?" she ventured. "Really. On a scale of one to ten."

"Bad."

Sophie exhaled. "Bad like Chicago bad? I have a doctor. A really great counselor who could talk to you at a moment's notice."

He hated this. How Sophie was watching, looking at him like he had some sort of hidden darkness that might return at any minute. A side he'd been building and hiding his entire life.

He wondered if she was right.

He didn't answer her question.

"Have you heard any updates? About Lilly?" he asked.

"No, sweetheart, I haven't."

Oliver opened his eyes. Sophie's little altar was against the wall in front of them. The sitting Buddha statue. The single flower in a vase. The framed saying, *All we want is to wake up.*

"What's it mean, anyway?" he asked.

"I don't know what it all means. I don't know why all of this is happening to you," Sophie said. "And I don't know why a little girl would follow you guys like that and just disappear in the woods—"

"No," Oliver said. "I don't mean about Puck. I mean the sign. *All we want is to wake up.* What does it mean?"

Sophie looked at her altar. She paused for what seemed like a long, long time. "Well," she said finally. "It's hard to put into words. Everything in Zen is like that. When you try to explain it, you fall far, far short."

Oliver studied the Buddha statue's smile. It was sly. A little mysterious. And for some reason mesmerizing. Even though Oliver's body hurt all over from the day, even though his mind ached with memories from that night—the brush shelter, the darkness, the cold—he liked looking at Buddha's smile. He didn't want to stop. Oliver looked at the single flower in the vase. It made him think of the koan the Zen priest mentioned. About Buddha twirling a flower and his student just smiling, understanding something that none of the others did. "Give it a try."

"Okay," Sophie said slowly. She stared at the ceiling, searching for words. "Buddha taught that one of the causes of suffering is that we are ignorant about the true nature of reality. We try to hold on, to force life to be constant, stable, comfortable all the time. We think everything is separate from us, that if we try hard enough, we can arrange it all to our liking. And hold it there." Sophie looked at the Buddha statue. "And that only then, when we finally arrange life to our liking, acquire what we want and get rid of what we don't, and stick it all in place, we'll finally be happy."

"Really?" Oliver turned his head toward his aunt. "That's kind of depressing. So the upshot is that we'll just . . . never be happy? Because life is a giant changing clusterfuck?"

Sophie smiled. "No. Just the opposite. That was Buddha's main concern: suffering. He was called the Great Physician because he wanted to treat deep dissatisfaction with life."

"But what does that have to do with waking up?"

True the Buddhist turtle chose this moment to emerge from underneath the white sofa. He slowly made his way toward Oliver, one loop of his pink ribbon undone and dragging along the carpet. He blinked his eyes. Slowly.

Up.

Down.

"We have to wake up from our ignorance about reality. We have to realize that in some ways, we tumble from one unsatisfactory experience to the next. Because we're always running, always thinking, always in the future or the past. Always trying to anesthetize what feels bad, to get what we think will feel good. And it will never stay still. And we suffer, over and over again."

Sophie stopped talking. She and Oliver sat there in the

quiet. He thought about Lilly. About reality. About Essa's question whether Oliver and Lilly were ever in the same one. Oliver thought about playing pirate ship with Lilly when they were kids, those moments when they were at sail on the same make-believe sea. He thought about her first delusion. The dryer. How he went along with it just to be close to her. So she wouldn't shut him out. So the distance between her world and his could shorten, if only for a moment.

He thought about that time with Lilly in Chicago, when he told her he didn't believe her, when he finally told her how he felt. That she was alone in the world she'd created. That her reality wasn't real.

But maybe his wasn't, either.

"So." Oliver looked up at Buddha's sneaky smile. "What's the answer?"

"The answer?"

"Happiness. If we're suffering under these delusions about life, where is it? Where's happiness?"

Sophie smiled again. She shifted a little closer so her shoulder was touching his. "That was Buddha's message: It's available to each of us. Right here. Right now. Moment by moment. Kalpa by kalpa—the smallest possible units of time. If we wake up. And we're mindful. The sounds. The colors. The breath. If we follow the Eightfold Path."

She didn't say any more. They stayed like that for a long time. Sophie's windows were open, and the night air wafted through her apartment. Oliver just watched it. Watched the invisible breeze dance with the Tibetan prayer flags hanging against the window. The red flag. The blue flag. The yellow. The white. The square of black outside, the warm glow inside. The sound of Sophie's breath. The sound of True's scaly feet slowly dragging across the carpet. Oliver's breath. The pain in his chest. The pain of loving Essa. The pain of the last night with Puck. The pain of being with Lilly. But never being with Lilly.

He stared at the flower in the vase.

What if Lilly went missing like Puck? He thought about Lilly sitting in the broom closet in the facility, telling him about clues in the *Chicago Tribune*. He thought about her being dragged back to her room by the guard. He thought about talking to her over FaceTime. How sad it was that he'd only see her a few times like that over the summer. How it wasn't really seeing her at all.

Then he thought about being home in Chicago. Always watching, waiting for her to spin out of control. Monitoring her for the subtle signs that delusions were building in her mind. Pretending to believe whatever she saw in the world, whatever pieces she was putting together.

"I miss Lilly," he said, still staring at the single flower.

"I know, sweetie," Sophie said. "I'm so—"

"But I miss her when I'm in Chicago, too." He kept his gaze on the flower, petal by petal. "She's not really there. Even when you're in the same room with her. You know?"

The homesick ache he'd been feeling, the guilt over being gone, over leaving her in the facility, wasn't really homesickness or guilt at all. It was the realization that he didn't miss Lilly any more out here than he did at home when they were standing in the same room.

A thousand miles or ten feet. How far apart they were didn't matter.

The distance between them was always the same.

Maybe Lilly was already missing.

Just like Puck.

Gone.

And maybe Oliver had been gone, too.

"Do you know any decent flower shops in Boulder?" he asked, turning toward Sophie again.

"Sure," she said. "I get a fresh gardenia for the altar every few days. You can have one."

"Good. Because I'm going to need it."

June 25

30

ESSA

Puck had been gone almost three days.

Essa closed her eyes. Across the kitchen table, her mother gently wept. Essa recited her gatha:

Fears are clouds drifting by a mountain.
Watch them. Tend to them.
But know
You're the mountain.

The pain came rushing at her heart from all sides. Like fat black cattle let loose from a pen, panicked, afraid, charging. It had been three days since Essa had last seen Puck, last seen her crouched on the ground by the campfire, arranging sticks into mountains and stones into the sun. Three days since Puck had slept tucked under Essa's arm, warm against the Mummy-Range cold, the summer-storm damp. Three days since the person Essa loved most in the world was near.

I'm not a mountain. I can't survive this storm.

She tried another one:

Breathing in, I know my breath is the wheel of the ship.
Breathing out, I know the storm will pass.

She brought her attention to her breath, forced it there like some unruly child. She realized her breath was coming in short, fast bursts. It wasn't even filling her lungs. Not really. She realized how shallow it was.

She realized she was crying.

This storm is going to kill me.
I'm going to go under.
She tried another one:
Escape doesn't work. It doesn't cure duhkha.
Stay in this moment. Present moment.

Her mother's cries grew louder. The light above the kitchen table had never seemed so cold, so stark. Had it always been that harsh? That bright? Had the green of the cabinets always been so sickening? Had the mismatched and broken tiles on the floor always been so cold against her bare toes?

Pain and fear rose up behind Essa, like giant mountains suddenly pushed up from the earth. She could almost hear the great groan of an earthquake, the plates moving underneath her.

This storm is going to kill me.
The last gatha. Again:
Escape doesn't work. It doesn't cure duhkha.
Stay in this moment. Present moment.
And one last thought:
Bullshit.

June 26

31

ESSA

"It's day four." Essa stood on Micah's front stoop. She glanced down at the reclining Buddha statue by the door. She eyed his smile.

Don't even.

"I know," Micah said. His deep brown eyes looked bottomless. Scared.

"It's going to kill me. The waiting."

Micah stepped outside and looked up. Essa looked up, too, as if news of Puck would fall from the sky. Like she could catch it in her hands. Like this would all be over. Just like that. A streak of good news racing across the night. A shooting star.

"I keep trying to think of something philosophical to say," Micah said, keeping his eyes on the sky. "I've been reading my books all night. There's nothing. Plato. Aristotle. They've got nothing."

"I'm done with philosophy," Essa interrupted. "Theology. Done with all of it."

"Just give me more time. There has to be something wise . . ."

"Wanna share?" Essa reached into her pocket and pulled out a cellophane baggie.

Edi-Sweets. 500-mg THC. 25 Individually infused 10-mg pieces. Keep from children. No resale.

"Essa, I don't think you should—"

"Oh yes, you should." It was Skye. Popping up behind Micah,

two long braids hanging over her shoulders. "Are those gummy cherries? Yes, please."

Essa raised her eyebrows.

"We've been listening to Dylan albums," Micah said sheepishly. He eyed the bag of edibles. "Essa, they won't help. Trust me. They won't—"

"Yes, they will," Skye said. "That's, like, their job." She sidestepped Micah and took Essa's hand. She gently led Essa off the porch and into the darkness of Micah's front yard. There was a giant trampoline just over a small hill, lurking in the darkness like some sort of UFO that had landed there, a black disc of stretchy fabric and springs. "We'll bounce it away. All of it."

Essa followed Skye through the hard, half-dying grass. Skye scrambled onto the trampoline and reached a hand out to pull Essa up. Essa lay there, flat on her back, staring up at the stars. Skye jumped a few times beside her, sent Essa's body shuddering.

"Pull out a few of those cherries," Skye said. "Being high on a trampoline is the best. It's so great. You feel like you're *so weightless*. It'll help. It will. About Puck and—"

"Here." Essa dug in her pocket and handed two gummies to Skye.

"No, no," Skye warned. She bounced down beside Essa, and rolled over onto her stomach, the trampoline bowing underneath her. "Just eat one. They take a while to kick in. Two can make you *loco*. That's when people jump out of windows and shit."

Essa knew that. She knew everything there was to know about pot and edibles and timing and getting high. She didn't care. She just wanted the pain to stop.

Skye popped a gummy in her mouth. Essa stared at the lone sugar-coated cherry left in her palm.

"I want to be bouncing when it kicks in," Skye said, her eyes bright. She stood up and starting jumping. Quick, small hops at first and then they got bigger and higher. Essa joined her, still clutching the gummy in her hand.

Up.

Down.

Up.

Down.

Essa didn't pay much attention to where she was landing. She didn't care if she bounced off, landed on the ground, cracked every bone. She just bounced. Higher and higher. Eyes on the sky.

Come home.

Come home.

Come home.

"Come down." It was Micah. "Let's walk."

"Sure," Skye answered. "But high walking is totally not as good as high jumping. Ha. Get it? High jumping? Isn't that a thing?"

"Just Essa and me," Micah said. "We'll be back." He helped Essa off the trampoline, and didn't let go of her hand once she was down. "This way," he said, leading her back toward his house.

They walked along a garden path to a picnic table beneath the kitchen window. Essa watched her feet move along the pea-sized gravel, listened to the crunch of it beneath her. It made her think about running through the woods, searching for Puck. Churning her legs as hard as they would go, leaves and brush flying up in her wake. Micah climbed on top of the table. He craned his neck, trying to see into his kitchen.

"She's not in there," he said.

"Who?"

"You'll see. Just give it a minute."

Essa climbed onto the tabletop and sat next to Micah.

"It's not you, you know," he said.

"What? What's not me?"

"Weed. Checking out. Running. What would Puck—"

"Please," Essa said. "Don't say her name."

"You think it's going to be a break," he said. "From how it

all feels. From reality. You think it's just going to hit the PAUSE button, you know? Just some relief. And as long as you don't smoke it as much as your mom does, like as long as you don't go crazy with it, it'll help. Right?"

Essa nodded. Closed her eyes as teardrops slid down her cheeks. She thought of how disappointed Puck would be. How ashamed.

"It doesn't help, Ess," Micah said. "I smoke and I'm all high and I'm hamming it up like I'm having the best time in the world." He looked up at the sky again. "But I'm not. The shit is still there. Sometimes getting high makes it worse. Makes me feel like it's going to eat me alive. Like it's working a hole in my heart. Like my chest will explode. Or let's say I have some awesome high. Sometimes I do. But after it wears off, it's still there. But worse somehow. Like while I was gone, the pain was doing push-ups—"

"Wait," Essa said. "The pain? You mean about Puck? You've been smoking way before she went missing, Micah—"

"There," Micah said, pointing in the kitchen window. "There she is."

Essa turned on the weathered wooden tabletop, got on her knees so she could see inside. Her breath hitched in her chest. Her throat knitted tight.

Moving around the kitchen was Micah's mom. His beautiful Thai mother with her graceful arms reaching to pull a coffee mug out of a cabinet. She had on her signature cherry-red lipstick, the gold bracelets she was never without.

But something wasn't right.

Her arms were too thin, almost reedy, like Essa could see the bones and muscles and tendons under her skin. And her thick jet-black hair was hidden, wrapped up in a scarf. Not a strand of it peeking out.

"I smoke because of that."

Essa furrowed her brow, confused. "I don't understand—"

"She has breast cancer, Ess," Micah said. "She's on chemo.

She's got medical weed to help with how sick it makes her. And don't judge that, okay? It's not all bad. Not everybody's an addict like your mom . . ."

"Oh, Micah," Essa said, shifting close to him on the bench. "Why didn't you tell me?"

Micah ran a hand through his hair, looked directly into Essa's eyes. "I kept thinking it would be over soon, you know? Like she'd get the surgery, get the chemo, and then . . . done. Like everything would go back to the way it was. But she's still so sick. And we don't know if the cancer will come back. If *she'll* really come back. The way she was. It's like I don't know if things will ever be like they were." Micah looked back in the window, watched his mom fill a teapot with water, set it on the stove. "And she keeps giving me all the Buddhist shit about—"

"Change?" Essa asked. "How it's the only constant. How nothing is immune. How it sucks."

"Duhkha," Micah said with a sad smile.

"Duhkha."

"And no offense, but it's why I've still been hanging out so much with you guys. At the End of the World." Micah looked down. Even in the darkness, Essa could see a flash of embarrassment on his face. "I haven't even really met anybody at CU. I go to class, I go home to help Mom, she takes her medicine. And I guess I take mine."

Essa saw such a small, pitiful sadness in his eyes. No Micah, Big Man on Campus. No Micah, Dormitory Cavalier. Just Micah, with his breath getting quicker, with tears pushing through.

Essa reached her arms around him.

"Getting high doesn't help, Essa," Micah said. "I promise. It's all still there when it wears off. It's all still there."

Essa pulled back.

"So is it hitting you yet?" he asked. "The gummy? You only took one, I hope."

Essa put her hand in her pocket and pulled it back out in a

fist. She opened her fingers, and there in her palm was a single sugar-coated cherry gummy.

"Didn't take it," she said, with a sad smile.

"And you know where you should go."

"I do. I totally do."

It was almost midnight by the time she reached the garden. The wildflowers were closed up in the darkness, curled tight, patiently waiting for the dawn. The water fountain was still tinkling into the small pond; the Adirondack chairs were still waiting in the lawn; traffic was still zooming down Arapahoe Avenue. Lighter. But still there. The light was on, casting a warm glow on the sign: BLUE SPRUCE INN.

Essa made her way through the sleeping garden and past the Buddha statue in the half-boat next to the Zendo. Out of habit, she kicked off her shoes and left them there, peered in the window. The room was dark. The zafus were all perfectly round and perfectly plump, waiting on meditators to come sit, to try to arrive in the moment, breath by breath, kalpa by kalpa. The incense on the altar was smokeless and cold, ready to be lit. The vase was empty, content to wait for flowers. She tried the door.

It was locked.

She knew it would be.

She took a few steps back and eyed the second floor.

Do I?

There was a wooden staircase that zigzagged up to a little covered porch and another door on the second floor. This one was painted a rich pine green.

I'm going.

Barefoot, she ascended the stairs, taking them slowly, as quietly as she could. The wide slats of the covered porch creaked as she walked onto them, and groaned louder still as she leaned toward the window.

A light was on.

The curtains were drawn, but they weren't opaque; she could see through them just enough to make out the light of a candle, the glow of a small desk lamp, and a silhouette. His silhouette.

She was trembling, rattled by nerves. She'd met with him in the Zendo before. He'd helped her write gathas. He'd worked with her on the sanctuary koan. She'd been a student during his Dharma talks. She'd had tea with the sangha in the garden.

She'd never been up to his apartment above the Zendo.

Alone.

At midnight.

I shouldn't be here. I shouldn't knock on his door.

She thought about going home, about carrying the pain and worry about Puck behind her like a ten-thousand-pound boulder. She thought about trying to sleep, trying to eat, trying to do anything. She couldn't sit zazen. She couldn't recite gathas. She didn't want to smoke or eat gummy edibles that would only make things worse. That would only let her little sister down right when she needed Essa most. There was only one thing to do—knock on the door.

She heard a shuffling inside, footsteps across the wooden floor, the lock turning.

"Essa?" The priest narrowed his eyes in the darkness of the porch.

"Hi." She opened her mouth to explain. To apologize for showing up at midnight, unannounced. For being there at all.

"Are you all right?" he asked softly, interrupting her before she could even utter one word of explanation. She shook her head.

His apartment was sparse. A long wooden table cut through the center of the room, its top well-worn. A small box garden of herbs sat in the middle. Little labels were affixed to the sides. *Dill. Basil. Rosemary.* A sofa and a wicker rocker were in the living room, where a painting of Bodhidharma hung from a nail. The portrait of the sixth-century Indian monk showed him wrapped in a white robe, sitting in full lotus, staring at a rock wall only inches from his face. His eyes were downcast and seemed submissive somehow. But his eyebrows and full bushy beard made him look cross. He was the one who brought Zen (Chan) to China.

"Jeff, who's here?" The priest's sleepy wife emerged from the bedroom, rubbing her eyes. Behind her, on another wall of the living room, hung their young son's artwork. Crayon renditions of boats, rocket ships, dogs.

"Hi, Clara."

"Oh, Essa." Clara crossed the room in her wrinkled nightgown, put her arms around Essa. "I'm so sorry," she whispered. "Is there any news?"

"No."

"I'm glad you're here. I'll make you tea." She glanced at her husband. "And let you two talk."

Essa eyed several zafus next to the sofa and headed toward them. They always sat on zafus when they had practice discussions. But the priest stopped her.

"Why don't you just sit in the rocker?" he asked. "It's a great one. I love to sit there in a storm."

"Thanks," Essa said, sitting down.

He sat on the sofa, folded his hands in his lap. Essa wanted to say that she couldn't survive without knowing her sister was okay, that she couldn't survive without her sister, period. She looked at the priest and wanted to say all that.

But she didn't.

The look in his eyes was a familiar one, and it silenced her. It was a look that only people who'd spent many, many hours meditating had. It was like his eyes were pools fed with clear running water. There were lazy fish swimming circles in the deep. Green reeds rolling gently with the current.

"Have you been able to sit zazen?" he asked gently. "Since she's been gone?"

Of course Jeff knew about Puck even though they hadn't

spoken. The whole town of Boulder did. Essa had seen Puck's name everywhere—on the news, on Missing Child posters, on the front page of the online *Daily Camera*. Essa shook her head no, wiped her eyes, tried to somehow shove the tears back in. "I can't sit."

"Please cry. Don't try to stop it," he said. He leaned forward on the sofa. "To deny what we feel is to be violent toward ourselves. Be kind. Let it come. Let the clouds come."

The tears came quickly then. Essa closed her eyes as a warm wetness coated her cheeks. Then she felt a delicate tap on her shoulder. It was Clara, holding out a cup of tea. It was in a sea-green clay mug with no handle.

"Drink this," she said. "Careful. It's hot."

Essa's tears slowed, and she took the cup in both hands. The tea had a strong smell she didn't recognize. She took a sip from the steaming mug, and a strong, bitter taste stunned her tongue. And something else. "It's smoky," Essa said. She took another sip. "Really smoky."

"It's lapsang souchong," Clara said. "It's strong and smoky and can't be ignored. It's what I drink when my mind is a storm. It brings me out of the wind and into the tea."

Essa loved that image. Coming out of the wind in her mind, the turbulence, the rain, the thunder . . . and into this small mug of hot smoked tea. Somehow the cup suddenly seemed like the safest place in the world.

"A teacher of mine used to say that sitting was the only way to truly calm your heart in times of trouble," the priest said. "Even if your crop fails. Sit. Even if you are ill, sit." He looked at Essa with his flowing-water eyes. "Even if a *child* is ill. Or gone. Sit."

At the word *child*, pain pierced Essa's chest. She thought she couldn't breathe. She thought she couldn't keep holding the cup of lapsang. She thought she was going to die. She thought of her mother, stoned and happy on Pearl Street. Stoned and happy with Ronnie.

"But why? Why be here when here is so awful?" She gripped the cup tightly, the smoky steam rising up to her nose. "What's the point?"

"There is no why," he said. "If you try to grasp a certain result, you'll miss it. But sit anyway. I think you'll notice joy there. Strength. A store of peace that will ensure you don't capsize." He looked at her again, and this time she saw sadness. A deep compassion that made her feel for a moment that he understood. Even though it wasn't his sister who was missing. Or his child. He understood. "If you sit, you'll remember that there is pain. Often unbearable pain. But the pain is a cloud."

"And I'm the mountain."

Her gatha.

He nodded. "Not detached from it. Not oblivious. Not numb. Don't push against it. Don't aim for a blank mind. For nothing. For no thoughts. Let them come, but return to your breath. When your mind is located somewhere else, in the past, in the pain, in the future, return to your experience. Your body. Say to yourself, *Just this. This very mind is Buddha.*"

"Just this." Essa looked into the darkness of the tea. "This very mind is Buddha."

"Kalpa by kalpa, comfort is available, Essa. Solidity. Safety." His eyes. So calm.

Kalpa. The smallest divisible unit of time.

"I almost got high," she said softly. "I just want . . . away."

"Escaping won't work," he said. "If it did, I would tell you to go." He smiled softly. "You don't have to act on your thoughts. You can feel them. And you can let them pass."

Essa watched the tea and its steam. Felt its warmth slowly fade. She put her cup down on a small side table. But before she stood to go, she took a breath. And then another. And then another.

Pain is a cloud drifting by a mountain.
Watch it. Tend to it.
But know
You're the mountain.

PART III

THE THIRD NOBLE TRUTH:

Duhkha arises; duhkha can cease.

What goes up can *come down.*

June 27

32

ESSA

In the morning, Essa walked out of her bedroom and down the hall. She was going to shower, get ready for another day in the mountains, helping search parties. Looking. She was ready to look forever.

Don't look in Puck's room.

Don't look.

Don't.

She did.

She saw the awards on the wall. The kites on the ceiling. The lumpy comforter on the bed. Essa felt like she couldn't take one more step. She thought her legs would give out from the ache, the pain, the sorrow. She sat on the floor in the middle of the hallway, her chest cracking open. Her heart spilling out.

She leaned against the pain, trying to shove it back. Memories of Puck came knocking, and she pushed hard against those, too. Puck swatting at Essa with a wind-sock fish at Above the Clouds. Puck running through the store in her tap shoes. Puck spinning on the stool in front of the computer with a pile of lollipop wrappers at her side. Essa tried to will them out of her mind, but the memories seemed to grow louder somehow. Sharper. Bigger.

She thought about what the priest had said: *To deny what we feel is to be violent toward ourselves. Be kind.*

She stopped pushing.

The pain rushed in.

She thought she couldn't breathe. She thought she couldn't survive.

Sit zazen.

Just sit.

Slowly, she pulled her legs underneath her; she straightened her back. She brought her attention to her trembling breath. In and out. In and out. Her mind spun into the woods, into the darkness. It watched Puck head into the forest to go look at stars on her own. It watched Puck get lost and not be able to find her way back. It watched Oliver trailing her. Oliver hurting her. Like he hurt his own sister.

Just this.

Just this.

This very mind is Buddha.

Gently, Essa brought her attention to the now. To what was actually happening in that very moment. She noticed things around her. The hum of the refrigerator coming from the kitchen. The rough, twisted carpet underneath her legs. The soft coolness in the back of her throat as her breath came in. And out. In. And out. Her heart slowed. The air seemed to slow around her. A stillness wrapped around her shoulders.

Pain is a cloud drifting by a mountain.

Watch it. Tend to it.

But know

You're the mountain.

It wasn't gone.

She wasn't fine.

But for just one kalpa, she felt solid. Still desperately sad.

But safe.

She opened her eyes.

Down the hallway, her mother's door was open. Her bedspread was sliding off the bed as usual. The rising sun was coming in through her mother's eastern window, casting a cool, bright light into the room. Memories of Puck crashed through Essa's mind again like waves, threatening to overtake her.

She brought her mind to her breath again. Kept her eyes open, but downcast, just like Bodhidharma in that portrait. She just looked. And breathed. For a few kalpas more.

Just this.

Just this.

Just this.

Essa noticed the dust motes floating in the ray of morning sun in her mother's room, slowly drifting and careening like tiny drunken flies. She saw a tissue crumpled into a ball on the floor. A stray sandal under her mother's bed. A small box.

A small box.

Essa unfolded her legs and crawled down the hall. She reached under the bed and pulled out the box. It was a wooden one. With pieces on the outside that slid this way and that.

A Puzzle Kite.

One of the wooden puzzle boxes Puck loved to solve. Her favorite thing from Above the Clouds. Inside would be a kite to put together. An owl. A horse. A princess.

Essa's hands flew along the outside of the box. The pieces clicked and clacked as she shoved them left and then right and then left again. Just like Puck's had, her tongue slid out of the corner of her mouth as her hands danced over the puzzle. She thought maybe it held the horse kite Puck had wanted. Maybe Essa could put the horse kite together and go fly it. And feel close to Puck somehow. Like they were both high in the sky. It was a piece of her sister. A kite she left behind.

Except there wasn't a kite inside.

There was a piece of paper.

With a drawing on it.

A wheel.

A wheel with eight spokes.

She recognized it. Pushing up from the carpet, Essa took the piece of paper and ran into Puck's room. The poster on her wall, the one that won first place in the social studies fair. The one about Eastern religions. On the left side was an image of the very same wheel. A wheel with eight spokes.

The wheel of the Dharma.

The text on the poster read, *Buddha gave his very first teaching at Deer Park, in Sarnath, northern India, and it contained the Four Noble Truths. It is said that with his first teaching, Buddha began to turn the wheel of the Dharma.*

Essa ran into her own room, fumbled as she reached for her cell phone beside her bed, and dropped it on the floor. She plopped down on the carpet and picked it back up with her shaking hands. She texted Micah and Anish. Come over. I think I found something.

"So you think she left this here? As a message or something?" Micah asked. He and Anish stood in Puck's room next to Essa, eyeing the drawing.

"Maybe," Essa said, her eyes wide. "What else do we have to go on?"

Anish looked up at Puck's poster. "So why is it called the wheel of the Dharma again?"

"Dude," Micah said. "You're from *India*. You're, like, from where Buddhism started."

Anish rolled his eyes. "A) I'm not from India. I'm from Fort Collins. B) India is roughly the size of another planet. I've probably been to .00005 percent of the towns in it. And C) my grandparents in India are Hindu."

"Parents?"

"Presbyterian."

"Right," Micah said. "Sorry, man."

Essa took the drawing from him. "Dharma is another word for Buddha's teachings. And he gave the first one in Sarnath. The wheel is a symbol for the Dharma. By teaching it, Buddha started turning the wheel, sort of . . ."

"Setting his teachings in motion?" Anish asked.

"Exactly."

"I don't know, Ess," Micah said. He put his hand on her shoulder. "I know you want her back. And so do I. But I think this is a stretch. I mean, you don't even know how long that box has been under there. It could've been there for a whole year or something."

"No," Essa said. "She stole a Puzzle Kite from the shop a few weeks ago. She thought the horse kite was in it. I know this was the box. This was the one. She must have just put it under there." Essa climbed onto her bed, glaring at the wheel. "Help me figure this out."

Micah and Anish exchanged looks like they thought Essa had completely lost it, but they had no choice but to help.

"Okay, okay," Micah said. "Let me see the wheel." Essa handed over the piece of paper. He studied it like it was a new kite that had arrived at the shop, a complex one with a new design he'd never seen. Like he had to figure out how to put it together piece by piece. "Spokes. Look at the spokes. There are . . ." He silently counted them. "Eight."

"Which makes sense," Essa said. "They stand for the—"

"Eightfold Path."

"That's the path Buddha laid out to relieve suffering," Essa said, turning to Anish. "To stop dhukha."

The three of them sat there for another ten minutes, just staring at it.

"Essa." Micah sighed. "I think it's just a Dharma wheel. I'm sorry."

The wheel blurred in Essa's vision as tears started to pool in her eyes. "Talk to me, Puck. Talk to me," she whispered.

"Wait," Anish said. "Let me see it."

Essa handed the drawing to him, and he held it up to the one on the poster. "This spoke," he said, pointing to the one on the left. "It's darker than the one on the poster, right? Come look."

Essa and Micah leaned it. "Yeah," Micah said. "But she probably just drew it with a different pen. The ink is just darker there."

"No," Essa said. She pressed the drawings close together. "He's right. It's darker. It really is. Just one spoke."

"What's it mean?" Anish asked.

"I have no idea," Essa said. She brushed her finger over and over again across her sanctuary tattoo. "Maybe I missed something? Micah, search under my mom's bed. See if you can find anything else. I apologize in advance if you find anything weird. It's my mom, after all."

"No problem."

Micah headed down the hallway, and Anish and Essa started to tear Puck's room apart. Her desk drawers were full of equal parts scripts for school plays, tangled kite string, and old homework assignments all with the grade of A. Essa looked under her bed and found candy wrappers, scented markers, a unicorn pillow, and Puck's tap shoes. Anish took Puck's closet and said he found nothing but clothes, shoes, a giant box of gumballs, and a mammoth tub of Jolly Ranchers.

There wasn't anything under her bedside lamp, under her carpet, behind her curtains. There was nothing but Puck's usual stuff.

"I found nothing." It was Micah, back from Essa's mom's room. He was standing in the doorway. "Well, not nothing. My hand brushed a pair of boxers under the bed. Which I can only assume are Ronnie's." Micah looked slightly ill. "Can I get an STD on my hand?"

"What about this?" Anish said. He was standing by Puck's study desk, holding something in his hand.

It was a compass. A cheap plastic one with a flimsy plastic red arrow. Anish moved around the room with it. It still worked. No matter where he turned, the arrow spun around to the north.

"What about it?" Essa asked.

"Maybe the wheel isn't just a wheel. Maybe it's directional. Maybe the darkened spoke is an arrow?"

Essa looked back at the drawing. The spoke in the due west position was the darkened one. She sat up a little straighter on the bed, hope rising. "Okay," she said slowly. "So assume it's pointing west. But west from where?"

Micah crossed the room and took the compass out of Anish's hand. "Well, if the wheel is a compass, then you should head west from where you found the wheel."

"Oh my god," Essa said, hopping off the bed. She raced to her mother's room with Micah and Anish in tow. "The box was there," she said, pointing under the bed. "Due west would put us . . . in Mom's bathroom."

They tore the bathroom apart. They found all her mother's herbal bubble bath jars, incense holders, and homemade soaps. Micah yanked open a drawer under the sink and started pulling out Q-tips. He threw them over his shoulder like they were handfuls of salt for good luck. Essa bent down and started picking them up as fast as he could throw them.

"I don't think tossing Q-tips around is going to—" She stopped when she saw something peeking out from underneath the bathroom vanity.

A mala.

It was the mala that Essa had found in the bathroom earlier, before their trek in the mountains. The one she worried her mom had bought for herself even though Puck had asked for it.

She leaned over and pulled it out. The beads were a little dusty from being on the floor. She held them up to the light and gently blew against them to clean them off. The brown tassel on the necklace's end swayed in Essa's breath.

That's when she saw it.

Something nested in the tassel. A tiny note, tied in among the string. She hadn't noticed it when she picked the necklace up earlier:

Sticks and Stones.

"Look," Essa said, holding it up for Micah and Anish to see.

"It says sticks and stones. A mala with a note, left due west from the Puzzle Kite box." Essa's heart pounded in her chest, in her ears, behind her eyes. Hope filled every cell of her body like chlorophyll filling a green leaf in the sun.

It's a clue.

It's a note.

She stowed away under a kite because she was planning to fly.

"You guys," Essa said, almost shouting, "this is real. This is it. She ran off. She planned it. She ran away and she wants us to—" Essa stopped talking. Her mother appeared in the doorway. She wasn't in one of her carefree skirts or tiny little tanks. She was in sweatpants, a huge old T-shirt with paint stains on it. Her hair was messy. Her eyes were puffy from crying. Essa knew right away from the look on her face. It was one of dread. Of horror. Of despair. She had something to tell Essa, and she didn't want to.

No. No. No.

"Mom." Essa swallowed hard.

"They found the man you saw in the woods. He checks out. Just a strange guy who's delusional, but harmless."

Essa looked up, hoping to see light in her mother's eyes. Maybe good news.

"And they found something else." Her mother's eyes stayed dark. Full of grief. "A shred of Puck's clothes," her mother whispered. "It was a mountain lion, Essa. They're sure of it." Her mom stepped close and held Essa's face in her hands.

"No," Essa said, her sobs coming quick. Choking. She was choking out the words. "She's okay. She is. Look." Essa held up the mala. "There's a note. 'Sticks and stones.' It's a clue . . ."

Essa's mom was crying, too. She was looking at her daughter with something Essa was sure she'd never seen before. Just like the priest's face—it was compassion. Or maybe pity.

"She ran away, Mom," Essa continued. She was shaking now. Hard. "She wants us to find her. She left these clues. She's a runaway—"

"Maybe she ran away," her mom said. She took the mala from Essa's trembling hands. "But if she did, she didn't get very far."

"No, no, no—"

"She's gone, sweetheart. She's gone."

June 29

33

OLIVER

"It's in the paper again today," Sophie said, clicking through the *Boulder Daily Camera* website.

Oliver couldn't bear to read one more detailed account of how a beautiful nine-year-old girl wandered away from her camp and was eaten by a mountain lion.

"The search is officially called off. And apparently Puck was the second child to be attacked by a mountain lion in the Comanche Peak Wilderness. Another small boy from Boulder was attacked and killed by one in the . . . wait, the date was just here." Sophie squinted at her laptop. "In the 1990s. He ran ahead of his family and was dragged off. They only found his shoes."

"I'm going to be sick." Oliver pushed away from the table and ran to the bathroom. He held his head over the toilet.

They found Puck's shredded clothes.

He heaved and nothing came up. And again. And again.

His phone jingled in his pocket. He didn't want to look. It jingled again.

Lilly.

FaceTime.

He wasn't going to answer. He couldn't. First he'd need to get out of the bathroom, get it together, act like everything was okay. His mom had told him that Lilly was home from the facility, doing better on her new medicine. Oliver couldn't tell Lilly what was really going on. It might send her spiraling into another episode. She might put the pieces together. She might . . .

He pressed the green ANSWER button.

"Hey," he said.

His sister looked back at him through his cell screen. She was sitting in his bedroom back in Chicago, on his bed. His pillows were stacked behind her. She'd drawn a cluster of spheres with red colored pencils and taped it to Oliver's wall. "I'm in your room."

"I can see that."

"And you're in the . . . bathroom?" She glanced at the bath towels hanging on the rack behind him.

"Um, yeah, I was just . . ."

"You're sick," she said. Her smoky blue eyes sharpened. She leaned toward the screen. She was holding a book and clutched it to her chest. She was worried. "Are you okay?"

Maybe the medicine really was working. Maybe she was getting better. But still, he was supposed to say yes, that he was doing fine. He was supposed to be calm. He was supposed to talk about the weather. He wasn't supposed to say anything that could upset her. That could set her back. He wasn't supposed to lean on her. Like a sister.

"No." He heaved again into the toilet. He couldn't help it. "Not okay."

"What's happened, Oliver? What is it?"

"I'm so sorry, Lil." The tears came next. "I'm so fucking sorry. For what I said to you. For what I did. Please forgive me. I'd die if something happened to you. I'd die."

"Oliver. Breathe. I love you. It's okay. I'm okay. You need to come home—"

"I will," Oliver said. The heaving stopped. He sat down on the tile floor and leaned against the bathroom wall. He reached up and pulled one of the bath towels off the rack. He ran it over his face, down the back of his neck. "I just can't come home yet. I can't leave her."

"Can't leave who?"

Don't tell her.

Don't tell her.

"Essa." He looked right at his sister. Like they were pirates in the same crew. Like there was a storm on the high seas he needed to tell her about so they could put their heads together and chart their course to safety. "I'm in love with her. But I screwed up. I really screwed up. She won't even talk to me. And her sister. Her little sister Puck, she . . . disappeared."

"I know."

He paused. His stomach tightened. "You do?"

"I heard Mom talking to Sophie on the phone. I looked up the news story online." Lilly looked better. She really did. Oliver thought her eyes looked *here.* Present. "I can't believe you guys were up in the woods like that. So scary. And they found her clothes?"

"Shreds of it." Oliver closed his eyes. "Hanging on a bush. Totally shredded. Just a few pieces." The tears came again. "I love you. You know that, right? And if something ever happened to you, I'd miss you so much. So, so much."

Lilly nodded. Then she held up her arms.

May 16

Chicago

34

OLIVER

"You're schizophrenic."

Except Oliver wasn't saying it. He was yelling it. That Lilly was sick. Unhinged. A maniac. That so much of what she believed wasn't true. That the whole story she'd just told him about their father planning to kill someone was a delusion.

He'd told her.

He'd left her reality for his.

Lilly ran into the bathroom and grabbed his razor by the sink. She pulled out the blades, slicing her fingers as she pried them loose. She pressed them against her flesh, over and over again. Back and forth, up and down. She seemed to know exactly what she was doing. She didn't make dainty little horizontal slices on her wrists. She made long, deep cuts up and down her forearms. She flayed the flesh, carved it like it was a rotten pumpkin after Halloween. Soft. Worthless. Ready for the garbage.

There was blood. So much blood. It splattered on the bathroom floor. It splattered all over the sink. The mirror. Just before she passed out, she said one last thing:

"Traitor."

Oliver's mother appeared in the bathroom doorway. He told her what do, his voice flat. "Call an ambulance."

After Lilly was admitted to the hospital, his dad left. His mother drank wine. Oliver went to his room. And lost it. Threw books. Punched the walls. Felt like the worst human being on earth.

His mom and Sophie made the Boulder summer plan the next day.

I almost killed her.

June 29

35

OLIVER

Now Oliver stared at the phone.

"Look, they're healing." Lilly was still holding up her arms, wrists facing the screen. The cuts were healed, but the scars were deep purple and blue. Slashes ran up and down her forearm, thin lines branching across her skin. "It's not your fault. Not really. I get it." Lilly played with a long strand of her hair.

They looked at each other for a long while. Were they together again? In the same moment, in the same world?

"I'm sick," she said.

"I know, Lilly. I know you are. And I'm so, so sorry."

"It's okay," she said. She reclined on Oliver's pillows. "I might be. But I think I know what causes it." Her blue eyes flashed bright. "They said they were giving me Risperdal in there. But it totally wasn't. The pill didn't look right. It wasn't the right shape. I think it was an experiment. They were experimenting on me. Seeing what they could do to my brain . . ."

She's not better.

Maybe good enough to be out of the facility for a little while. But she wasn't better. She was just in a new delusion.

He had the urge to go back to his old habits. To ask her about the medicine. To agree with her that it was probably an experiment, a poison, a test. He started to tell her that he'd help track down the doctors. He'd help her make it right.

But he didn't say any of that.

He thought about telling her that she was wrong. That they were giving her the right medicine. That the doctors cared for her. That they were trying to help her. That she was schizophrenic. And would be. Forever.

He didn't say any of that, either.

He wanted to be with her like they were when they were kids. At sail on the same sea. It was all he wanted.

"Lilly," he asked, "can you hold on?"

She nodded, and he got off the floor. Phone in hand, he went to Sophie's living room, to the little altar. He pulled the single white flower out of the vase by the Buddha statue. He sat down on the sofa and held the flower up to the screen.

"Do you see this?" he asked. He twirled the stem.

"Yeah," Lilly said, looking confused.

"It's a gardenia." Oliver was so sad, so tired. But he sniffed the flower. Looked back at Lilly. "It smells so sweet. And it's beautiful, right? See how these petals fold over? And look at the middle. So perfect. What's it look like? To you?"

Lilly still looked a little confused, but went along. She leaned toward the screen, studied the flower. "Like paper. Like a paper sculpture. A featherweight paper flower."

She opened her mouth to say something else, but stopped. Oliver kept the flower in his hand, kept holding it up for her to see, kept twirling it. Around and around. They watched for a few beautiful moments.

Just the flower.

Just him.

Just her.

Just this.

He twirled it one more time.

And smiled.

She did, too.

For one beautiful kalpa.

He felt the koan.

Buddha was surrounded by his students. He held up a white flower and twirled it, saying nothing. No one understood the meaning of this wordless sermon except Mahākāśyapa.

Whose only response was a smile.

Mahākāśyapa understood the Dharma gate, the mind of nirvana that does not depend on words.

For the first time since they were little, he felt like she was near. That she was here. That he didn't have to miss her, because she wasn't gone.

Lilly leaned back. She looked away from the flower. "I thought of something." She held up the book she'd been holding. Oliver could see its misty green cover, the sea-blue typeface: *The History of Fairy Folklore.*

Oliver prepared himself to hear the details of another delusion. Another paranoid story. Another world. He feared their moment together was over.

"They found shreds of her clothes, right?" she asked.

"Yes," he said slowly. "That's right."

She opened her book to one of the dog-eared pages. "I saw Puck's picture in one of the articles I read," Lilly said. "And I felt something. Sometimes I feel like I'm a real-life fairy. With wings. With magic. And Puck looked like one, too."

She's gone again. Totally and completely gone.

"And the thing about fairies," she continued, "is that they like to leave fairy dust behind them. So you know where they've been. So you can follow them wherever they go."

She looked at Oliver like he should understand.

He did.

"So you think . . ."

"Yes. I think."

PART IV

THE FOURTH NOBLE TRUTH:

The Eightfold Path

*The path of peace. The cessation of duhkha.
Enlightenment.*

Right View
Right Thinking
Right Speech
Right Action
Right Livelihood
Right Effort
Right Mindfulness
Right Concentration

June 30

36

OLIVER

I'm at your door. That's what his text said.

All Oliver saw were ellipses in response. Essa was typing back. But no message came through.

Can I come see you? He tried again.

More ellipses. More nothing.

I have something really important to tell you.

He waited. And waited. She didn't text back.

But then she opened the door.

He'd never even known someone who'd lost a sister before. Or anyone before. He wasn't sure how to act. What to say.

"Hi," he said. He jammed his hands into his jeans pockets.

"Don't say you're sorry for my loss and you can come in," Essa said. "If I hear that one more time, I swear I'm going hit someone."

He'd been wondering if she'd look the same after a loss like that. And she did . . . mostly. Her hair was still long and wavy and hanging over her shoulders. She was still wearing the same type of thing: a skirt. A tank top. Her tattoo was still there. She hadn't had it removed or changed.

But she was different.

She seemed smaller somehow. Like someone had chopped her spirit in half, stolen the campfire light from her eyes for good. She took up less space.

He followed her down the hall and thought she was headed for her room.

She was headed to Puck's.

"I stay in here now," she said, sitting on the floor. "I feel close to her here, you know? I like to look at her kites at night. I like to think of her flying them, wherever she is. Even though I don't think of it like . . . a place, really."

Oliver sat down across from her, bent his long legs into a pretzel shape that he was getting much better at holding. He didn't know what to say. So he decided to say that. "I'm sorry I didn't know what to say. After. I've never known anyone who disappeared and—"

"Died. She died." Essa said it defiantly. Like she was almost angry. "I'm tired of people stepping around it. Just say it. It's real. It's what happened."

"I'm sorry." Oliver blushed. Maybe coming here was a bad idea. Maybe she wasn't ready. Maybe he was making things worse. "I'm not very good with words."

Essa paused. She pulled her hair over one of her shoulders and looked at him, her head cocked to the side. "That's not why I haven't talked to you." She started playing with the hem of her long skirt, pulling the fabric through her fingers over and over again.

"Oh." He was at a loss for words. Again. "You probably haven't wanted to talk to anybody. I'm sure it's hard—"

"I thought you hurt her."

"What?"

"I thought you did to her whatever you did to your sister." Essa stretched out on her back, stared up at the owl kite. "But it wasn't you. It was some beast."

"What are you talking about?" Oliver's eyes were wide. "What do you mean, what I did to my sister?"

"Well, you hurt her." Essa leaned up on her elbows. Glowering. "Didn't you? Before you left Chicago to come here? That's why your mom shipped you out here. That's the stuff you said you needed to get away from."

"No." Oliver spread out on the floor next to her. He looked up at the owl kite, too. "She was having a delusion, Ess. About my dad being some sort of criminal or something."

Essa rolled to her side and faced him. "Keep going."

"And that night, I just couldn't go along with it again. I couldn't do it anymore. And our parents were fighting, and Dad had filed for divorce over the stress of it all . . ." Oliver sighed, remembering. Shook his head. "And I just lost it. I told her that she's schizophrenic. That none of it was true. That she was paranoid. Delusional. That she was causing the divorce. That it was awful, and then she . . ."

Oliver paused. Essa was looking at him so intently.

"She tried to kill herself," he said. "She ran into the bathroom and took my razor and cut her arms. Her wrists." He motioned where she cut. "There was blood everywhere. And it was all my fault—"

"Oh my god." Essa rested her hand on his arm where he'd said Lilly had cut herself. "That's what you had to tell me. I'm so sorry I thought you hurt her . . ."

"That's not what I came to tell you," he said. "I talked to my sister. And she said something. About yours."

Essa furrowed her brow, looked confused.

"She saw Puck's picture. She looked up the story," he said. "And she had this idea. She thinks the clothes . . . the shreds they found. That maybe—"

"If you're going to say something that makes me hope, don't. Don't unless—"

"She thinks Puck dropped the pieces of clothing on purpose. A trail. So we could find her."

Oliver couldn't be sure, but he thought he saw a tiny light in Essa's eyes. Not bright like a flame or even a small spark. But there. A tiny, persistent glow, like an ember he just found in a fire he'd thought was out.

● ● ●

The pieces of clothing were in a cardboard box at the police station. There were a few shreds of Puck's unicorn T-shirt. A piece of her shorts. Essa clutched them close. She never wanted to let them go.

"But what now?" she asked. "Do we figure out exactly where they found each one? And go there?"

"I don't know," Oliver said. "Can I see one?"

Essa carefully handed him a piece of T-shirt. He flipped it over and over in his hands. It was dirty and stained brown. A tiny clump of mud still clung to it. He brushed it off.

And saw something.

"Look," he said. He brushed it again and again, trying to get all the dirt off. "There. See that?"

Essa peered at the fabric. "Is that a stain or . . . ?"

"Writing. A number?"

"One zero eight?"

"Yes. Essa, yes. A hundred and eight." Oliver put his hand in the box and pulled out another piece. "It's on this one, too. A hundred and eight. And an N. What's one-oh-eight N?"

Essa shook her head. "But I thought this before. I thought she ran away. But even if she did, they think a mountain lion dragged her . . ."

"But if she wrote on these clothes and left them on purpose, then they weren't shredded by a bear or a mountain lion or anything else on four legs. They were shredded by *her*."

"Oh my god." Essa looked at piece after piece. She found 108 N on nearly all of them.

"Is it a coordinate? Is this some orienteering thing?"

108

108

108

"Malas," Essa said. "There are a hundred and eight beads on a mala. It's like a Buddhist rosary. Puck wanted our mom to buy her one. And I think Puck left one behind. With a note that said, 'Sticks and stones.'"

Oliver's eyes lit up. "So a hundred and eight. And she's on foot. Maybe it's one hundred and eight miles to somewhere?"

"She can't be planning to walk a hundred miles."

"So steps? It's a hundred and eight steps. From where she left?"

The ember in Essa's eyes grew to a flame. "Maybe that's where the next clue is. A hundred and eight steps from our old shelter."

"So we should—"

"Call Micah. And get in the Jeep."

37

ESSA

The search team had recorded the coordinates of their campsite. It was a long hike in, but Essa, Micah, Oliver, and Anish made it just after three o'clock.

"Okay," Anish said, sitting on the ground. "We're here. And this time, we've got shit-tons of food, water, flashlights, and batteries. Plus, I brought ten lighters, five maps, and an emergency beacon."

Essa scanned the woods. She hated being here. She hated seeing the aspen trees, the brush, the dead leaves underfoot. She used to love the way the forest smelled. Now it smelled like loss. Like fear. Like death.

"All we know is one-oh-eight N," Essa said. She pulled one of the shredded T-shirt pieces out of her hiking pants pocket. "Our shelter was against this tree." The support beam still leaned against it, a few pine poughs still hung from the bark. So maybe a hundred and eight steps north from here? Or a hundred and eight feet?"

They measured it in all different ways. They walked 108 Puck-sized steps. 108 Essa-sized steps. 108 Micah-sized steps. They went 108 feet north. Then tried south, east, and west just to be sure. They looked up in the trees at those spots. They dug in the ground.

Nothing.

Micah pulled a fire pan out of his pack. "I'm going to build a fire," he said. "We can sit and stare at it for a while."

Essa started scraping along the ground with her hands. She overturned every leaf pile, every stick she could reach. "There has to be something," she whispered. Tiny beads of sweat started rolling down the back of her neck.

"Help me collect some pine sap?" Oliver knelt beside her. He asked it softly, gently. "Some kindling?" He held out a hand for Essa and stood up.

She looked up at him. His hair had gotten longer since he lived in Boulder. He'd gotten sun on his face and arms. "You know, you almost look like an outdoorsy guy," she said with a sad smile.

"Maybe I am," Oliver said, grinning.

They collected small sticks and twigs for kindling. Oliver scraped off a fresh glob of pine sap from a nearby tree. They stood by Micah as he started to build the fire. Essa thought about that last night with Puck. How Micah had built a fire in the firepan. How Essa had boiled a cup of pine needle tea and burnt her finger.

But then a painful memory came.

Puck, hunched over a few feet away, making art on the ground. Puck asking Essa to come see it, and Essa forgetting all about it. Forgetting to go see what might be Puck's last art project ever.

Maybe it's still here.

Essa walked a few paces away from Micah's burgeoning fire to look for Puck's artwork. If it was still there, she wanted to take a picture of it. She could frame it. Hang it on the wall. She looked and looked, and her heart sank. It was gone. Probably washed away in an afternoon storm or dismantled by a curious raccoon.

But then her foot struck something.

A stone.

A small circle of them.

She'd found it. Puck's forest artwork on the ground. Two

mountains made of sticks with a stone sun above it. One of the mountains was barely recognizable; the sticks had gone askew. But it was Puck's work to be sure. Mountains and the sun made of sticks and stones.

Sticks and stones.

"You guys, come here." Essa waved them over. "It must be a hundred and eight steps north from this! The clue in Mom's bathroom was *sticks and stones*. And look. This is what she made that last night. And told me to be sure to come see it."

"Sneaky, Puck. Sneaky, sneaky, sneaky," Micah said, wiping his ash-covered hands on his pants. "I'll count off the steps. Oliver and Anish—you guys dig. Essa, you take the trees."

They followed Micah 108 steps and stopped. Essa scanned the tree cover above them. She narrowed her eyes and studied every branch, every pinecone, every twisted trunk. She was looking for a note, another mala, for anything out of place.

Talk to me, Pucky. Talk to me.

"I found it!" Anish was pulling something out of the ground. It was buried and covered with a pile of leaves. He held it up, wiping off the dirt.

It was a clear cellophane bag.

From Pure Buds.

"Edibles?" Micah asked, reading the label.

Anish opened it up. "Nope. A note." He slid out a piece of paper and read it. "Puck + Ayden equals . . . a bunch of circles. What the hell?"

"Let me see." Essa held the note. "She had a crush? On a boy named Ayden?" She clutched the paper. "She didn't tell me," she said softly.

"I've seen that before," Oliver said, looking over Essa's shoulder. "When I started at Above the Clouds. It was in the storage room. On the computer desk."

"She was planning this at the beginning of the summer? And she knew some boy named Ayden back then?"

Essa thought back to the night they first met Ronnie. When

Puck ran ahead and ate one of the chan seeds he'd held out for her. When Essa discovered that Puck had stolen the Puzzle Kite. When she reminded Puck about sneaking stuff on the computer.

I made her promise to tell me everything.

I made her promise.

"I have no idea what this means," Essa said. She looked at Micah, a desperate feeling started to build. She felt shaky. Unsteady. "I didn't really know her like I thought I did."

Micah walked over. "Don't say that. You know her well enough to get this far. Let's make some dinner. Refuel. We'll figure it out."

"And put up a tent," Anish piped in. He ran back to the fire and picked up the tent bag. He looked at Essa, his fake smile an obvious attempt to distract her and cheer her up. "Which is carefully tucked and perfectly folded in this handy-dandy tent bag." He held the large canvas bag, its seams bursting from the pressure of the tent inside. "No brush shelters tonight, yo."

"Excellent. Let's eat and stare at a fire," Micah continued. He started to walk Essa closer to the flames. "Then we'll get some sleep. Maybe something will hit us in the morning?"

Essa nodded and watched as Anish struggled to pull the tent out of its bag. He yanked the drawstring open. Oliver grabbed one end of the bag while Anish started pulling out folded-up poles and canvas.

The tent bag.

Essa looked back down at the note. And the cellophane Edi-Sweets bag. "Maybe the note isn't all there is," she said slowly.

"Huh?" Micah asked as he poked at the fire.

"The bag. From Pure Buds. Maybe it's a clue, too."

Micah's eyes got wide. "And who would know about something to do with Pure Buds?"

No, Essa thought. *Please, no.*

But she knew the answer.

"My mother," she said.

"Exactamundo. The Queen of Edibles herself." Micah forced a smile, tried to look upbeat. "This is great. Maybe she'll know what this is about right away?"

"Have you met my mother? The woman who is spaced out ninety-nine percent of the time? Who can't get to work on time? Who never listens? Who pays more attention to weed brands and boyfriends than to her own daughters?"

"Hey," Micah said, dropping another stick on the fire, "if it's up to me, I'm going to choose to be optimistic."

Essa sighed. "But if it's up to my mother, I can't be."

Essa's mom was in bed. A lumpy mound under her purple velvet bedspread.

"Mom." Essa nudged her shoulder. Clicked on her mother's bedside lamp. They'd driven all the way from the wilderness. It was the middle of the night.

"What time is it?"

"I need to talk to you."

Her mother didn't respond. Essa put her bag down and stared at the ratty carpet. She got down on all fours and peered underneath, just to make sure Micah hadn't missed anything. Another box. Another note. Another . . . something.

"What are you doing?" Her mother's head was hanging over the side of the bed as she stared at her daughter, blinking in the bright light of her bedside lamp.

There wasn't anything under the bed. Except Ronnie's boxer shorts.

"I'm trying to ignore Ronnie's disgusting boxer shorts and—"

"They're under there?" Her mother huffed. "That's all the bastard left."

Essa paused and looked up at her mom. The disappointment on her mother's face made it clear: Ronnie had taken off.

"Said he couldn't handle everything. With Puck," her mom said. "That there was bad energy." She ran a hand over her face, like she was trying to wipe away her exhaustion. She shook her head. "But why are you looking under there in the first place?"

Essa put her head close to the floor again, scanning the darkness and the dust bunnies under the bed, willing something to be there. There wasn't. She sat up. "I was looking for what Puck might have left behind."

With that, Essa's mom pulled the covers back over her head, like a heavy lead blanket during an X-ray, as if the purple velvet could stop any harm from coming through.

"Mom." Her mother didn't stir. Essa sat back on her heels, reached up, and slowly pulled up the covers. Their eyes locked. Essa took a breath.

Tell her.

"I think she could be alive."

Her mother's eyes widened. Like her velvet shield had failed her, like it hadn't managed to keep the danger on the outside. "Essa, you've got to stop. If she ran, she didn't make it, honey. She didn't—"

"A mountain lion didn't shred her clothes. She did."

Her mother sat up. She was wearing a new necklace. A long gold chain with an open locket. Puck's picture. "What do you mean, she shredded them?"

"She wrote a message on each piece of fabric. And dropped them in the woods like breadcrumbs." Essa stared at her sister's picture. At the intelligence in her eyes. She wondered what other mysteries lay behind them. Other boys she'd had crushes on. Past runaway plans that maybe she'd never acted on. More ideas for treasure hunts that lead to her. "They led us to this." Essa reached in her bag and pulled out the Edi-Sweets package from Pure Buds that Anish had unearthed. She pulled out the note. "'Puck plus Ayden equals circles.'" She locked eyes with her mom. "Does any of this mean anything to you? The note? The bag? I'm thinking she left this clue for you. That maybe you'd understand."

"You're serious? You found this?"

"Yeah, by the campsite. In the woods." Essa ran a finger over the Pure Buds label. "She left clues, Mom. She wants to be found. Maybe there's still time."

"Ayden," Essa's mom whispered. "Ayden."

"You recognize it?"

"She said something."

Essa stood up and sat on the edge of the bed. "What did she say? Was he a boyfriend? A crush?"

"I can't remember . . ." Essa's mom reached over to her bedside table, fumbling for her multicolored glass pipe. "Hand me the lighter, will you?"

"No."

Her mother rolled her eyes and reached for her pipe and lighter herself. She pulled them into her lap. "Essa, I need to—"

"When?" Essa said. "When did Puck mention Ayden?"

Her mom shook her head. "I was with Ronnie. It was late. We were in the kitchen making bread with some seeds he brought."

Essa sat there, eyes wide, waiting for her to go on.

She didn't.

"Mom, think." Essa's voice was climbing. "What did she say?"

"Puck came in the kitchen. Said she couldn't sleep and that she wanted to wait up for a piece of bread." She stopped, leaned over again, and pulled open her bedside table drawer. She took out a small bag of green buds and loaded her pipe. "This will help me remember." She held the lighter over the bowl, circling the flame, wrapping her lips around the end of the pipe, drawing in a breath, drawing the heat over the dried green knot, sending a thin line of smoke snaking into the air. She rocked back and forth as it hit her. Her face softened, relaxed. Her shoulders eased down a little. She softly closed her eyes. "I don't know. I can't . . ."

"Think. Think hard. What was Ronnie saying? What were you saying? Did Puck say why she couldn't sleep? Had she been drinking too much Kool-Aid or—"

Essa's mom opened her eyes. "She said she'd heard a sad story. At school, I think."

"A sad story? About what?"

Her mother kept rocking back and forth. Back and forth.

You don't remember.

Essa glanced back at Puck's picture in her mother's locket. "Were you high? When Puck came in?"

Her mother's answer was a whisper. And a nod. "Yes."

Essa stared at her mother's bowl. The blackened bud against the bright colors of the glass. The smell of burning. The smell of forgetting. The smell of escape.

"You say it will help you remember," Essa said slowly. She twisted the Edi-Sweets bag in her hands. "But it's what helps you forget."

"I'm sorry, I—" Her mother stopped and reached into the drawer again.

"Just stop, Mom. Don't smoke anymore. You're already . . ."

"I'm not getting more," she said. She ran her hands through the junk in the drawer. She brushed aside pens and old rubber bands. ChapStick and bookmarks. Crystals and pennies. "Here." She held up a photograph.

Essa leaned in. It was a photo of a young woman in high-waisted pants. She had cropped hair and was wearing pearls. She was holding a small child. A little girl. Essa recognized the look in the child's eyes. "That's you," Essa said. "And is that . . . my grandmother? Holding you?"

Her mother's eyes were turning redder by the second. Glassy. She nodded. "You never got to meet her. But growing up, she was so strict with me, Essa. So strict." Her mother looked up at the ceiling like her memories were plastered there, a collage over her head, a lifetime to watch as she fell asleep each night. "She wouldn't let me do anything. Talk to boys. Go out with friends. Nothing. It was awful. So awful." Her mom looked back at the pipe in her lap.

Her mom was high. Her voice had that familiar faraway sound to it.

It made Essa sick.

She stood to go.

I don't want to listen. I want to find Puck.

"I just never wanted to be like that, you know?" her mother asked. "So strict. So cold. I told myself if I ever had kids, I'd be fun. Chill. The cool mom."

Essa looked at her mother, so pitiful there in a heap of purple velvet. With a bowl in her lap. With a faded picture of the past. "That isn't what kids want, Mom. Not really."

"Yeah? Well, what is it that they want?"

"They just want your attention. Your complete and undivided attention. For you to be with them when you're with them. To be here when you're here. You don't have to be rich. You don't have to have a fancy Boulder house. Or a villa in Aspen. But wherever you live, you have to be there. Just . . . *there.*"

"I'm always here. I—"

"You aren't. You forget everything. You never pay attention. When Puck talked. When she told you things."

Her mother hung her head, stared again into her pipe.

"And now this clue," Essa said, holding up the Edi-Sweets bag and the note about Ayden. "This could lead us to Puck. It could save her life. And it's up to you. And you don't remember. She left this for *you.*" Essa stopped. She heard Puck's voice in her head.

What Puck said about why she liked Oliver when she first met him.

"He took me seriously. About my dragon. He was paying attention."

What Puck said during the fight with their mother on Pearl Street about the mala. How Puck had explained to their mom three times what the beads were.

"See, Essa? She never listens."

What Puck said, standing in Above the Clouds with tears in her eyes when Essa busted her on the computer. When Essa said their mother would be so mad if she found out Puck was ordering stuff online again.

"She won't even notice. She's too busy making out with half of Boulder."

What Puck said when she was sitting on her bed working on the Puzzle Kite, hoping it had the horse kite inside.

"I told her five times I wanted the horse kite. And she kept saying she'd buy it. But I could tell she wasn't even listening."

"Oh my god," Essa said slowly. Her mother looked up from her pipe. Her glassy eyes red-rimmed with tears.

"What now?"

"They're all for you," Essa said. She locked her clear eyes on her mother's foggy ones. "All the clues. She left them for you. They're all about things you weren't paying attention to. She wanted you to find her. To teach you a lesson about . . ."

Essa stopped and dug in her bag. She fumbled for the Puzzle Kite Puck had left under her mother's bed. She popped open the top and took out the drawing of the wheel of the Dharma with the darkened spoke. In front of Old Tibet, Puck had said that each spoke stood for a step on Buddha's Eightfold Path. Essa ran into Puck's room, turned on a light, and looked up at her sister's poster. The Dharma wheel on it wasn't labeled. Essa crouched in front of Puck's bookshelves, searching for a book on Buddhism. She found one and flipped to the index in the back.

"The Eightfold Path," she whispered, running her finger down the page. "There." She turned to the section. There was a drawing of the wheel of the Dharma. With eight spokes. The first spoke pointing directly north was Right View, the first step. Moving clockwise, the next spokes were Right Thinking, Right Speech, Right Action. The spoke pointing directly south was Right Livelihood. Then Right Effort.

Essa stared at the next spoke. The spoke pointing directly west. The spoke that Puck had darkened on the wheel she left under her mother's bed. The spoke that was the very first clue, that pointed west to her mother's bedroom, to the mala and the clue about the sticks and stones:

Right Mindfulness.

The step on Buddha's Eightfold Path that was about paying

attention. Being aware. The teaching that suffering—dhukha—could be eased by bringing our minds and our bodies to the present moment. Out of the storm of our thoughts of the past and the future and what we have or don't have and into the present. Into the cup of smoky lapsang tea. Into the breath. Into the awe of something as simple as a paper towel. The tree it was made of, the water that fed the tree, the sun that turned its leaves green. Awe. Awareness. Presence. Peace.

Right Mindfulness.

"Essa."

Her mother was standing in Puck's doorway, pipe in hand. She held it out. "I'll stop. I will." She looked at Essa, begging. "Just find her."

July 1

38

ESSA

Mrs. Connelly was picking up a pile of scripts that had fallen on the auditorium floor. They were for the school's first production of the next school year: *Peter Pan*.

"Essa," Mrs. Connelly said, nearly dropping the scripts in her arms. Her short gray hair was in tightly permed coils, and she was a wearing a T-shirt that read, KEEP THE DRAMA ON THE STAGE. UNIVERSITY HILL ELEMENTARY SCHOOL DRAMA CAMP.

"I'm so sorry for your loss," she said, tears welling in her eyes. "I could barely finish the drama camp without Puck. We are all so sad. They brought counselors in to help the kids understand."

Essa smiled weakly. "Thank you. And I never got to thank you for letting her do the camp for free."

"Of course," Mrs. Connelly said. She held up a script. "I had already pegged her for the roll of Tinker Bell next year."

Essa imagined Puck in a fairy costume, her blonde hair in a high ponytail, her feet in little green shoes. She'd be perfect. And she'd love it. Essa looked up on the stage and imagined her sister there, flying back and forth. The dusty red stage curtain was partly open. A few kids dashed back and forth behind it.

"Um, I was wondering," Essa began. "About your students. If you had one named Ayden in the camp this year? With a weird spelling. It's A-Y-D-E-N."

Mrs. Connelly put the scripts down in one of the auditorium

316 🍂 Emily France

seats. "Ayden," she said slowly. "No. We had a Cayden? And a
Jade. But no Ayden."

"What about in the rest of the school? Is there an Ayden at
all?"

"Oh gosh, I wouldn't know . . ." Mrs. Connelly looked puz-
zled. "Why do you ask?"

"It's just that Puck told my mom a story about someone
named Ayden. A sad story. But my mom can't remember it."
Essa stopped. "We think it may have been Puck's boyfriend. She
wrote 'Puck + Ayden' on a note. We'd just like to know, that's all.
None of us knew she had a crush."

"Puck? A crush?" Mrs. Connelly flashed a sad smile. "Well,
that little stinker. I never saw her with a boy, if that's what you
mean. And she certainly wasn't a flirt. I think she intimidated all
the boys in drama camp anyway."

Essa smiled. "She was smart." She reached in her bag and ran
her hand over the Puzzle Kite box. "Smarter than any of us even
knew."

"I'm so sorry—"

"Thanks," Essa cut her off. She suspected Mrs. Connelly was
going to say she was sorry for Essa's loss again. Essa couldn't
stand to hear it one more time. "I hope *Peter Pan* is a hit."

"Thank you," Mrs. Connelly said, her face still filled with pity.

Essa took one last look at the stage. The one her sister loved
to be on. The one she might never be on again. Essa turned and
made her way slowly toward the auditorium exit.

"Wait," Mrs. Connelly called. She hurried down the aisle,
waving for Essa to stop. "Ayden. I just remembered. We did a
unit on safety in the city. And one on wilderness safety, too.
We're a downtown school in the mountains after all." Students
on the stage behind her started giggling. Mrs. Connelly glanced
over her shoulder at them. "Anyway, I've got to run. But Ayden.
You asked about him?"

"You know him?"

"Not personally. But he was a student here in the nineties.

He went hiking with his family and family friends, and . . ." Mrs. Connelly paused, like she didn't want to say the rest.

"And?"

"And he disappeared. They finally ruled that he was taken by a mountain lion. They only found his shoes."

At the mention of a mountain lion, memories flooded Essa's mind. The sound of something dragging along the ground outside their shelter the night Puck disappeared. The thought of Puck's clothes being ripped to shreds by sharp claws and teeth.

But a mountain lion didn't shred her clothes. She did.

"It hit Puck really hard, that story," Mrs. Connelly said. "She talked about it. How sad it was. That no one was paying close enough attention to Ayden."

"Do you know anything else about it?"

Mrs. Connelly shook her head. "I'm afraid not. Sorry I can't be of more help."

"Thank you," Essa said. "You've helped more than you know."

Essa hopped in the backseat of Micah's idling Jeep. Micah, Anish, and Oliver had been waiting outside the school. "Can one of you rich kids with the unlimited data plans hand me a phone? I need to search the Net for Ayden."

"Here." Oliver handed Essa his cell. "So she knew something?"

"Yep. There was a kid who was a student here in the nineties named Ayden. He went missing in the woods. Mrs. Connelly heard Puck talk about it."

Essa searched for "Ayden" and "Colorado." The hits were all over the place. There were sites about men named Ayden who were long dead and gone. Burial records from the early 1900s, funeral announcements in the *Boulder Daily Camera.* She scrolled down.

"Here it is," she said slowly. "Ayden Beech. He was six. Ran ahead of his family while they were hiking and disappeared."

She stopped. Looked at Oliver. "In the Comanche Peak Wilderness." She handed Oliver the phone. "Read the rest; I don't think I can."

Oliver read the article out loud. "'There was confusion in the hiking party. The group split into two. The group at the front thought Ayden was back with the others. And the group in the back thought he'd run ahead to the front.'"

Essa pictured a little kid racing along the trail, alone between the two groups. Everyone thinking they knew where he was, but no one really did.

They weren't paying close enough attention.

"No one was paying attention," she said slowly. "That's what gave Puck the idea to run away in Comanche. To make her point about mindfulness."

"Ayden," Oliver said. "He wasn't her boyfriend . . . he was her inspiration."

Essa couldn't get the image of Ayden out of her mind. No one realized he was gone. Until it was too late.

Maybe it's too late for Puck, too.

"Come here," Oliver said, next to her in the backseat. He pulled her close, and she rested her head on his shoulder.

"Show me where you saw the Ayden note. In the shop," Essa said. "It's all we've got."

39

OLIVER

"It was right here," Oliver said. They all stood in the storage room of Above the Clouds. Anish was searching the room for anything else Puck could have left behind and Micah was searching the front of the store. Oliver pointed to the spot on the computer table where he saw the Ayden note. "I'd just started working here. It was my first day. And I saw all these lollipop wrappers on the table, and this little white note in the middle of them. 'Puck + Ayden.' And circles. It makes sense now. The circles must be—"

"Dharma wheels," Essa said.

Oliver sat down at the computer. He looked at the tabletop. Under it. On the sides. Looking for another note. Another clue. He didn't find one. He looked back at the darkened computer screen and moved the mouse, waiting for the screen to light up. He typed in the password.

"Here," Anish said, holding out a handful of lollipops. "Eat one of these. Keep your strength up."

Essa smiled. "Thank you."

"Ugh," Oliver said.

"What? You don't like these flavors?" Anish stared at the candy. "There's bubble gum, apple, cherry. The only one I'm missing is grape."

"No, no. The password isn't working. Is Jan around?"

"I'll go see." Essa pushed open the swinging storage room door. She was back through it in minutes with Jan in tow.

Oliver hadn't seen Jan in a while. She was still wearing a flowing white top, a long necklace. He got a kick out of remembering the first time he met her. How he thought she might be some sort of Yoda figure. Always saying something wise. He remembered how foreign Boulder seemed. How sleepy. How small.

Now it felt bigger than any place he'd ever been. Full of koans. And Zen priests. And Essa.

"Password trouble?" Jan asked, swooping onto the stool.

"Goflyakite isn't working," Oliver said. "I tried it three times."

"I changed it. Too many people knew it." Jan smiled. "You're gonna love the new one."

They all peered at the screen as Jan typed in the new code: *BadasstheDragon.*

"I love it," Essa said.

Oliver smiled, thinking of Badass with her flaming blue scales and giant open wings. Jan hit enter and the screen lit up just as the storage room door swung open and whacked against the wall.

"Kite club's here." It was Micah. "They need fifteen winders. And ten pieces of line laundry. Preferably the giant squid. I don't even think we have three." Micah pulled a cardboard box down from the shelf and started rummaging through it. He cast a glance at Jan. "And please notice I'm working off the clock, out of the abundant kindness in my heart."

"Noted," Jan said. "I will hang your employee of the year plaque as soon as possible."

Micah looked at the computer screen. "You find Puck's kite app?" he asked.

"No, I want to look up the news stories on Ayden," Oliver said. "That kid who went missing in the nineties."

"Wait," Essa said, looking at Micah. "What kite app?"

"Thought that was what you were looking for," Micah said, pulling winders out of the box. "Puck was all proud of herself because she installed it without my help. I tried to help her, but she wouldn't let me." He crossed the room and pointed at the screen, to the kite icon in the top corner. "Puck and I made a deal. If she would help me memorize all the dragon inventory, I would help her install stuff on the computer. But she did this one on her own. She said she loved it."

Essa looked at the icon. "I remember," she said. "Puck said it was a game. With kites. *With really pretty kites.* Open it. I want to see."

Oliver moved the cursor toward the game icon. The little white arrow hovered over the kite, and he double-clicked.

It wasn't a game.

The kite icon changed. The colorful canvas drawing disappeared, and in its place was a black box.

Oliver double-clicked again, and a program opened up.

Puck's screen name appeared on the right-hand side, *Pucknow*. Icons of little houses lined up underneath it. One had a star on its roof. Oliver clicked it. A chat log popped up. A long one. Conversations that went back months.

"It's a veil," Micah said slowly. "Man, that girl is sneaky."

"A veil?" Essa asked.

"It's a way to disguise an app. You give it a fake cover—a veil. I've seen one that makes an app look like a calculator icon. But when you click it, it's something else entirely. I've never seen one that disguises something as a game . . ."

Essa looked ill. "The last time I caught her on the computer in here, I tried to open her last browser page, but I couldn't. I thought she was shopping on the Internet again, signing up for another candy-of-the-month club or something. But . . ."

"You couldn't open up her last web page because she wasn't on the web." Micah narrowed his eyes at the screen. "She was in this chat app."

Oliver scrolled and scrolled. Puck had been chatting with so many different people. Mostly about plays and dragons and wanting to take tap classes. But then something caught Oliver's eye. A chat dated Saturday, June 17. The day of his first kiss with Essa near Gold Hill. The day that Puck's mother announced the plan to marry Ronnie and move to Portland.

■ ■ 👤+ 📞   ⚙

> It's time.
>
> Pucknow · Sat, June 17, 4:45 PM

You Sure?

Hoverracer · Sat, June 17, 4:45 PM

> Mom is marrying that creep.
>
> Pucknow · Sat, June 17, 4:46 PM

NO WAY.

Hoverracer · Sat, June 17, 4:46 PM

> Yup. Right after she told me, I hid the box and the mala. The first two clues.
>
> Pucknow · Sat, June 17, 4:47 PM

Tell me where you're going.

Hoverracer · Sat, June 17, 4:47 PM

> Nope. But I'm leaving from the woods. I've been studying orienteering like a champ. I'll be fine. Can't wait to see the look on my mom's face when she finds me. Ayden never made it, but I totally will.
>
> Pucknow · Sat, June 17, 4:48 PM

You SURE?

Hoverracer · Sat, June 17, 4:48 PM

> 😃 Yup. And PROMISE you won't tell. If you do, you'll ruin the whole thing.
>
> Pucknow · Sat, June 17, 4:49 PM

Promise

Hoverracer · Sat, June 17, 4:49 PM

Essa looked like she was going to be sick. Like she was going to vomit all over the keyboard, the screen, the mouse.

"Hoverracer," she said slowly. She looked at Oliver. "It's probably some kid who has been in the store."

"We'll find him," Oliver said. "It can't be that hard to track him down."

"But he doesn't know where she is. She didn't tell him."

Essa shook her head in disgust and walked away from the screen while Oliver scanned the rest of the chat. Puck had been complaining about her mother, how she never paid attention. How she smoked pot all the time. How Puck tried to explain Zen to her. How her mother never listened.

Then Oliver saw the worst thing.

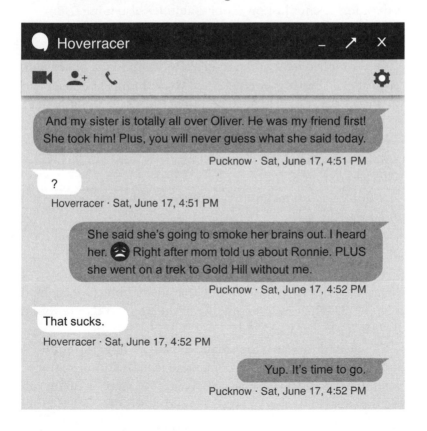

Hoverracer — ↗ ✕

> And my sister is totally all over Oliver. He was my friend first! She took him! Plus, you will never guess what she said today.
>
> Pucknow · Sat, June 17, 4:51 PM

> ?
>
> Hoverracer · Sat, June 17, 4:51 PM

> She said she's going to smoke her brains out. I heard her. 😣 Right after mom told us about Ronnie. PLUS she went on a trek to Gold Hill without me.
>
> Pucknow · Sat, June 17, 4:52 PM

> That sucks.
>
> Hoverracer · Sat, June 17, 4:52 PM

> Yup. It's time to go.
>
> Pucknow · Sat, June 17, 4:52 PM

Oliver hoped Essa would stay across the storage room, that she wouldn't come back over and read the last part.

But she did.

Oliver remembered when Essa had said she wanted to smoke. It was obvious from the look on her face that she did, too. The day that Essa's mom broke the news about Ronnie, Oliver and Essa had been watching Puck out the kitchen window. Puck was throwing rocks angrily at the fence. Essa said if she didn't get out of there soon, she was going to smoke her brains out.

Now, Essa stared at the screen. "Puck was listening," she said. "She heard me. I knew it." Essa looked down at the dirty storage room floor. "That's why she ran away when she did. Because our mom was letting her down. And so was I." She looked at Oliver, eyes wide. "It's not just my mom's fault. It's also mine."

"Don't say that."

"But it's true."

Oliver looked back at the screen. He scanned the chat again. About Puck studying orienteering. About hiding the mala and the Puzzle Kite box. He looked at what Puck said about Ayden:

Ayden never made it, but I will.

"Wait," Oliver said, his back straightening on the stool. "Ayden never made it . . . where? Where was his family hiking? Where were they going?"

"I think she just means that Ayden didn't survive and she will and—"

"But what if that was her destination? *Ayden's* destination." Oliver typed Ayden's name into a search box. "Here it is," he said slowly. "Ayden Beech." Oliver silently skimmed the rest of the article until he came to a line that made him stop. He read it out loud. "The group was hiking to the Bennett Campground . . ." He looked at Essa.

She leaned forward, the smallest spark of hope in her eyes. She pulled up a map of the Comanche Peak Wilderness, traced her finger along the Comanche Trail. "We were breaking off the trail west to Brown's Lake," she said slowly. "For Puck to get to Bennett Campground, she would have to go north to catch Beaver Creek Trail. That would lead her straight to it."

"And she wrote N for north on the clothes she left. The Edisweets bag was buried a hundred and eight steps north, but maybe she was also . . ."

"Headed north to the Beaver Creek Trail. As long as she made it to the trail, finding the campground would be easy."

Oliver looked back at the screen, at the news story about Ayden. "Ayden never made it, but . . ."

"Maybe Puck did."

40

ESSA

Essa showed the cops the chat log and by the time she made it to Bennett Campground, there were five police cars and one ranger's Jeep already there. The cops were scouring it all: the tent sites, the bathrooms, the park.

There was no sign of Puck.

Essa and Oliver stood in the parking lot. Watched the wind scatter a few paper cups across the pavement. Mountains loomed in the distance. Campsites were tucked along the creek, some on hillsides with views. Others surrounded by trees.

Puck, were you here?

Did you make it this far?

Essa felt unsteady. Not solid. Like the bottom had dropped out beneath her. She saw the campground bathhouse off to her right and went in, thinking she could at least splash some water on her face. That maybe it would make the world stop spinning.

Inside, there were five sinks with mirrors and a long line of bathroom stalls. She leaned against the counter and turned a sink faucet on cold. She let the water run over her hands. It got colder and colder. She splashed some on her face.

It's too late.

She's gone.

She thought about Puck in the bathroom underneath the Boulder Cafe. Hiding in a toilet stall. Doing a vault into the middle of the room. She thought about Puck practicing kicks in the mirror.

I'm afraid this pain will kill me. I can't survive this storm.

She turned off the water and walked to the paper towel dispenser. She yanked out a wad.

But stopped.

Be mindful.

Be here.

It's the only way you won't capsize.

She looked down at the paper towels in her hand. Brought her attention to them. Puck was right; they were plants. They were trees. They were water. They were the sun. Gently, she put them back in the dispenser.

Just this.

Just this.

This very mind is Buddha.

She walked to the electric hand dryer and pushed START. Just like Puck would have. As the hot air blew over her wet hands, she brought her attention to her breath. Thoughts kept racing through her mind. Puck cold and hungry in the woods. Puck forever lost without a trace.

She didn't push the thoughts out. She felt the sadness, the fear. But then watched them like dark clouds overhead. She had to survive this. She had to.

She brought her attention to her breath.

In.

Out.

In.

Out.

That's when she saw it. Carved into the electric hand dryer. Scratched into its white enamel surface:

Ess G.H.Mine

Even though she couldn't decipher the whole thing, the first word was unmistakable.

Essa.

Her breath came quickly then. She tried to slow it down, but it was no use.

The last clue is for me.

"Oliver." She screamed it as loud as she could. He came running into the bathroom. "What? What is it?"

"Look," she said, pointing. "She was here. She scratched this message."

"What's it mean? "

"I have no idea." Essa stared at it. Ran the letters through her mind over and over again.

"Have we seen those letters somewhere before? If this clue is for you, it has to be about something you forgot or weren't paying attention to."

"It was on the hand dryer, which is totally for me. I almost wasted about a thousand paper towels when I was chasing her around the Boulder Cafe."

What else did I forget?

What did I do wrong?

They slowly walked back to the parking lot. Essa looked ahead as the bright sun lit up the evergreens in the campground. The broad teardrop leaves of aspen. The boulders scattered in groups of twos and threes, huddled like children on a playground whispering secrets. The sun cast it all in a golden glow.

A golden glow.

Gold.

"Gold Hill," Essa said slowly. "G.H." She thought about the orienteering trek they did. How Anish had dropped Oliver and Essa in the woods near Gold Hill, how they'd had their first kiss. How Puck had been so mad when they found her underneath her comforter at home later. Devastated about the Portland news; furious that Essa and Oliver hadn't invited her on the day trek like they'd promised. "Gold Hill Mine."

"So she's in the Gold Hill mine somehow?" Oliver asked. "But how would she get there from here?"

"No," Essa said, scanning the hillsides surrounding the

campground. "Remember what Puck told you? About the Gold Hill mine?"

Oliver smiled. "They got the gold out of streams. There is no real mine in Gold Hill."

Essa nodded.

So there must be a real one here.

The opening of the abandoned mine was a mile from the bath house, a large gaping square of black up a hillside. Essa ran as fast as she possibly could.

Be there.

Be there.

Be there.

She reached the mine completely out of breath. She peered into the darkness. Giant wooden beams still held the earth open, dried cobwebs hung in corners and swayed in the cool breeze blowing from the deep. She heard dripping water.

"Puck!"

Inside, her eyes adjusted and she saw something on the floor. A flash of blonde, like a gold coin found at the bottom of a fountain.

Puck.

Eyes open.

Completely awake.

Essa knelt, wrapped her arms around her tiny sister, pulled her close. Her skin looked sallow, dry. "Are you okay?"

"I'm cut," Puck said, her voice weak and small, like a baby marmot calling for its mother. She held up her arm. She'd stripped a large piece of pine bark and strapped it to her forearm. "Tripped and fell on the way here. But knew how to make a pine bark Band-Aid." She smiled and slowly blinked her eyes.

Up and down.

Up and down.

"But you're okay?"

Puck nodded. "Told you I'd make a good survivalist."

Essa smiled as tears ran down her face. "Did you have enough food? Are you hungry?"

"Starving," Puck said, her voice sounding weak again. "I forgot my backpack in our shelter. But if I went back in to get it, I knew I'd wake you up. I've been stealing food from campers at the campground, but haven't been able to for . . ." She stopped talking and looked around her, like she'd forgotten where she was. She saw Oliver arrive at the mouth of the mine, the ranger in tow. "Where's Mom? Did she find me? Is she with you?"

A familiar pang filled Essa's chest as she watched Puck look for their mother and realize she wasn't there.

"No," Essa said. "But Puck, she heard you. Loud and clear." Essa rocked Puck back and forth in her arms. Back and forth. "She saw all the clues. What you were trying to tell her. She understands what you meant about listening, about being present." Essa put her lips close to her sister's ear, gently whispering. "And so do I."

Essa saw the tiniest spark of victory in her sister's eyes, a warm campfire glow.

July 3

41

ESSA

Even though Puck had been home for two days, Puck and Essa still slept in Puck's bed together, curled up close just like they were the last night before she disappeared. Essa thought of nothing but the feel of Puck's warm body next to hers, the smell of her hair, the sound of her gentle breathing just as she fell asleep. It didn't take any effort—to be completely absorbed in the present.

Her Zen teacher said that was how you could spend each moment. Like you've been gone and are suddenly home.

Just this.

Just this.

This very mind is Buddha.

Their mother knocked on the door. Asked if she could join. Puck nodded, and the three of them squeezed in bed together. One giant pretzel.

"You know how many buddhas are in this bed?" Essa asked softly.

Puck nodded that she knew. "But tell me anyway," she said.

Essa looked into her sister's bright blue eyes. Their mother reached out and softly stroked Puck's cheek.

"Three," Essa said. "It's just that we don't always know it. Or act like it." Essa thought of the Zen priest's compassionate eyes. What he said about not being violent toward yourself. Being kind. "So have a little compassion for us when we're not in the moment."

"We're trying," their mother said.

"Well," Puck began, "you know what I think Buddha would say to that?"

"What?"

"Don't try too hard, or you'll miss it."

And she smiled.

They all did.

42

OLIVER & ESSA

"I can still feel the Ghost Train Haze," Oliver said. "Are my lips melting? I mean, really. Look closely. And why did you let me order that again?"

They'd left Cheba Hut and were walking toward Arapahoe Avenue, toward Saturday zazen.

"Because you seemed so excited to suffer again," Essa said, smiling. She took his hand and swung it back and forth as they walked. "And you would've hated the Robert Plant, anyway. It's pretty healthy."

"True."

As they got closer, they could hear the hum of Arapahoe. The hustling cars. A few horns. The laughter of two girls sitting on the porch of a Naropa building.

The garden outside the Zendo came into view. The warm light shining on the Blue Spruce Inn sign. The empty Adirondack chairs. The swaying closed blossoms of wildflowers. Just as Essa was about to open the gate and step into the garden, Oliver stopped her.

"Can we walk a little? This way." He pointed down the street. There was a bench under the cold, stark glare of a streetlight. Litter was cluttered about.

"Sure," Essa said, confused. "Down there?"

"Yeah."

Essa shrugged and took Oliver's hand again. They walked to

the bench and sat down. Essa draped her legs over his lap, and he pulled them close. She put an arm over his shoulders, her mala beads cool against the back of his neck. He looked in her eyes and softly ran a finger over her sanctuary tattoo. The blade of grass.

"So the koan," he said, "about the sanctuary. I think I know what it means."

Essa raised her eyebrows and smiled. "But you're not supposed to understand them with your mind, you're supposed to—"

He interrupted her with a kiss. Long. And slow. And gentle.

"It means when I kiss you, I kiss you," he whispered. He kissed the place just under her ear. "And when I touch you, I touch you." He ran his hand over her cheek, down her neck. "I guess what I'm saying is . . ." He stopped. Leaned his forehead against hers and looked into her eyes. "This is a good spot for a sanctuary."

She smiled the most beautiful smile he'd ever seen. It was the smile by the bonfire when they first talked about their sisters. It was the smile when she asked him to follow her to the Zendo for the first time. It was the smile after they first sat zazen and the one after the Dharma talk. It was all of them. All at once.

She cast a glance around them in the cold streetlamp light. At the litter on the ground. The cigarette butts. The empty paper cups. A broken beer bottle. She felt the warmth of his hands holding her. The rise and fall of his chest as he took each breath. The softness of his lips as she kissed him again. And again.

Just this.

Just this.

This very mind is Buddha.

"You know what I think?" she asked, pulling back.

"What?" He pulled her closer.

"The sanctuary is built."

And she smiled.

They both did.

Author's Note

I first heard the koan about Buddha silently twirling a flower—the story Oliver uses to finally connect with his sister—during a Dharma talk in a Boulder Zendo. It struck me in a way I cannot describe, but it profoundly impacted my life, just as it did Oliver's. Later, I would learn that it is often called the Flower Sermon, and it is a foundational Zen story. It inspired this novel.

Although *Zen and Gone* is a work of fiction, it is filled with factual references to the historical Buddha, the main tenets of his teachings, and several practices used in the branch of Buddhism known as Zen.

The historical Buddha is thought to have lived sometime between the mid-6th and mid-4th centuries, BCE. Born Siddhārtha Gautama, he was a member of a wealthy family in what is today southern Nepal. His father attempted to keep him from witnessing the harshness of reality (struggle, sickness, death), but when Siddhārtha was finally exposed to these things, he renounced his privileged life and set off to find a way to ease the suffering inherent in the human condition. From physical suffering to existential suffering, the Great Physician was concerned with finding a cure for deep dissatisfaction with life, for dhukha in its many forms.

For forty-nine days, Siddhārtha meditated under what became known as the Bodhi tree, which Puck accurately describes as a *ficus religiosa*. The Buddha emerged, claiming he had gained insight about the true nature of reality and the suffering that delusion causes: he had reached enlightenment. The Four Noble Truths that begin each section of this novel are some of the main ideas the Buddha shared in his first teaching in Sarnath, India. The first clue that Puck leaves under her mother's bed—the eight-spoke wheel of the Dharma—is an actual Buddhist symbol used to represent the Buddha's teachings and his eightfold path.

Right Mindfulness is the aspect of the eightfold path that serves as Puck's primary focus. If you'd like more information about mindfulness, a great authority is Thich Nhat Hanh, one of the most well-known Zen masters in the world. Nominated for the Nobel Peace Prize by Dr. Martin Luther King Jr., he has written many books—some for young people and children—that touch on the topic. My favorite is titled *Happiness: Essential Mindfulness Practices.* He also founded Wake Up International—a global community of young people who are committed to practicing mindfulness. Participants are Buddhists and non-Buddhists alike, all with the goal of creating a healthy and compassionate society. For more information, check out www.wkup.org.

Lastly, there are many branches of Buddhism; the one that Essa and Oliver encounter in Boulder is Zen, and in particular, Soto Zen. Zazen, gathas, and koans can all be used in Soto Zen practice. Zazen is the meditation that Oliver attempts in the Zendo with Essa. Gathas are short verses that help direct attention back to the present moment. Koans are riddles or stories that are intended to confound the rational mind, to bring a student into a direct insight about reality. While they are emphasized more in the Rinzai school of Zen, they are used in the Soto tradition as well when helpful.

As for the wilderness portions of this novel, the game my characters play is not true orienteering. Orienteering is an organized sport in which participants navigate between checkpoints with compasses, maps, and an official timer. For more information see Orienteering USA, www.orienteeringusa.org.

My characters do use actual wilderness survival tools such as the brush shelter, deadfall trap, bow and drill, root rope, rock-and-stick compass, and pine needle tea. However, Essa, Oliver, and Micah harm the woods in many ways—digging up roots, pulling down branches, etc. In reality, when not in an emergency situation, please practice Leave No Trace principals when in the great outdoors so that it will be here to enjoy for many generations to come. For more information see the Leave No Trace Center for Outdoor Ethics, www.lnt.org.

Finally, my characters find themselves in an emergency situation in the woods mostly due to their lack of preparedness. For more information on wilderness safety see the National Forest Service, www.fs.fed.us.

Acknowledgments

I will always believe that I write the books I need to read. This novel was no exception; I wrote it during the most challenging time of my life. Crisis after crisis kept hitting my family over the course of drafting. The practice of zazen and writing this story helped me find joy in the storm, kalpa by kalpa. And the great news: we didn't capsize.

I would like to thank Gary Hardin, an ordained Soto Zen priest and Head of Practice at the Boulder Zen Center. Thank you for your gentle guidance, your time, and your instruction. You have helped me experience joy and be present with those I love in ways I never knew were possible. And to the Sangha who stopped burning incense during zazen just because I had morning sickness, thank you for your kindness.

To my wonderful editor, Daniel Ehrenhaft, thank you for believing in this story from the very beginning and for your kindness and patience as it came to life. Your guidance and your confidence in me have transformed my writing. Thanks to managing editor Rachel Kowal for going through my novel with such care and attention. Thanks also to the entire team at Soho Teen; I'm so honored to be one of your authors. And special thanks to Juliet Grames, Paul Oliver, Abby Koski, and Rudy Martinez for their support, kindness and general badassery. Come back to Boulder! We have so many restaurants to conquer. And thanks to Paul and Abby for the epic filming adventure in the frigid Denver Botanic Gardens.

This novel would not exist if it weren't for my indomitable agent, Jennifer Unter. The pep talk you gave me in the eleventh hour of drafting saved the day—and the story. Thank you for believing in me and for shoring me up in one of my toughest hours.

Thanks to the wonderful new owners of the Tattered Cover, Kristen Gilligan and Len Vlahos. Launching my first novel at your magnificent bookstore was a dream come true. Your presence and words that night sparkle in my mind as one of the greatest memories of my debut year.

Thanks to the entire kid lit community of writers in Boulder, Colorado. You are my people. And special thanks to Melanie Crowder for her all-around wonderfulness.

For always reading and never letting me give up, thanks to my critique partner of 15 years, Tara Thomas. I cannot imagine writing without you.

Thanks to my Boulder teen advisors, Berit, Rowan, Griffin, and Colter. You are the coolest, and I'm so lucky to know all of you. Thanks to Wendy for telling me all about The End of the World and her escapades as a Boulder teen. And thanks to the city of Boulder, Colorado, for inspiring me, for being my favorite place on the planet, for being home.

And to my dear friends who surrounded my family with love and brought us dinner every night for two solid months during the worst of the storm: Josie, Joanne, Pam C., Mark, Joyce, Marion, Mary, Olivia, Linda, Liv, Kate, Sylvie, Lisa C., Maggie, Lauren L., Jimmy, Scarlet, Patti, Ann, Sarah, and anyone I'm forgetting! I will treasure your acts of kindness and love for the rest of my life. Heather, we will never forget the call from your husband, "Heather said something about a baby and a dog?" Thank you for rescuing Nala while we brought our baby into the world! We love you. And Joanne, sister-friend, your wit and your wisdom have saved me so many times. I love you to the very tips of my toes. And to Pam Stormo, a joy, a genius, a master of the now, how I miss your light. I will love and stick close to your beautiful family forever.

Thanks to my parents, my sister, my in-laws and the rest of

our family who came to our rescue in so many ways. I couldn't have written another novel without you.

Finally, to my husband, thank you for never letting me give up on my biggest dreams; spending my life with you makes me so profoundly happy. And to my son, being your mother is the greatest joy and honor of my life. Oh, how I love you!